Her Name is Gatekeeper

by

Laurel Thomas

Her Name is Gatekeeper

Cover Art by *The Wild Rose Press, Inc.*

The Wild Rose Press, Inc.
PO Box 708
Adams Basin, NY 14410-0708
Visit us at www.thewildrosepress.com

Publishing History
First Edition, 2025
Trade Paperback Print ISBN 978-1-5092-6362-2
Digital ISBN 978-1-5092-6363-9

Published in the United States of America

Dedication

Take your gift, beloved, and let it defeat your fear.
Your courage might just become a gate of freedom for others.

Prologue

Dragons are often misunderstood. Blazing rivers of fire, charred destruction – all that. Certainly, I enjoy a good flame. It warms my heart as it controls the masses. My spew is most often calculated. It must be said that I am a bully at the core.

Until one day an almost regret, an almost sorrow crept uninvited over my overwhelming greatness.

A little girl stood outside the city gates. The wall behind her housed Darras, a territory that belonged wholly to me. The Nayeli culture boasted a thriving slave trade, oppression of the weak and vulnerable, all cloaked in the name of prosperity. What more could a venerable serpent like me desire?

I craved a grand entrance when I could get it. So, I flew overhead, swooping low to let a foreshadow of my heat waft through the clouds. I expected the little one to dash back inside to the safety of those massive walls.

Instead, a tangle of brown curls covered one eye when she lifted her head and stared at me, an intruder in the rosy sky of early dawn. With only a crinkle between her brows, she tossed away the lock like an unruly distraction and planted her feet into shifting desert sand.

She held a mangy cur, cradling it like a baby. She didn't run, only stood as though she waited.

I plunged through the desert air and blasted a grove of acacia trees. A nearby spring of water did nothing to save them.

The girl watched as limbs collapsed into ash. Then she opened her mouth and sang.

Lift up your heads, O gates, lift them up ancient doors.

The gatekeeper must come, and she will not fail.

Why did I pause, as if requesting her permission to enter? My breath had consumed a myriad of stony walls. The towering wall that stretched around Darras, center of my illustrious worship, would not deter me.

I wanted those city gates. I would have them.

Perhaps you haven't heard. You've lived in obscurity on your trek, winding your way unseeing on this blue-tinged planet.

I didn't need a fanfare. The truth was enough.

My name was Gatekeeper.

Gatekeeper of all.

Chapter 1

The gown was blue like the sky Giselle Basir never saw often enough. Soft, flowing sleeves grazed her elbows, unlike the countless tunics she wore year after year that were uglier than unwanted baggage. She paid for it with money she borrowed from the kitchen coffer. Or stolen, depending on how you looked at it.

A dress wasn't the best for her daily lurch down the city walls, but she'd make it work. The gates were locked this time of day, so she couldn't exactly walk out the front door. Fleeing the Gemini Inn to the outside world, even for a little while, was worth a bounce down granite stones.

She tied the rope kept under her bed to the base of the gnarled dresser. Knotting the other end around her waist, she climbed onto the windowsill and sat, perched like a desert sparrow.

Sand dunes wavered silently across miles of desert in every direction. A camel train approached in the distance like a thin rope. Escape traveled closer with every plop of those hairy hooves and the drivers who led them.

Not until later, though. She needed to see the sundial one more time.

The first leap never failed to take her breath away. Thirty feet was a long way down. Still, it was proof that the walls of Darras couldn't hold her. She sucked in a breath. "Don't look, you ninny." Then stuffed a yowl of pain when her knee met stone with a whack.

Her stomach listed with another jump, a couple more bounds, and a final leap as she finally landed on the sandy desert floor.

Gray sky retreated in streaks of rose and orange over the horizon. A lone desert lark sang from a stony outcropping, happy for this moment of stillness, too. Nearby, a grove of date palms waved fan-like leaves over a spring where deep gurgles barely etched its surface. According to Papa, the city of Darras once stood on the shores of a massive lake. Papa wasn't one to lie, but still…

The sundial stood outside the sprawling limbs of an ancient olive tree. Fingering its metal rim, she steeled her heart against a rush of grief. Papa set its stylus the day she was born, sixteen years ago. It was their favorite meeting place, first thing in the morning when the desert rested, and the air was fresh and cool.

Now, on yet another day in the trade hub of the Nayeli people, Papa was still gone, and she was done waiting for his return. Resolve settled inside as she knelt at the sundial. "I'll find you," she whispered. "Somehow."

"Entrada." Clank, clank. Bang. "Yo! Entrada!"

Guttural voices intruded into her moment. The first round of camel drivers finished their all-night trek and waited for entrance through the city gates. One of them, a grimy sand warrior ready for breakfast, banged his fist against the metal doors.

Duty called.

She hurried to the gates, elbowing her way through the crowd. "Chronos!" she yelled. "Wake up, already."

Chronos, the night watchman, was no doubt sound asleep. He stepped in after Papa left to open the city gates each morning and close them at the end of the day. Not actually a gatekeeper, he was more like an occasional gate watcher. Not a very good one at that.

The burly man appeared from an open window overhead, rubbing his eyes and cursing. "Shaddup. I be here." He jabbed in her direction. "You, Giselle Basir, won't be commandin' me. I din't care who your daddy be."

"Oh, hush and do your job."

In moments, the massive gates pitched, then slid into recessed stone walls.

Chronos wobbled on bowed legs as the camel drivers rushed in like a horde of unruly schoolchildren. "Yo. They be a smelly lot."

"Don't be such a cranky butt. They're tired and hungry."

"That be my concern? Fie. Best be getting inside before them hoodlums take over the kitchen." Deeply etched lines crinkled his face into a craggy smile. He jabbed a gnarled finger at the guard who took his place. "Oi! Watch out for Aaron, here."

Blond hair billowed out of the young man's plumed helmet. He held a hand to his chest and bowed low to Giselle. "Save me a dance at the masquerade?"

She laughed with more than a little defiance. Today, on her first day as a full-fledged citizen, she was invited with the rest of Darras to the annual gala where rich and poor alike celebrated in the lavish palace. The freedom of not being recognized brought plenty of drama, from what she'd heard.

Mother's usual aversion to her daughter doing

anything but work didn't bode well for an invitation, which might have stopped her before.

Not today. She had a plan, and it didn't include compliance.

Her mother, Ursula of Basir, appeared as if she'd called her name. Black hair gathered in long waves at her back, and she was dressed in a richly embroidered robe. She bowed slightly to the camel train owners. With a graceful sweep of a manicured hand, she motioned them inside the inn and then turned to Giselle. "Where is your...Never mind. The dining room. Now."

Their words ripped each other apart the night before, but Mother sure didn't carry any scars. Did she even remember it was her birthday? Giselle pasted on a placid face, refusing to hurry after the woman who disappeared into the inn.

Unknown ancestors had built the Gemini into the walls at the city's entrance. In Papa's eyes, the inn was a magical place of divine protection. Those stones were no sanctuary. They were a prison with Mother as chief jailer.

A short, stocky camel driver smiled a crooked grin at Giselle as he strolled inside with the same rolling gait as his flat-footed animals. Slaves tethered by long connecting twine sat cross-legged on the ground as they pulled dried meat and bread from pouches at their sides.

"Good morning." She nodded to one of the slaves whose grizzled beard had seen many years. His hands and feet oozed with angry sores along with sand-blasted skin. "Hang on. I'll fill your water skins." Hoisting the lid off the well nearby, she lowered a wooden bucket until it plunked against the water.

The bucket grew heavy as it filled. One pail filled

three skins, the next filled three more. By the time each vessel was full, her arms complained and sweat rolled down her temples. Still, anyone who'd traveled all night over sand dunes had a right to fresh water. No matter who they were.

"Danke." Blond hair straggled over a young man's forehead and into his eyes. His fair skin was mottled pink, with shades of red and brown. Had he been taken from a wife and child who waited for his return? She wanted to ask, wanted to know what had led him to this desert outpost as its captive. Any attention from her wouldn't bode well for his life, though. She'd slip a tray of flatbread to the men after the morning rush. And bring a jar of healing ointment they kept in the kitchen.

Servants carried dried lamb, cheese and bread to waiting customers in the large, timbered dining room. She headed for the kitchen at the far end of the room and ran smack into Louis, the cook.

"A table in the back needs more bread." Louis stood back and looked her up and down. "Hey, rice dress."

Louis was about her age as far as she could tell. Mother hired him after their aged kitchen manager ran away with a gypsy chieftain. Giselle scanned the young man's lanky frame which stooped a bit as if to bring the world into better perspective.

His hair was the color of sand, sometimes golden, sometimes tinged with red, depending on the light. It dangled into a wrinkle between brows that made him look perpetually confused. Or plotting. She wasn't sure which.

Was he…cute? Did she…

No. Just no.

Would she miss him?

7

That squinty gaze through eyes the color of heaven spoke of unauthorized capers that made life bearable. Louis was her only real friend in this desert outpost. It didn't matter that she didn't know where he'd come from or what brought him to the inn. He made her laugh. That alone made him a refuge of sorts.

Yes, she'd miss him.

Enough not to leave?

No.

Her stomach growled with the aroma of fresh bread. "I can see the empty table, thank you very much. Where were you when I needed your help with that rude merchant yesterday?"

"Doing my job." Louis waved a platter of bread under her nose. "Fresh out of the oven. The cheese is under a towel." He laid the dish on an oaken serving table and crossed his arms. "You're welcome."

Louis was irritating, but his food was amazing. And timely. Giselle slathered soft cheese on the warm bread and took a bite. Then held her belly in pleasure.

"Delicious, right?" he asked.

She rolled her eyes. "You know it is."

"Here. Turn around."

"Why?"

"Just turn around. It's your birthday. Right?"

Giselle kept her neck craned to watch him. He loved practical jokes, and it would never do to be snared in one of his tricks. He might douse her hair with flour and call her granny. Instead, Louis drew a delicate silver chain out of his pocket. A small key dangled from it as he placed it around her neck.

She touched it to be sure it was real. This was no ordinary key. It looked like an artisan had taken a grapevine, released a key inside, and covered it with silver.

"I dub thee Princess of the Gate," he said, fastening it around her neck.

Giselle looked up, startled. "What?" Papa repeated a prophecy since she was little. 'The breaker, who opens a way through the gate, bursts through doors of bronze and bars of iron.'

Not that she understood it. Those words were as empty as the place Papa left.

Louis stood. with that wrinkle deepening between his eyebrows. He'd face the heat of her mother, as well as the lion's share of work, after she left. Now he was giving her a sweet gift?

"You're supposed to say thank you."

"How did you know?" She wanted to blurt out the plan. Then again if he knew it meant leaving home, he'd try to stop her.

"I have my ways. This is a momentous birthday. Besides, I saw another gift in the kitchen with your name on it. It looked a mite practical."

Giselle knew without seeing the present. A new tunic from Mother. Her yearly replacement.

Louis side-stepped another servant. "Better get back to the kitchen."

She stood for a minute in the middle of the breakfast rush, grasping the necklace.

The key Papa had carried wasn't to show off his important position as gatekeeper. Guards searched from the battlements of the city walls day and night. With a single alarm, he rushed to close the gates to potential intruders. The safety of the city depended on his vigilance, and he never let them down. This necklace was a reminder that she was his daughter.

Not that she was like him.

Only days ago, she heard of a range of mountains where evil Magi kept their captives as slaves. There was nothing at the inn to hold her any longer. The camel train she chose traveled to the furthest Nayeli city. She'd take the adventure from there.

A rotund merchant walked through the back entrance, followed by a weaver of fine cloth. The marketplace beckoned from the open door, just as bustling and full of stories as their inn. The Gemini was open to Darras, as well as the rest of the world. They just had different entrances. The back doorway was open to any citizen who could afford a meal in the cool shelter of the inn.

"Louis." Her mother skirted a group of tradesmen on her way out the back door. "I'm leaving. Take over in the kitchen."

She peered at her mother, ruler of the Gemini Inn and her life. Would she miss her?

Not a chance.

Mother went to the palace at this time every week to deliver trays of pastries special to the king's heart. It took five servants and a wagon away from the inn during their busiest time. They traveled on the boulevard that led past homes built in semi-circles around the city's interior, through the marketplace, and to the far end, where the palace and temple stood side by side. What King Abusari wanted, he got hand delivered. The royal endorsement made Louis's baked goods famous, and business thrived.

A caravan from Egypt arrived with grimy, tired travelers. Sweat rolled under her arms and down her waist as Giselle hurried from table to table. She groaned when a shout broke through the chaos.

Trouble. Just after Mother left.

"Make way, make way!"

A flutter of rich fabrics appeared at the door that opened to the city. It couldn't be the king. Mother was still at the palace. The musky fragrance of oud permeated the air as she opened the door.

Oud was a rare aroma at the Gemini for good reason. Ordinary people couldn't afford perfume worth a year's wages. This visitor was some sort of royalty.

A square-faced priest who led a contingent of other clerics bowed slightly. "Good day, most excellent innkeeper." His mouth twisted into what could be a smile. Or an attempt to prove he was friend, not foe. "We seek entrance for the Highly Esteemed Servant of the Eternal Gad El Glas."

Ramaz, high priest of Gad El Glas? He didn't need permission in this city. Or anywhere else, for that matter. The entire Nayeli kingdom trembled at his presence. Wind gusted in with a plume of dust as the attendants parted way, allowing a man wearing a silken black robe to walk through. He paused at the doorway, as if waiting for a personal invitation.

Giselle opened her arms in welcome. She never saw the high priest inside the inn, or anywhere other than presiding over glittering ceremonies in the temple. When everyone fell to the ground in the dining room, her mind rushed back to the present. She was standing in the presence of the Highly Esteemed One. In a single move, she landed on her knees and toppled to the floor.

A stale piece of bread rested by her nose. Her necklace dangled against the tile. She smelled manure, probably camel dung. Would her new dress stink all day?

Then again, the floor cooled her sweaty body. When she peeked up, Ramaz raised his hands.

"Please. Be seated," he said, as if in benediction.

After an awkward silence, customers scrambled up and retreated to their meals. Giselle rose, too. Words stuck in her throat, and all she could do was point at a long plank table. A servant pulled out a chair and the priest settled himself.

Where was Louis? She cultivated a fish wife's shout guaranteed to bring him out of hiding. Then again, this was the one and only time she was called upon to serve the most influential man in their city. She smiled and lowered a tray of food on the table.

The priest's gaze followed her movements. "Hello, Giselle."

The Highly Esteemed One knew her name? If only she had a veil to cover the face Mother declared a forever open book. Fear threatened to paralyze her limbs and trail into her mind. She had to say something. Anything.

Constant work at the inn made her and Mother infrequent worshippers. Darras was a large city, though. Surely, they weren't missed. Were they in trouble?

"Giselle. That's your name, is it not?" His voice was rich and soothing against the chaos of his arrival.

Obviously, the man presided equally well over the holy and unholy, no matter where his feet tread. Giselle nodded.

"I thought so. Thank you for your hospitality." His dark eyes scanned her from head to toe.

Giselle tried to rub a smudge from the middle of her tunic, but it spread into a large blob.

The crow's feet around the man's eyes crinkled as he smiled. "What a lovely necklace."

Her hand rushed to grasp the ornate key. The high priest's manner was so attentive. Unlike the usual customers she served all day. Her heart began a slow thaw at his gentle tone, rare for a man of such stature. "Thank you. Sir. Today is my birthday."

"Ah. Sixteen? Full rights of citizenship in Darras. Is it true that you help your mother run the Gemini? Since you were a child?"

"Yes. Sir. Your…" She wasn't sure how to address him. Your Majesty?

"You welcome the world into our fine city with excellence. It hasn't gone unnoticed."

Giselle blushed with pleasure over the priest's words. He was far too important to be here, eating with commoners in their inn. Yet he took precious time out of his day to honor a nobody like her. She reached over to fill his cup with water.

A servant grazed her arm and whispered. "We're low on bread."

Now of all times, they ran short of the very bread that made them famous. Too late to whip up a fresh batch and Louis was nowhere in sight. She'd scrounge up whatever she could find in the pantry. When he suddenly appeared at her side, she hissed, "Where have you been?"

"None of your business." He notched one thumb toward the kitchen. "There are twenty-four rounds of flatbread, two legs of lamb, five barrels of ale, and forty-two customers. Tables three, six, and nine are done eating and ready to leave."

"How do you do that?"

Louis just looked at her. "What?" He shrugged and handed her a stack of circular loaves.

It was like he memorized everything in the busy kitchen, divided it by some unknown number and came out with the right amount of food, no matter how many hungry customers waited.

He lifted his hand, the first two fingers crossed.

It was their sign.

Only they knew what it meant. Sometimes the signal warned of an unruly customer or fight brewing. Often, it was support after a confrontation with Mother. It didn't mean anything to others. To her, it meant, "I'm here. No matter what."

The high priest and his company sat, quietly talking, as she exited the kitchen. Ramaz saw her and lifted his hand. She picked up a filled tray from the serving area and hurried to his table, avoiding the gaze of the square-faced priest who sat next to Ramaz. Embarrassment still stung from her unholy mess of a greeting.

"The food was delicious, and I'm refreshed. We appreciate your service."

Giselle curtsied and tried to gather empty plates without disturbing the priestly entourage.

"May I ask about your birthmark?"

Her hand rushed to the crimson stain on the inside of her forearm that throbbed without notice. She was supposed to keep the star-shaped blotch covered. Was it infected somehow?

The high priest's kind attention melted her defenses. Suddenly, she needed to explain why the birthmark was unique even though she kept it hidden. "I. My father had the same mark. Before he…." Her lower lip trembled.

"Oh, holy one. Have mercy." The voice jolted her to attention.

Mother stood, as unmoving as a pillar etched in

marble. Except that stone was too simple, too austere to describe the woman whose skin was bronzed ebony. Her amber eyes flashed like shards of glass. Her words were no plea. Couldn't she show respect?

Ramaz didn't stand, although he smiled. "Ursula of Basir. I've enjoyed a chat with your daughter."

"Indeed." Mother's response was like a stab. "You've honored the Gemini with your presence. How may I serve you today?"

"I received precisely what I came for." The high priest's gaze left Mother and returned to Giselle.

Her mother bowed with a tiny hitch in her otherwise graceful form. "May your day be blessed, O Esteemed One."

The priest raised his hand, and the clerics stood to their feet. "Indeed. It has already been truly exceptional." His black robe trailed over golden slippers.

An unnatural hush lingered in the usually chaotic dining room. A command sounded, and Ramaz and his company filed out the back entrance.

Mother's face was unreadable as she nodded toward the kitchen. "Follow me."

Louis was there, waiting.

"What? We don't have time for this in case you haven't noticed." She'd long since given up being civil.

Louis and Mother faced her like an unlikely, but impassable wall. Louis was her friend, and yet he stood beside Mother like an ally.

Mother lowered her head and studied her hands.

Her mother was never at a loss for words. Certainly not now, standing in the kitchen where they'd worked side by side for as long as she could remember.

The flash of memory, a moment long forgotten,

flooded her mind. She was a little girl, begging Papa to take her on one of his journeys.

He gathered his cloak and water skin as Mother prepared a cloth bag of food. "Not this time, little gnome. Meet me at the sundial on the morning of winter solstice. I'll be there."

The memory was so real, Giselle half-expected to see Papa walk into the kitchen with a hearty, "Shalom, my beauties!" She turned to her mother. "I remember…"

A strange reality pulled her out of the past. The kitchen was deserted. Odd in the hectic day that had shifted from morning to afternoon without her notice. The scent of evergreen drifted around her like a memory. There were no trees like that in Darras. Only once, long ago, had that fragrance filled her senses.

Mother's chest rose into one long breath as she turned to Louis. "Prepare the horses. We leave tonight."

"What? No."

Her mother's voice lowered several decibels. "You *will* leave. Tonight, after the gates have closed."

"Your life is in danger." Louis chimed in, strong and certain. Without warning, her teasing friend morphed into someone she didn't recognize.

Enough of petty rebellions, stuffed into her already aching gut. Droplets of spit flew into the air like tiny propellers. "You! You are *not* my commander. You're supposed to be my…" She choked on the word that came out anyway. "Mother."

She whirled to face Louis. "And you. I'd call you snake, but that would mean you have a backbone."

If it were bridges that needed burning, she'd incinerate them all.

Chapter 2

Giselle planted her feet, ready for a battle. She wasn't a trembling little girl anymore, vying for her mother's attention. She was leaving, all right. On her own terms.

A servant stuck his head inside the kitchen. "There's a fight brewing. A big one."

"I'll go." Louis hurried out.

More shouting followed by a crash from the dining room. First, Giselle and then her mother rushed into the dining room, where a man thundered. "Magi scum!"

"Peace, friend." Louis held his hands out, as if he might stop the rage spewing over the dining room.

"There is no peace with these maggots on earth, much less appearing in the revered city of Darras." The man puffed up like an indignant toad. It was Sir Damien, an ironsmith and frequent customer of the Gemini. Her eyes scanned the large room. No one looked threatening. A man, shrouded in a hood and traveling garb, sat hunched over a flask of ale at his table.

"Sir Damien. This man isn't harming anyone." Louis spoke in an even tone.

Giselle scanned the stranger. His dusty tunic was the same as any traveler who stopped for a break on a long journey across the desert. A tangled strand of dirty brown hair covered one eye. He wasn't Nayeli. Nothing about him appeared hostile, though.

Not that she'd ever seen a Magi. Once she peeked over a tight circle of kids as an old man at the marketplace whispered stories of glowering fiends who crept in through windows and devoured young children as they slept. She woke up screaming with nightmares until her mother discovered their source and wouldn't let her go back to the vendor's stall.

Magi were filthy thieves who lusted after Nayeli treasure. Darras was on constant guard from their invasions – especially from infiltrators who came to spy out their land. She couldn't bear to think that Papa had been taken captive, held in one of their dungeons. Or worse.

No. He was alive.

Somewhere.

His heart had been her North Star. Its brilliance was still in the heavenlies, set in place long before her world began. It led weary travelers when all other landmarks were obscured by darkness. She was always Papa's tiny satellite, pulled away only by unexplained journeys that kept him from the inn and from her.

Last week, a dusty camel trader droned about a wall extending around the Nayeli kingdom. Only the dreaded Magi knew how to cross the uncrossable and enter the mountains beyond.

Maybe Papa had been whisked away. Maybe he was there, waiting.

Sir Damien's words pulled her back to the present.

"So high and mighty." The man blustered. "Pretending we don't know what they're up to. I'll show 'im." Hoisting the heavy table in two arms, he tottered for a moment with the weight of the oak table. Then, hurled it toward the stranger.

Louis pushed Giselle out of the way with such force that she fell, sprawling to the floor. She sucked in a breath. The table wobbled midair, then shifted as if it had a will of its own. It landed yards in the opposite direction of the man's table and splintered against the tiled floor.

The stranger pulled back against the wall and finished a draught of ale.

Sir Damien's barrel-chest rose in alarming jerks as he stared at the table that had refused its target.

Mother faced Damien, fully in charge. "This man has come to the Gemini as our guest.

"You. Ursula of Basir. Of all women. Your husband rots in a Magi prison, and you defend them?"

"Stop." Mother drew herself up in a regal stance. "You refuse to acknowledge our refuge, which welcomes the outside world. You will leave. Now."

It was true. The Magi held Papa. No wonder he hadn't come home. Why wasn't Mother drilling the merchant for information instead of booting him out of the inn?

Damien's bluster shifted from uncertainty to outrage. He twirled around, commanding everyone's attention as he delivered a message for all. "The Gemini is no friend of the Nayeli. Or of mine. I'll not darken these doors again." He pivoted and stomped out the rear entrance.

Giselle glared at Mother. "How could you? You don't care that Sir Damien knows something about Papa?"

The stranger stood. He bowed his head to Mother and exited quietly through the front entrance.

One by one, customers left by the door to the market. Some left with a backward glance, others with eyes to the ground. In minutes, the dining room was empty.

Mother stuffed a stray lock of hair behind her ear and strode out the back door, her shawl dangling off one shoulder. "I'm going back to the palace. Handle things here."

Giselle stood, ready to scream at the woman already out of earshot. Gnawing on a ragged fingernail, she tasted dirt. She spat on the floor and shouted loud enough to clear the already empty inn. "Don't. Tell me. What to do. Ever again."

Evening light diffused in colors of rose and gold through windows that opened to western skies. She almost forgot.

Every adult in the city would be at the masquerade. She'd find Sir Damien and convince him to tell her what he knew. He wasn't her enemy, even if Mother treated him like one.

She was going.

As soon as she figured out what to wear.

The gown she was so proud of was torn from her leaping jaunt down the city walls and stained with who knew what from her stint on the floor. People spent months planning their costumes for the most coveted palace event of the year. She had one dress and a few shapeless tunics.

Mother, on the other hand, had a closet full of gowns fit for a leading business owner who was no stranger to the palace. Some girls raided their mother's closet. She hadn't been in Mother's room since Papa left.

No time like the present.

Silken shawls drooped over the ornate vanity. A ledger filled with facts and figures rested, open, in one corner of the room. Papa's woolen mantle hung over the bedpost. She buried her face into its comfort, looking for, but not finding his scent.

She'd often padded down the stairs at night when she couldn't sleep. A wavering light in the library meant he was still awake. Or, more likely, wrapped in a worn quilt, sound asleep with his face pressed against the upholstered chair and book dangling from his lap.

She missed his booming voice as he joined camel drivers and sojourners, besting their stories with adventures that made her heart pound and skin tingle. Mother shushed him when he came to the good parts. In her eyes, Papa was far too much – too loud, too boisterous, too undignified. His laugh could wake the dead, she said.

They needed some waking up in this empty place called home. Joy picked up and left their world shrouded in hues of ash.

Giselle steeled herself and opened the closet. She touched one gown, then another. A shimmer of gold appeared stuffed in the back. She caught her breath as she fingered the silken fabric, then dropped her hand. It was too fine. Besides, she never saw Mother wear it. Returning the gown, she remembered the folded tunic on the kitchen counter.

This wasn't stealing. It was payback.

In one motion, she slipped off the blue gown and stuffed it under the bed. Raising her arms, she let the dress settle over her head and billow over her frame in gentle waves. Then dared to look into the mirror.

What was she expecting to see?

Papa wasn't anywhere in the narrow chin that jutted out like the horny toad, ready to run at any moment. Her curves defied Mother's slender form, and unlike raven locks, her own curls looked like an abandoned bird's nest. She planted her feet for a short twirl, just to be sure there wasn't something, somewhere like the only two family members she'd ever known.

Nothing.

Clearly, she'd fallen to earth, proving that not everyone belonged where they landed.

Crystal vases filled with brushes, and jars of ointments lined the vanity in neat rows. Giselle dabbed a long brush into a pot of dark kohl, then stroked a broad line on her upper eyelid, curving it slightly at the edge. She lined the other eye and backed away to get a better perspective. Not bad. Even her nose looked straighter.

An earthen vial of almond oil filled the air with its sweetness when she removed its lid. She swept it through her curls until they fell into sleek waves and perfumed her neck with long strokes. Scarlet ointment stained her lips and highlighted cheekbones. With every stroke of color, nondescript features became a mysterious beauty.

Amazing.

All she needed now was a mask.

Chapter 3

Wind whistled through the maze of stone-walled corridors as Giselle hurried through the darkness.

Ridiculous. She barely knew these alleys in daylight, much less at night. Mother's demands at the inn successfully kept her out of whatever fun the city offered. Tonight, she planned to say *yes* to whatever adventure beckoned.

The low, haunting melody of the flute-like *ney* sounded through a shuttered window. At night, the true magic of the desert came to life. Searing heat transformed into cool breezes, and every living thing emerged from hiding.

There were a few nocturnal visitors no one wanted to meet. The Arabian wolf or even a rare caracal prowled outside city walls. Occasionally, a hooded cobra slithered in search of prey. Even now, jackals barked and howled from the hills beyond Darras.

Her heart bounced to her stomach and back when an owl swooped from a tree above and nabbed an unsuspecting mouse.

Who needed a masquerade, anyway? Her mother would be there. She'd call her out as a thief. Worse, if they *had* welcomed a Magi into the Gemini, the last place she needed to be was at the palace.

She stood quietly in the darkness. Velvety light of a full moon shone overhead, and countless torches lit the palace in the distance. She breathed deeply, letting her heart settle. Fear could shout all it wanted to. This time, it wouldn't ruin her fun or her journey to find Papa.

When a cat yowled from a vendor's stall, she hiked up her gown and sprinted the rest of the way to the palace.

Pale granite walls shimmered in torchlight. Sweat trickled down her back by the time she stood outside the massive entrance. She was late, so at least no one was around to tell her she was too stinky to be part of the festivities. When the lacy mask slipped on her nose, she sighed in relief.

She forgot. No one would recognize her with the mask. She'd search for Sir Damien, and no one could stop her.

It was a thought of pure liberty. Before she could change her mind, she rushed through another set of doors where a thousand lights stopped her in her tracks.

Giselle stood, blinking, at the top of a sprawling marble staircase. Chandeliers spanned a vaulted ceiling towering over a wonderland where fantastical creatures danced or chatted in tiny circles.

She never considered what to do once she arrived at the masquerade. Knowing everyone over sixteen was invited hadn't prepared her for the massive crowd pressed into every corner of the enormous room. Was she going to wander around like a lost child?

Her world extended only as far as the Gemini Inn. The scene before her was bigger than her wildest dreams. Then again, it was only a matter of time until Mother recognized the golden gown and ruined an amazing night. She spun on her heels to leave when crimson-clad attendants appeared on each side and escorted her down the stairs.

A breeze shifted the air as a masked couple whirled by in dance. Light danced across the stucco ceiling where trapeze artists hurtled over revelers. A clown juggled apples as he wound around the outskirts of the crowd. Being invisible was an unexpected bonus.

Until a faun looked up from its conversation and stared. An Egyptian queen whispered to a man whose black and white suit was painted in the perfect halves. A tabby cat, with long tail and furry ears, pointed in her direction.

She was imagining things. She searched the crowd for the burly ironsmith but couldn't pick him out of the throng of costumed revelers.

Warm cinnamon and nutmeg wafted from a table loaded with food. Just as she wondered if she needed permission to eat, a hefty woman dressed in folds of purple silk elbowed her way to the table. She loaded her plate full of tiny crimson cakes, stuffing in bite after bite like a ravenous squirrel.

Giselle nibbled on a tartlet of fresh raspberries and cream and sighed in delight. No one looked appalled, so she polished off three more pastries. Moving down a line of table after table, she stopped at an enormous unicorn ice sculpture that overlooked crystal glasses filled with clear bubbling liquid.

Its scent was sweet, far from the bitter ale they sold at the Gemini. There had to be a catch.

This was too good to be free.

She looked around again, took a sip, and then scanned the drink in wonder. It tasted like fresh blackberries on a summer day. Finishing the drink in one gulp, she hid the glass near a pile of napkins and grabbed another. And another. A buzz overtook her brain, and she didn't care if Mother appeared. This magical place said yes to anything her heart desired.

A court jester caught her eye across the room. Dressed in bright red and gold plaid, he wore curved satin slippers resembling scimitars. His mask was a leering grin with equally creepy eyes. Ebony feathers shot out above the mask and waved back and forth as he bobbed from one person to another.

Eww. He reminded her of a regular at the inn who guffawed at his own jokes, then sniggered like he enjoyed his own nastiness. The man whispered in one person's ear and laughed in a coarse jeer at others. He angled through the crowd in her direction.

People surrounded her on every side. There was no escape.

The jester slinked around bystanders until he reached Giselle. He leisurely scanned her from head to toe. "Ah, the innkeeper's daughter. Don't you look lovely." The man's voice revealed a smirk she couldn't see but knew was there.

Pastel macarons scattered like coins as she backed into the table. He knew her. How was that possible? Surely the mask kept her from being recognized.

Hot air breathed on one side of her face as the man leaned in. "Are you afraid, little one? Of me?" Metallic fabric brushed her shoulder.

Dread seeped over Giselle like a smelly blanket. Her birthmark throbbed with such heat she longed to tear away her sleeve. She couldn't run, couldn't punch the man. He might be someone she knew. Then again, this man was no friend. She whirled to face him. "Leave me." She mustered her deepest tone of voice. "Now."

"What if I don't?" The man crept closer like a snake looking for a warm place to coil.

Giselle pulled her hand into a fist. She could hit him. She'd never hit anyone, but something inside her told her she could, and she could do it hard, hard enough to knock him to the ground. Was this the part of her that was her father's? The side that had a quiet, violent streak within. Or was it the side of her that loved to shock her ever-refined mother? She didn't know but hoped this man would take one step closer.

Suddenly, the jester retreated. A way through the crowd appeared. Giselle looked around in surprise. A silent plan on her part wouldn't scare the jester. Her heart jumped as an angel appeared at her side.

He was a man dressed in shimmering black with silver wings. This creature was not Cupid with a bulging tummy and chubby arms. Sinewy muscle streamed down his bare arms, and a filigreed mask pressed over silken curls. Wings extended over his shoulders, keeping him at a distance from lesser beings.

Her knees weakened. Perhaps he was a messenger sent from an unseen divinity. Not that she would know. She heard about sacrifices at the temple. Their god wasn't one to rescue.

This man, on the other hand, smiled down at her as if he knew her. And liked her.

The jester melted away into the crowd as the man bowed and guided her to the center of the ballroom.

The crowd opened before them.

It was only the atmosphere of this carnival. Still, uncertainties melted away in the man's arms. Like the fact she didn't know how to dance. When she stumbled on the hem of her gown, the man lifted her into a twirl as if it had been his plan all along. Unlike being stripped by the jester's stare, this man held her as if she were a newly discovered treasure.

Couple after couple made way for them. Most costumed revelers ignored her and openly stared at her regal dance partner. Why wouldn't they? She peeked up from time to time, trying not to look like what she was – a swooning teenager.

The mask was exactly what she needed it to be. Who needed reality? Tonight, she was a mysterious beauty of undetermined royalty who waited for this moment and for this man all her life.

When the orchestra paused for a break, the angel-clad man pulled her into a quiet corner where servants appeared with trays of drinks and morsels of food. He bowed slightly to each one and offered her a crystal glass.

She sipped furiously from the glass as her leg brushed his, hoping that it didn't put her brain into more of a spin. Then again, a little magic fuel might keep this fairy tale from disappearing as quickly as it arrived.

Lifting his mask, he rested it for a moment on the crown of his head. "Apologies. It's hard to breathe with this thing." His face looked both worn and youthful. Black hair curled around the back of his mask. It was his eyes that made her shiver with equal parts of joy and terror. They were darker even than her own. And intent, as if he studied a gemstone. "What is your name, lovely one?"

Giselle swallowed hard and hiccupped. She tried not to squeak. Still, her voice came out like a strangled camel. "Giselle."

"My name is Makir. Your name means promise, I

believe."

She tried to think of something riveting, but nothing came to mind. It was only a matter of time before the celestial man discovered she was an uninteresting mortal.

A trumpet call came to her rescue. Dancing couples whirled to an abrupt stop as each instrument in the orchestra hushed its melody. Trapeze artists dropped from their bird's eye perch and retreated to corners of the room. A man dressed as a rooster stood, hands behind his feathered back and head bowed.

Makir lowered his head and shifted on the bench.

Another trumpet blared, and then another and another. The sound ricocheted through the ballroom as an unrelenting summons. A uniformed herald marched in with maidens carrying multi-colored banners on each side. The man extended his arms to the crowd and shouted. "King Abusari of Darras, divine benefactor of the Nayeli people."

King Abusari entered the massive foyer as though it was a stage, swishing a patchwork of brocade and velvet fabrics that traveled in the wake of his short, squat body. His jewel-encrusted crown towered overhead as if to compensate for his missing height.

"My friends," the king said with an expansive tone. "Welcome to this night of revelry. I'm honored to serve as your High Regent and King." A deep breath shifted his rotund body in a show of immense pride. "May I introduce two illustrious guests to our festivities."

At his words, a woman appeared and stood beside the king. She was taller than him and commanded a presence that overshadowed the stubby monarch. Her gown was designed entirely of black and white feathers that clung to her statuesque frame. A crown of silver spikes rose above black plaited hair, and a porcelain mask adorned with jewels covered her face.

When King Abusari bowed, she lifted the mask. Her eyes narrowed as she searched the crowd below. In minutes, her gaze landed in Giselle's direction, then to Makir.

Suddenly, the crowd retreated around her and the angelic dance partner. The man nodded slightly to Giselle, then strode through a silent pathway. Feathered wings brushed the ground as he ascended the staircase.

At the top of the stairs, he bowed first to King Abusari and then took his place beside the woman. When a chorus of trumpets cleared the air of any other noise, a herald proclaimed, "Queen Naifa, Queen of the Eastern Mountains, and her son, Crown Prince Makir."

Giselle stood frozen in shock. The court jester's voice hissed from behind. "Better run while you can." When she twirled to face him, he disappeared back into the crowd.

This evil man chose her as his target, even though she didn't recognize anything in his sinister ways. An absent person poked through the festivities of that evening like an answer. Mother never missed a masquerade, yet she was nowhere in sight.

Giselle sucked in a trembling breath.

What if the jester heard about the confrontation with Sir Damien? That was it. He knew her and Mother were in trouble. This wasn't about being an innkeeper's daughter. This was about being *the* innkeeper's daughter.

She stood, wavering, as King Abusari extended his hands benevolently over the crowd below. "Please. Enjoy."

Everyone scrambled back in place. Musicians rearranged sheet music and tuned stringed instruments into a tangle of chords as discordant as the atmosphere around them.

Makir scanned the crowd as he chatted with the king. Was he looking for her? Her heart jumped. Maybe tonight, her fortunes truly changed.

Hope swirled like an unaccustomed phantom through her mind. The next minute, it found wings and raced away.

This whole evening was only a tiny reprieve. Unlike the masquerade, her life at the Gemini Inn was no fantasy. The dazzling prince wouldn't be interested in someone like her, far from the alluring beauty he imagined. Underneath the stolen dress hid a gnome, not a princess, who cleaned up people's messes and was never brave enough to venture out of a life she hated.

Even more terrible, according to Nayeli law, she was a potential traitor.

Elbowing her way through the crowd, she dashed into the night air. A maze of hedges stood before her like a leafy stockade. She was thoroughly lost in its devilish puzzle until torchlight flickered through the hedges and footsteps sounded on the pavement nearby.

With one more turn, the roadway spread out before her. She almost burst out of the hedges until a man and woman peeked out from a narrow alley. Black tendrils of the woman's hair fell out from an embroidered mantle.

She knew that cloak.

Her mother looked straight at her. Not with a maternal look of love. This was pure terror. Grabbing the man's elbow, they retreated into the shadows.

Giselle stood in the street, dumbfounded.

Mother recognized her, then ran away as if she carried the plague.

Her reaction meant one thing. She was hiding the stranger Sir Damien accused of being Magi at the inn that afternoon. Her mother knew the man was a hated enemy all along. Not only that, she defied Nayeli law by helping him escape.

That crime meant execution. Authorities weren't picky about arresting co-conspirators. Any family member would do.

Their world was poised to fall apart, and Mother added to the ruin. Clearly, her daughter was a worthless pawn. If she thought leaving would chink the stone of the woman's heart, she was wrong. There was no reason to linger, no reason to stay for a family that didn't even exist.

She'd find Papa. There was no grid for anything without him.

Hiking up the golden gown, she ran through the night, sticking to alleys and back roads until she reached the Gemini. She dashed up the stairs to her room, and jabbed clothes into a cloth bag. Her gown fell to the ground in one motion, as if suddenly tired. An almost clean tunic was fine for tonight.

She had to hurry. The camel trains were ready to leave. It was time for her, too. With a long breath of regret, Makir and the masquerade faded into a mirage, lovely, though best forgotten.

Before checking her conscience, she hurried to Mother's closet and pried open a slat of wood. The money chest opened to coins of all sizes and shapes. Some were Nayeli, and others were from travelers around the world who paid with their own currency.

The staff, including Louis, pocketed wages at the end of each week. Not her. She was less than an indentured servant.

She grabbed fistful after fistful of coins, stuffed them into a pouch, and tied it around her neck. She closed the chest and replaced the wooden plank.

Papa's cloak hung on the bedpost. It was the lowest form of stealing. Right now, she needed it more than Mother. She wrapped herself in the mantle, stifling tears as she hid the coins.

The kitchen was quiet. Louis must have gone out for the night. She gathered bread, cheese, and dates into a pack, then filled a waterskin. Her breathing thrashed around like an intruder lurked nearby. Or like she was leaving the place called home.

She was a child here. According to Papa, she toddled between busy servers, snitching fresh bread, and charming customers with a toothless grin. Years later, it was the battlefield where she and Mother waged war.

Peering around the deserted inn confirmed what she already knew.

It wasn't much of a home anymore.

She'd miss Louis's smiles and funny ways. Her heart would always wonder what might have been with the handsome prince. The rest was a knot of pain better left behind.

The lead driver, wrapped from head to toe in fabrics to shield him from desert sands, bowed. It was odd that she didn't recognize the man, even though only his eyes peered from under a dusty turban. She knew most drivers whose treks made Darras a stopping point.

She slowed her steps, longing to run back to the safety of the Gemini. Instead, she blurted out, "A passage. Please."

The man scanned her briefly, without expression. "Twenty drachmas."

It was an outrageous price, and he knew it.

She turned away and scoured the money bag. Selecting a few coins, she hid the pouch beneath her tunic. "This is all I have."

His hands, mottled by blazing sun, pocketed the money and yelled a command.

She'd heard that voice before. Impossible, though.

Taking her place at the end of the line, she knew one thing. There would be no riding. The cash bought her a slave's passage. She'd have to find a way to keep up, even though her legs were already jiggly with fatigue.

Night creatures scurried through the dry brush, and a hoot owl called a warning. Events of the day tumbled around her mind. Pieces of life for the last sixteen years sent out tentacles to draw her back. She steeled her insides.

City walls towered behind a giant fortress as she trudged behind a baying camel. There were no tearful goodbyes, no signpost that shouted, "You're free."

She didn't feel liberated. She felt afraid and alone.

Something skittered across her foot. She turned, expecting a hare to leap out of the brush. Instead, calloused hands covered her mouth and dragged her into the darkness.

Chapter 4

Bright light pressed against Giselle's eyes. It didn't matter. She was too tired to open them. She wanted to speak except opening her mouth and forming words was impossible. Her mouth was so dry she couldn't spit, much less speak.

A donkey brayed, loud and complaining in its pen.

No. Someone was laughing.

Shadows bobbed here and there through patches of light until a face appeared with unruly black eyebrows that arched into a single line. A woman dressed in an assortment of checks, plaids, and paisleys picked her teeth with a long fingernail as hoop earrings swung back and forth. "She's a purty one, fer sure." Her voice boomed louder. "Hullo, dear. Me name be Carnation."

"Leave her alone. She'll be in dreadful angst when she comes to her senses." A man who sounded like a professor spoke in clipped consonants and plump vowels.

The aging gypsy queen leaned in to study Giselle's face. "She don't look skeert. Only a mite stupid."

"I'm. I'm not. Stupid." Giselle sat upright and bumped into Carnation's nose. She tried to rub her eyes, but her hands were bound. "Where am I?" She sputtered before gathering more words. "Who are you?"

Now that she could see better, the elderly man didn't look like a cultivated gentleman at all. He looked ragged and hungry.

"Important questions that require an answer," he said. "Ferdinand Porcellio, at your service. This is my friend, Carnation Penelope Theodosia Hester." He took a deep breath to replenish his lungs and pulled on his ring finger, as if by habit. "We do wish we could take you back home. Unfortunately, that is not to be."

A fleeting thought crossed Giselle's mind. Her mother twisted the finger where she still wore her wedding ring. Was the old man a widower? He and Carnation weren't exactly a matched set.

"Ignore Ferdie." Carnation's chin jutted out in indignation. "He sez fourteen words when one will do. We be needing bargaining potential and ye were available."

Giselle had seen Ferdinand somewhere. Was it yesterday? Last week? Something had stolen time and taken her with it. In a moment, she remembered. "I saw you outside the Gemini. You were a slave."

"True. Circumstances have changed radically since your very long nap." He sighed so deeply his narrow shoulders rose with the effort. "Carnation and I are free, although not as liberated as we will be when we obtain money for travel. That's where you come in."

"How? I don't have anything to give you." The heaviness of coins against her chest was gone. The money pouch was gone. Whoever captured her also robbed her blind. She had nothing left to bargain for her freedom.

Carnation's brow crinkled in sadness. "Ah, but you do. You have a price on yer head. A fine one, at that." She lifted a water skin to Giselle's mouth and let her drink.

Giselle gulped the water, then turned to the bedraggled gypsy. "You're going to sell me?"

"Did you think we was going to eat you? We ain't cannibals." The woman flumped out her skirt like a schoolgirl at her first dance.

"That would be correct." Ferdinand spoke decisively, as if relieved to be certain of this fact. "Renegade slaves, yes. Flesh-eaters, definitely not."

"I have a fam…" Giselle stopped mid-sentence. Ferdinand and Carnation probably had families, too. That hadn't kept them from being captured and sold. "But I am…

"Special? Of course." Ferdinand shrugged, half-apologetically. "Perhaps you can explain what makes stealing someone from home and breaking his back in the salt mines wrong for you and right for us?"

Carnation adjusted a tangled scarf against her brow with a hand pocked with painful sores. "He talks so high and mighty. Me, I'm a plain talker."

"Agreed," said the old man. "You talk. And talk. And talk. All night, you talked."

"Hush, now. Didn't see you on that bag o' bones camel all night – jest to babysit girlie here."

"You…" Giselle stammered.

"Held ye in my lap like a wee one." Carnation tried to hold her pride but couldn't. "Had a little help sleeping, ye did. Ferdie here had a potion just right for traveling across the desert all night and not stirring up a fuss."

"You drugged me?" That explained why her brain was as stuffed with cotton as her mouth. Betrayal by this genteel old man stung. Then again, she was snatched outside the gates of her city. Evidently, there weren't any rules when it came to absconding with an innocent citizen.

"A gift, although, in truth, it was administered without your permission. You didn't seem to mind. You slept like the proverbial baby." Ferdinand glared at Carnation. "Would you rather have walked on shifting sand for hours without a proper cup of tea?"

Giselle struggled to bring her thoughts into a full sentence. A small feat when what she really needed was a plan. Moving her body for a real escape was out of the question. She could barely lift her head.

She tried to beg, to reason, to plead, but her words fell out like a bag of rocks. "I'll...work for you. I can cook, clean. My mother and I run an inn. I have skills." She finally blurted out a weak coup d'état. "Besides, we never owned slaves at the Gemini. Papa wouldn't allow it."

"Good for Papa. Nayeli's wealth would be nothing without the slave trade. We stood on your platforms. Our families wept as traders dragged us away. Our bodies ached with labor. A network of tyranny extends from your fair city like tentacles to the world outside."

"How did you get away?"

"We paid mightily for the first leg of this journey. To Nayeli thugs, sadly."

Neither of her aged captors seemed dangerous. They didn't have the meanness to carry out her kidnapping, unlike the men who lounged in the distance.

One sharpened his dagger in long, even strokes against a flint. The other man gnawed on a piece of dried meat and washed it down with crimson liquid that trickled down his beard. He nodded in her direction. She looked away quickly, sorry that she'd made eye contact.

"Be kerful of those two, lovey." Carnation's

warning was low and whispered. "Criminals, they be."

"Necessary for our escape last night, though. And for navigating our way to Apamea." Ferdinand was equally subdued, keeping his head bowed. "We'll be rid of them as soon as we arrive at our destination."

"The camel drivers? Are they…"

Ferdinand shook his head, and Carnation examined her sandaled feet.

Giselle remembered the drivers' loping gait. They grinned as they entered the Gemini, tired and ready for a break after their night-long journey across the desert. They were used to dangers along the dry highway of sand. After all, they carried slaves, loads of salt, and other treasures to the Darras market year after year.

This was no caravan. With only a few camels, they were mere nomads, alone in the desert and without protection. The whole scenario was scary enough without being held as a slave. Did they know how scary?

Heat rose in waves from the dunes outside the oasis. A wave of dizziness overwhelmed her, and she leaned her head against her knees.

Ferdinand offered her another drink of water from his skin as she leaned against a palm tree. "Rest while you can. Evening will come soon enough, and we'll travel with it."

"Untie my hands. Please."

Ferdinand glanced at the two men and shook his head. "The camels. I must tend to them. Forgive me." He practically ran toward the small herd tied nearby.

She hated the thought of being left alone. Instead, she followed Ferdinand, hands still bound but grateful for his gentle presence.

A man with blond hair, tied back with a leather

thong, loaded heavy chunks of salt. His arms strained as he hoisted the pillars onto seated camels and tied them on. His fair skin was mottled, battered by desert sun.

She recognized the sunburned hands that took her payment the night before. And silenced her scream as he hauled her into the darkness. He stole her money. The water skin and food she packed from the inn were gone, too.

This man, disguised as a camel train driver, was part of the plot to rob and abduct her. If he hadn't murdered the innocent drivers, he hadn't stopped the ones who had.

Carnation noticed her gaze. "That be Erik. He'll be going home, like the rest of us. Most of us, anyway. He don't want to come around. Embarrassed, he is."

"He's not used to being a lawbreaker. Or a captor, for that matter." Ferdinand knelt to hug a pillar of salt and tugged. The load didn't budge. He sighed in frustration as if an old enemy bested him.

"No need to be embarrassed. He's a perfectly good liar and thief." These people weren't friends. They grabbed her on purpose and schemed to take her to the nearest slave platform. If they thought she was an easy target, she'd prove them wrong.

Carnation half squatted by a tower of salt. Digging her feet into the sand, she pushed with ample hips until it toppled over one end. She threw up her hands and muttered an undefined curse.

Erik motioned Ferdinand and Carnation away as he took over the job. He lifted one load with long, sinewy arms that strained with the weight.

He tricked her. They all had. They planned to sell her for the highest price at the first slave market. Why should she help? Then again, if someone untied her hands, she could run away at some point.

Holding her chin high, she faced Erik. "If you untie me, I'll help."

Together, they hoisted the first pillar and balanced it over one of the camel's backs. Over and over, they lifted salty towers over the hairy beasts, avoiding their broad, flat teeth that could take a hard nip. She was exhausted and drenched with sweat by the time they were done and ready to leave.

Carnation and Ferdinand tethered the camels one after another into a line as Giselle plopped down under the shelter of an acacia and dangled her feet in a pool of water.

Erik handed her a battered water skin. It was her own. "Not too fast," he said as he offered the water. "Take your time."

Giselle slowed down to sips and studied her abductor, who gazed over the vista of sand dunes that extended in every direction around them. "Are you a murderer or mercenary? Or both."

Erik took a long drink from a crinkled water skin. His tone softened. "Erik Vallen, once a fisherman from the north country. Now a freed slave."

"You forgot captor and murderer." Only the chirp of a nearby desert sparrow sounded in the stillness. "How did you end up in the desert?"

Finally, he spoke. "I'd just said goodbye to the polar night. Light rose from the horizon for the first time in two months." He glanced up, then back to the ground, refusing to keep eye contact. A learned behavior when a prolonged stare could bring a beating.

"I knew the danger of the elements, blizzards, sudden storms on the fiords. I kissed my dead sister good-bye. But I never knew sun that beat like the drums of our captors. I'd never worked in the salt mines, my very breathing steeped in salt, with thirst never quenched."

Mines appeared out of the sandy haze of the desert. They were cut from ancient seabeds.

Salt was their only preservative for food in the arid climate where there was no ice. Their desert was the chief natural source of rock salt, its most desirable form.

"I've heard of the mines but never seen one."

"A steady stream of slaves is essential. Most die within the first year. Not to worry, though. Salt is as valuable as gold. What's a life compared to all that cash? Gold wins every time."

Foreign languages murmured beyond the stalls of exotic spices and silks at the marketplace. Bare backs strained with salt pillar after salt pillar outside as slaves loaded them onto waiting camels. She'd never questioned whether it was wrong or right. It just was.

The sun began its downward journey as they finished a meal of dates, flatbread, and water. Erik handed her the skin of water, food, and money pouch he'd taken. "You'll need these. No stops on the way to Apamea."

When one of the Nayeli men lashed his whip into the air, Ferdinand and Carnation pulled themselves from the ground and took their places beside the line of camels. Erik moved ahead, sandwiching Giselle between them.

"Take heart, dearie," Carnation murmured. "Tis' a long night, though not forever."

Forever changed in one decision to run away from home.

By now, work at the Gemini slowed, and Mother retreated into her room without much of a goodnight to anyone. Louis would still be in the kitchen, finishing the day and preparing for the next morning. They'd had a towel fight the last time she tiptoed in for a quick snack.

If only she had the strength to muster up more rage. She chose to leave for her own survival and to find Papa. That didn't keep her heart from aching in countless ways. Anger and fear traded blows whenever she thought about Mother's possible arrest and execution.

This couldn't be the end. After all, her hands were free. Night was coming. She'd escape into the darkness, rest until morning, and return to Darras.

As if in answer to her thoughts, Erik tied her hands, then took his place between her and the Nayeli men.

She spit on the ground. "A pox on you."

Her heart pounded and calves ached with each slough through the deep sand. Erik tried to help her up when she tripped, but she jerked her hand away. "Don't touch me." She didn't need help from her captor. She'd get free despite him.

That night was a never-ending night with only the plop, plop of camel hooves, and poofs of sand as she walked. Her feet hurt, and thirst pounded against her throat.

A light breeze lifted a lock of her hair. Temperatures dropped as night replaced dusk. Giselle shivered, wishing she could wrap her arms around her chest. Her mind spun with plan after plan. She needed a weapon. At the very least, she'd find a sharp rock to sever the rope that bound her to the camel and the rest of the train.

She chewed on the rope, salty with dusty grit. Just a little longer. She was startled and hid her hands when

Erik turned and pointed overhead.

"Look."

The Milky Way wavered through the stars in a brilliant haze. Louis. Stargazing on the roof at the end of a long day. A pang of regret that had its own voice.

A dim outline of Ursa Major glimmered near the familiar Polaris. She called her mother the Great Bear, making her presence known even in the night sky. Mother knew by now that she was gone. Would she care?

"Seems odd to admire the sky when you're leading me to a slave platform. Are you Magi?"

"No. Although, I'm acquainted with their lore." Erik kept his eyes on the sky. "An old man and fellow captive taught me his knowledge of the stars. Turns out the Magi don't permit slavery. They believe each person carries a gift of infinite value. Like the stars, that gift carries a symbol or clue of its presence. People are ignorant – or choose to use people for their own purposes because it's convenient." He turned to her with an appraising glance. "He gave me hope."

"What happened to him?"

"He died one night when we were driven hard across the desert. 'Seek the sign of the Magi,' he said. 'You'll be safe with them.'" Erik pulled a sticker from his heel and kept walking. "The nearest city is north of here. We'll be there by morning."

She wasn't planning to be sold. She'd escape long before that happened. Still, a question nagged like a pesky fly. "What is it like standing there, waiting to be...bought?"

"Have you seen animals on the platform?" His voice faltered. "It's like that. Is he young? Can he bear heavy loads? Is she pretty? Then, of course, some are gifted in special ways. Like Magi. They bring a premium price."

"There's nothing special about Magi."

"Where have you been hiding? In a hole?"

"Magi are deceitful liars. They hate the Nayeli. We hate them."

"Of course, you're right, being Nayeli and all. History tells a different story of counselors to kings, sought out for their wisdom. Their gifts are tied to the heavens. They are *sent ones*, commissioned to bless the world around them."

"That's not what I've heard."

"You heard wrong. Their gifts are greatly coveted. They are a target for many a treasure hunter hoping to merchandise what they carry."

"What kind of gifts do they supposedly have?"

"The ability to see the unseen, for one. For another, the power to unlock doors impossible for others."

"I've never met one. Well, maybe once. How can you tell a person is Magi? The man I saw looked pretty ordinary."

"Sometimes there's a sign in their bodies, as though their very cells affirm the gift. Like, the eyes of a seer might appear as starbursts surrounded by blue sky. Each person is a treasure cloaked in mystery until you care enough to ask. Their goal is to help, not to harm. Unlike the lies you've heard."

"I see you didn't adopt Magi ways. You're selling me to finance your flight. What did it take to sell your soul?"

"Being a slave for ten years and in the mines for far too long." He spoke simply. "The Nayeli perfected slavery for that very reason. This is only payment for time and suffering. I have no way to escape without money for food and travel. You're Nayeli. Someone will take pity on you."

"You're scum."

"True. You're worth far more than me."

There was no reason to waste her breath. The man refused to argue.

A shadow moved around the outcroppings of sandstone and then disappeared. Nayeli lore spoke of dragons that lurked outside their kingdom. She needed a good one right now to swoop down and blast her abductors. Still, the tales she'd heard were only myths whispered on nights to scare children. "Be good, now. The dragon watches for naughty children."

Whatever.

When a weird hum rose and swirled around the dunes, she whirled around, longing for someone, anyone to run to for safety. Terror rose inside as the dunes sang a strange dirge that whispered, then roared and whispered again.

No one around her seemed to care. Nothing interrupted the gentle plodding feet mingled with camel's hooves. She squeaked out a question. "What's that sound?"

Erik's voice was full of wonder and not a bit afraid. "The sand dunes sing as they shift. Perhaps they speak a message to us."

A mystic.

Great.

The only message she needed was how to get out of these bonds and away from there. She wasn't sure how far they were from the nearest city. There was a constant stream of trains back and forth from Nayeli cities, though. She'd find one.

At daybreak, Grecian columns of Apamea broke the horizon, looking more like ancient Athens than a desert kingdom. The sun rose beyond the sandstone walls, washing them in deep rose hues.

The knot finally untangled with a mix of spit and gnawing. Her mouth was sore, and jaws ached, but she was free. She kept her hands tucked away under her sleeves and pressed the water skin against her chest. All the better to run fast.

Erik stood, peering back to where they'd just traveled. "Look."

Rusty brown clouds filled the western sky and boiled toward them. Taking a long step back, she almost stumbled over Carnation and Ferdinand, who appeared at her side.

Furious cloud banks like that often raced toward the Gemini. Everyone, slave or free, hurried for cover when waves of dust and sand tumbled toward the city. At the inn, they drenched sheets with buckets of water and fastened them over each window, top and bottom. Then huddled in the kitchen, the only room without windows, as winds roared outside, and sandy dust grew in piles on the dining room floor. Even afterward, grit lingered against her teeth and made her stomach churn.

This storm was so huge it had its name in their desert land.

Haboob.

A strange name that didn't sound sinister. Unless you had no shelter.

Like now.

Chapter 5

The Nayeli brutes lost no time. They didn't stop to unload the camels they led. Instead, they ran toward Apamea, long legs sprinting around sand dunes until they were only specks in the distance.

Ferdinand and Carnation held on to each other. Erik planted his feet, a feeble stance against the massive sandstorm.

There was one plus, although it didn't matter much right now. They inherited a couple of extra camels and the goods they carried. The camels would do fine in the storm. Nostrils closed, long eyelashes, and even an inner eyelid protected their eyes. They were made for survival in the desert.

Unlike them.

Nothing stopped her from running away like the two Nayeli men. She rubbed her freed wrists, knowing she could outrun the storm if she left now. She'd worry about hiding once she made it to the busy city.

Carnation twirled around and grabbed her arm with Ferdinand in tow. "Oi! The hounds of hell be comin' fer us."

Ferdinand placed a frail arm around her shoulder. All three crowded around as if she was their deliverance.

She wasn't. Why should she care? She owed them nothing.

A memory rose of another sandstorm years before.

Bells in the watchtower had pealed in warning. Papa hurried to close the massive gates before debris filled the city's entrance. They hung water-soaked fabric over every window and doorway. She struggled with a blanket at her bedroom window when an old woman appeared outside the towering walls of Darras.

Where had she come from, and why hadn't she run for shelter? Maybe she was deaf. The woman's mouth opened in a cry the howling wind swallowed.

No one knew she was there. No one heard her. Except Giselle.

She hurried down the stairs and burst into the kitchen where customers and servants alike had taken cover. "There's someone outside!"

Papa doused one towel and then another in water. He wrapped one around his nose and mouth and dangled the other over his eyes.

Mother spoke softly. "Basir. No."

He pulled away from her grasp. When Giselle tried to follow, he handed her, kicking and fighting, to Mother who held her with an iron grip. When her mother left to tend to a frightened customer, Giselle wrapped her face in a scarf and sneaked out the door.

The wind was a roar outside. Suddenly, she was afraid. Papa could be blinded by the wind-driven debris or struggle to breathe as sand filled the air. She had to make sure he was safe.

She pushed against the door with all her strength and fell onto the tiled portico. Sand spattered in hard pits against her skin. She pulled the scarf tighter and crawled toward the faint outline of Papa's figure, bowed low as he crept toward the gates. Grit filled her mouth and crunched against her teeth. Howling wind swallowed her words when she yelled. "Papa! I'm here!"

Papa looked like a dark phantom as he leaned against the metal lock and pushed. Once the doors opened, rushing sand would build its own wall. An open gate was an entrance for the wrath of the storm.

Suddenly, the metal doors cracked open with the suck of a giant's breath. A body fell inside.

Giselle couldn't close her eyes in time to unsee the aged woman's face. Sand spilled out of grey eyes and gaping mouth. It flowed from her wrinkled face and down her neck like a dusty stream. Limp gray hair spun in a wild dance in the wind, as if somehow, somewhere, life went on.

As she knelt, frozen in place, Papa strained against the weight of the doors. Suddenly, Mother appeared and dragged her back inside the inn.

She'd never forgotten where mounds of sand buried an old woman just inside the city gates. Papa coughed and heaved grimy phlegm for days. Two weeks later, he was gone.

Giselle rubbed her wrists as Carnation wailed in Ferdinand's arms. Erik stood, stoic, beside them. If they didn't find a safe place soon, sand would pelt their skin like buckshot and blind their eyes. Tree limbs, dried mesquite, and who knew what else would plummet out of nowhere. Carnation and Ferdinand's old lungs would fill with dust.

She understood their fear. They didn't know the desert and couldn't defend themselves against the fury of a sandstorm.

She felt the same horror when they captured her.

Time was running out. She had to run now.

She glanced back to Carnation in Ferdinand's

stooped embrace. They had no idea what to do. Even Erik looked around, scanning the perimeter as if somehow help would show itself.

The air was full of twirling silt. The memory of the old woman's lifeless eyes returned, as if to haunt her. Or to give her an answer.

She couldn't leave. Carnation. Ferdinand. Erik. They'd never get home. No one would know they died in the desert, buried in a grave of sand without markers or any trace of the people they'd been. Their journey just began. It couldn't end now.

No reason to hide her freed hands any longer. "I need your headband. And your sash."

Red curls swirled with gray spilled out over Carnation's eyes as she ripped off both fabrics and handed them to Giselle, who soaked them with water from Erik's battered water skin and handed them back.

"Wrap them around your nose and mouth. Use this one for your eyes."

Erik helped Ferdinand until each of them had a wet layer around their mouth and nose and another over their eyes. Together, they tethered the camels around a small grove of mesquite trees.

The air was too full of dust to take a deep breath without coughing her guts out. She covered her face, partly shielding her eyes with a piece of fabric she'd torn from the hem of her tunic.

Erik ran toward a large sand dune. "We can hide on the other side."

"No. We'll be buried there. Help me find a hole in one of those stone outcroppings ahead. The higher, the better."

"Remain here, Carnation. I'll help Erik." Ferdinand

tried to pull himself out of Carnation's grasp and lurched forward into the sand when she refused to let go.

Giselle yelled over the rising wind. "Stay with Carnation. We'll be back."

They looked old and abandoned. The wind blew harder as sand rose around them like twisting pillars.

The storm barreled closer. If it hadn't taken so long to decide to save three people, they'd have more time. She and Erik scaled one last hill of rocky outcroppings.

"I found something!" Erik pointed to the leeward side of a group of stony pillars.

It didn't matter how big it was. It had to work.

The sky grew dark. Wind blasted their faces and pushed them back as they raced to Ferdinand and Carnation. Carnation hid under the wild skirt and her pantaloons flapped in the wind like a gypsy tent. Erik retrieved Ferdinand, who fell to the ground with the force of the gusts.

Erik and Giselle made the last climb, with Ferdinand and Carnation in tow. A rock shard flew by like a leaf in a gusty breeze. It smacked Giselle's arm so hard that blood trickled over her forearm and spread over the birthmark like a crimson web.

Erik glanced at the wound, then into her eyes so quickly that Giselle couldn't say for sure he even noticed she was bleeding. Surely, he wasn't worried about a flesh wound when their lives were at the mercy of this storm.

Giselle dragged Carnation to the top of the sand dune that surged like a wave under their feet. She helped the old woman lower her behind into a small cavity. "Here. Sit right here."

Erik came alongside Ferdinand and positioned him next to Carnation. He tugged Giselle's sleeve. "Get in.

Now."

"There's no room for you." Three of them would fill the space with no room left for Erik's tall, lanky body. "Ferdinand. Let Erik sit first. You're lighter. Hurry!"

Ferdinand crawled out on his hands and knees as Erik sat down, then positioned the old man across his chest and legs.

"Carnation. I'm sitting on your lap!"

"Me yap?"

No need to wait for permission. She lowered herself into the pillowy softness of the gypsy's ample thighs.

Stacked on each other, they pressed their backs against the wall of the tiny stone fortress so that only their legs dangled outside as wind roared overhead and around. They huddled together quietly except for Carnation's moans and Ferdinand's low shushing to comfort her.

Sand and debris that hurtled from behind would've buried them if they faced the other direction. Shadows descended like Papa's woolen cloak she used to cover her head and face. Why didn't she left when she could?

Fear screamed along with the storm that was determined to destroy them. She was stupid to think they could escape. She'd die here and Mother would never know. They'd all suffocate, buried without a trace.

On and on winds roared as they leaned into the rock and each other, pressing faces into each other's chests, as sand and hopelessness spilled over their legs like a heavy blanket.

Time tricked them. Somehow it joined the storm and morphed into a shadowy bulge where minutes and hours disappeared. When the winds finally slowed, giant plops of rain pelted the sand. Lightning crackled in jagged webs throughout the sky, and rain became torrents.

Death hadn't really left them. It only transferred its power to electricity that crackled in the air.

No one moved. Carnation sucked in a gasp as the sky became scarlet, as if it bled.

Brilliant blue snuck into the horizon, then filled the sky. The very heavens mocked them. When stillness came and stayed, Erik scooted Ferdinand aside and rose to scan the horizon. "It's over."

They helped Ferdinand and Carnation with creaking joints and groans until the four of them stood together like desert grass, quaking in a gusty breeze.

They were battered and soaked, but alive.

They could see. They could breathe.

They survived.

Carnation hurtled herself in a giant hug around Giselle's waist. The old woman bounced her up and down against the ground, shouting and laughing, "Thank ye. Thank ye, dearie."

Ferdinand waved his hands overhead to prove that the world had righted itself. "Let her go, Carnation. You'll asphyxiate her."

"We won't be selling ye as a slave. No." Carnation sang over and over. "We won't, we won't."

Ferdinand smiled and bowed to Giselle. "She's right, my dear. We'll take the extra camels to Apamea and sell them along with the salt. We have plenty to share. Isn't that true, Erik?"

Erik was silent.

Ferdinand looked uncertain. "You're able to manage the salt dealers, Erik. You know the prices. Correct?"

"We're outta here!" Carnation grabbed Ferdinand

into a happy jig.

Erik studied the vista over Apamea. Finally, he spoke. "We need sleep. We'll leave at first light."

Daylight faded and it was getting cold by the time they changed into whatever dry clothing they could find in the camel's packs. They huddled under a lone tamarisk tree for shelter. Ferdinand and Carnation were already trading loud snores as Erik fed a wavering flame with soggy brush.

He paused his work only long enough to glance in her direction. "How'd you do that?"

"What are you talking about?"

"We wouldn't have survived without you. Who taught you what to do? Brothers?"

"I learned from my father."

"Ah. A camel train driver. I need him to show me a few of those tricks."

"No." She paused and took a breath. "He was the city gatekeeper." All was still as even the desert came to rest. "No need to beg for what he knew. He's gone."

"Where did he go?"

"I don't know." She wrapped Papa's cloak around her aching limbs, too tired to sleep. "It's my fault he never came back."

Chapter 6

Sandstone columns towered at the entrance of Apamea. Giselle half-expected to see Greek warriors standing at the helm of chariots poised for war. Nayeli flags with the familiar dragon crest lined a wide boulevard into the city.

Erik glanced at her from time to time, no doubt still impressed by her skills. One thing for sure. He wasn't peering at her in silent adoration. An all-night trudge across the desert, a sandstorm, and driving rain hadn't helped her wild mop of curls and sandblasted skin.

"I be so very, very hungry." Carnation pointed at lines of vendors and their stalls that beckoned ahead like a shopping spree waiting to happen. She jiggled her share of the money from the sale of the salt. "But not fer long."

Vendors pressed in on each side as they approached. "Jameela," one cried out after another, pulling on her sleeve.

Slaves trudged by, carrying an elaborate litter and with it a musky fragrance that immediately melted into a thousand other aromas. Erik maneuvered her around a brawny merchant who argued over a side of lamb. As he ambled along, he stood taller, and his limbs seemed to fit better. The load of slavery was gone.

She understood for a few tortuous hours what it felt like to lose freedom. Her heart softened. She didn't know where to go from here, but for now, she'd eat and rest long enough to figure it out.

Ferdinand headed to an assortment of hand-carved pipes, and she and Erik followed Carnation's swishing behind them to a fabric booth. A shopkeeper saw them coming and draped layers of soft fabrics over her arm. She and her multi-colored gown moved together like a wisp of desert wind. Giselle studied her dirty tunic.

The jangle of coins at her side were her share of the camels Erik sold, as well as money from the salt. Erik returned her money pouch, too. She couldn't help gloating. "Those criminals didn't expect us to survive. They deserve to lose out on the cash."

"The camels aren't the only treasure they seek."

She hadn't thought about that. "Nayeli thugs. You paid for your freedom, and the criminals try to recapture you? How low is that? They're the worst of the worst."

A soft tunic and trousers that looked woven from smoke called her name, along with a simple headdress to cover her hair. "Good enough?"

Erik nodded. He fingered the silky fabric of an indigo-washed scarf and bowed slightly as the shopkeeper stepped closer.

"Oi, you've picked my finest." She lowered her voice and lifted narrow eyebrows. "Said to be crafted by fairies. Some say it even hides the one who wears it."

Giselle snorted. This woman was determined to make a sale. She nudged Erik and whispered. "She just wants more money." Pulling up a wall inside, she turned away. As she did, she snagged her sleeve on a nail where other fabrics hung.

How embarrassing. She was fastened in place in front of a woman she was trying to get away from.

"Let me help." The woman unhooked Giselle's

tunic and eyed her necklace. "A key? Only one race of people craft anything so exquisite. Are you Magi?"

"No!" Giselle pulled out money for the clothing and slapped it on the counter. When Erik spun around to study her, she hissed. "Stay if you want to. I'm paying for this and then leaving."

The woman carefully folded the garments and placed them with the headdress into a small fabric bag. "My name is Leonore." The shopkeeper's caftan shifted and became muted hues of a rainbow.

When Giselle turned to exit, the woman slipped a small dagger into the bag. She leaned in, ignoring Giselle's confusion. "Only a gift. Trust me. It completes the outfit."

"No. Wait. I can't…"

The woman left to wait for another customer as Giselle wondered what had just happened.

Before she could decide whether to return the knife, Carnation brushed past them like an excited child, decked out with clinking bracelets and streams of necklaces that rang like a hundred bells every time she moved.

"So much for hiding from our pursuers." Erik tried to scowl, although his mouth turned into a crooked grin.

Ferdinand was in a similar state, half-beside himself with an ornate hand-carved pipe and pouch of fragrant tobacco. His crowning glory was a richly brocaded turban and robe that made him strut like a wealthy sultan. "What about you, Erik? What is the desire of your heart?"

"Food."

A line of stalls ahead filled with aroma of Moroccan spices and skewered lamb. Like Carnation, she was very, very hungry. The first bite of lamb filled her taste buds with a warm, seasoned taste of home. She moved to the next booth, lamb in one hand and pastries filled with ground dates and pistachios in the other.

Erik found thickly sliced meat and sandwiched it in crusty bread. He patted a place beside him on a bench and started eating. He polished off not one, but three slabs of meat and bread. He paused to admire the last bite of meat, as if trying to recall the last time he had plenty to eat.

Giselle placed a pastry in each of his hands where they disappeared one after the other into his mouth. After mowing through all the food, he finally spoke. "There's a sea creature at home with tentacles. It tastes like salty breezes on a summer day. And swims like this." He waved his legs in and out like desert grass. Finally satisfied, he settled himself into a cross-legged seat on the ground. "You said it was your fault that your father didn't come back. Why?"

She was too exhausted to guard her words after the storm and blurted out more than she meant to say. The Erik she knew when she trudged with hands bound in the desert didn't deserve an answer.

Now, she saw with different eyes. She judged him with the hardness of one who had never been a slave, who was free to return to family and the city she knew as home. Her work at the Gemini was far from the labor he experienced and that few captives survived.

The real Erik was transforming from the slave he'd been for so long. Besides, he was heading home soon, and what he knew about her didn't matter. She hesitated, then blurted out the truth. "I wasn't there when he needed me."

"Weren't you a kid?"

"I didn't…You wouldn't understand."

"If you mean understand family, you're right. I don't."

"You will, though. When you get back."

"I'll go back sometime. Not to family, though. I left years before I was taken as a slave."

"Ferdinand said…"

"What people think they know is their business. Not mine to correct."

"Surely, you had someone in your life."

"Not one I wasn't glad to leave. There was no one left to protect after my sister died. I went in search of fortune and never turned back."

"You left everything for money?"

"What else guarantees security? Money meant power to build a life of my own. It still does." He stood abruptly, ending the conversation.

Ferdinand and Carnation paused with their mouths full as Erik walked toward them. "I've got some business. Want to check out that spring?" He pointed toward a pool beyond the market surrounded by acacia shrubs.

"A proper bath. Lovely!" Ferdinand took Carnation's hand and off they went.

He was kind to search the area for their safety. Giselle trailed behind Ferdinand and Carnation as Erik waved and headed in the opposite direction.

When the aged ones left the pool for their own patch of shade, she stripped off the first layer, hiding it and the money pouch under a stand of desert brush. Sand squished between her toes, easing her aching feet as she entered the water. When her footing gave way, she ducked under the water and then floated, willing her body to relax. She closed her eyes to the sunlight that filtered through the trees and rested. She was safe. Life was looking up.

With wrinkly skin and clean clothes, she was as fresh as new hope. She pulled the tunic over her hips and slung the money bag around her neck. With almost an afterthought, she tucked the knife into one pocket.

Camel trains traveled to and from the outpost called Apamea. Soon, she was on her way to find Papa. She had plenty of money for passage on a train going toward the mountains she'd heard about in the west. Trailing behind a line of stinky, plodding camels was a small price.

The two old friends sat practically nose to nose against the base of a coconut palm.

Carnation wagged a finger in his face. "I win, ye' bag-o-bones perfesser. Tis a *murder* of crows." She spit out murder and joined it with crows as if the two words proved an important point.

Giselle stood overhead, hands on her hips, half-amused and half-worried that they'd gather a crowd. "Carnation. What in the world are you arguing about?"

"It be our game, girlie. Ferdie thinks he knows more than me, a mere gypsy woman with no schoolin'."

"A parliament of owls." Ferdinand blurted out the phrase with gusto. He clapped his hands, as if his answer was a final victory.

"Not so fast, sir. A rhumba of rattlesnakes."

"A congress of salamanders."

Back and forth, they bantered, hardly taking a breath.

Carnation leaned closer to badger her friend. "Hush, now. A bask of crocodiles."

"A generation of vipers."

"Ah, now ye be beat." Carnation crowed with certain victory. "A wisdom of wombats."

"Humph. I'm not done. Gaggle of geese."

"Everyone knows that one. It don't count."

On and on they bickered.

It was best to leave them to their game. Giselle pulled damp hair into a knot, wrapped it with the simple headdress and hid her old tunic under a pile of brush. She sighed, contented. She was clean and camouflaged enough not to be recognized. It was time to find Erik.

Several large buildings surrounded an open square in the city's business district. Erik's familiar form stood near a broad wooden platform. He gestured to a portly man dressed in a priestly robe who held out a what looked like a leather pouch bulging with coins.

She'd seen that square-faced man before. He was part of the retinue that led the high priest, Ramaz, into the Gemini that fateful afternoon. What was a priest doing outside of Darras? The same ornate litter they saw earlier that day disappeared as its carriers scurried around the corner.

Although there were many travelers on those routes, a priest offered protection for a single woman. She hurried forward, then remembered who she was greeting. She bowed low in respect. "Sir. My name is Giselle Basir. I met you at our inn, the Gemini. You came for a midday meal?"

The man's gaze looked hungry. He didn't look so holy, after all.

Erik whirled around. His cheeks flushed, then lost all color. He grabbed the pouch and stuffed it into his tunic.

He didn't recognize her. After all, she was clean and in her nomad disguise. She pulled back the headdress and let her curls spill out. "Erik. It's me. Ferdinand and Carnation are resting by the spring." She turned to the priest and bowed again for good measure. "What brings you to Apamea, sir?"

In one motion, the priest yanked Erik's tunic and pulled him close.

Was he sealing some kind of deal?

Erik looked up in surprise, then crumpled to the ground, clutching his stomach as blood gurgled through his hands.

Bystanders hurried about, absorbed in whatever business seemed more important. No one stopped or cared that a man was just stabbed. She watched, paralyzed, as the priest retrieved the bag of coins from Erik's grip. He wiped the blade of a wide dagger on a patch of grass, then stuffed it back into his waistband.

Disbelief stole her words for seconds. "Help! Someone!" Tearing off her turban, she held it against Erik's stomach. "Stay," she whispered as if her words were enough to save him. She fumbled with the fabric as blood soaked through it faster than she could stop it.

Erik struggled to speak. "Worth more than I knew…"

Holding him in her arms, she shushed him like a tearful child. "Don't talk. I'll get help. I'll…"

Erik's breath rasped with a final word. "Run." His eyelids fluttered once, and he was gone.

The marketplace outside the warehouse bustled with customers and shouting vendors. Even the priest turned away, as if business called him elsewhere. Glancing in her direction, he raised one hand in a silent salute.

Now he was calling for help? Guards charged from a warehouse and rushed in her direction. They weren't coming for the priest.

They were coming for her.

It was too late to do anything except run. She sprinted toward a neighborhood of sandstone dwellings where children played on a broad, dirt-packed road. Her heart pounded as fast as her feet twisted and she turned to throw off the pursuers, who gained ground no matter where she ran.

It couldn't be true, but there was nothing else to believe. Erik sold her for a bag of cash. The priest murdered him and took the money back. So much for freedom.

She forced her legs to move, angling in and out of houses, dodging children, and stray dogs, as shouts of "There she is!" closed the distance between them.

A cloaked figure ducked out of an alley and overturned a large basket of potatoes in the path of men closing in. One tripped and fell to his feet, cursing. Her anonymous helper stuck out a long foot and tripped the other. Both hurried to get back on their feet and resumed the chase.

She headed toward the busy market, hoping to lose her pursuers in the crowd. She'd leave the city, grab one of the camels, and ride away. Somewhere. Anywhere. Away from a city that shined brightly only to draw her into a trap.

A wagon of vegetables plummeted from an alley into another group of pursuers. The men regrouped and climbed around the overturned wagon. A man dressed in homespun browns wove in and through another market stall. She ran too fast to figure out who'd decided to help her escape.

Leonore's booth of fabrics stood tucked away from the other stalls. She could hide behind the silks that served as curtains from the outside. Would the peculiar shopkeeper betray her?

The woman's arms were waiting as she fell into them. "I haven't done anything wrong."

Leonore didn't hesitate. When Giselle moved to a rack of hanging fabrics, she stopped her. "No. Here." The woman pushed her behind an opaque curtain of blues and golds. She held out a soft brown tunic and sandals. "Change into these."

Her new clothes were soaked in Erik's blood. They fell to the ground into a pool, as Erik had. She glanced at Leonore, then held out her arms to receive the new clothes.

"Stay behind these fabrics. I'll keep a watch outside."

Giselle peered through a crack in the wooden booth. The men scattered throughout the market, making a chaotic mess in stalls, tossing goods aside and forcing themselves into back rooms. They showed no sign of giving up. Why had a whole horde come after her?

Leonore peeked inside. "Who are you?"

"My name is Giselle. I'm no one. I don't know why they're after me."

Panic overtook her, and she felt fear just as terrible as the men who searched for her outside. It was the vendor's peculiar comment about her necklace and her conversation about the fabrics.

Leonore was Magi.

Evil plots spun in the woman's mind who appeared so friendly. No wonder she hadn't trusted the woman.

Her booth was a trap, not a refuge. She had to get out of there.

When the sound of pursuers faded away, and there was no sign of anyone from the booth, she bound out.

"Giselle. Don't." When Leonore reached for her, she slipped out of her grasp and ran to an alley behind the stalls.

The sun was an enormous orange sphere that descended on the horizon as she sped full tilt toward the city's entrance. Soon, the camel trains would leave on their all-night desert trek. It didn't matter where they were going. She had plenty of money to pay for a passage.

She almost reached the tree-lined boulevard when someone cried out. "There. By the entrance."

A fresh burst of adrenalin fueled her exhausted body, and she ran with all the speed she had left in her tired legs.

It wasn't enough.

In moments, she was bound and dragged back through the market. Her feet trailed against the sandy ground, and blood trickled between her toes. Vendors threw garbage at her and hurled insults. A woman held her child close and shouted. "Fie! A pox on Magi scum."

She sucked in deep breaths and searched for Carnation and Ferdinand. They couldn't have been in on the scheme. Her voice rasped. "I'm Nayeli. This man has taken me wrongfully."

The priest hissed a command. "Take her to the warehouse. Guard her with your lives – if you value your own." He scanned her without pity. "You were difficult to find, Giselle Basir. Your friend sold you out right before I moved on to the next city."

"Who are you? Why have you taken me?"

"My name is Anton. Gad El Glas smiled upon my search." He looked smug, pleased with his catch. "Your gift has come of age." He smiled grimly as a guard bound her hands. "How convenient that you're ignorant of that fact."

Chapter 7

What began as a beautiful day in a lovely city ended here, in a dirty warehouse as a slave of an attendant of Gad El Glas. Not Ramaz, but certainly someone with authority. Why had a random priest named Anton seen her as his personal prize? She only met him the day he accompanied Ramaz into the Gemini.

Betrayal turned into a short-lived treasure for Erik. Even knowing that he sold her out didn't erase the image of him dying in her arms.

Only one thing was clear. She was the plunder in a war she didn't know existed.

The next morning, small cries and whispers echoed in semi-darkness through the slats of a dirt-floored warehouse. Shadowy figures huddled in groups. Her hands chafed against the rope that bound them. Ordinary sounds became stabs of fear, and the stench that filled the room threatened to empty her stomach.

Someone belched, then cursed at some unknown obstacle outside the door that led to the slave platform. Heavy boots stomped over creaking wooden planks. A coarse laugh sounded, along with a low snarl of a dog. A crying child hurtled her back in time.

Papa was gone weeks after he promised to return, and she ran into the desert to search for him. By the time Chronos led her back to the inn, her mother's face was red, and chest heaved.

"Stop acting like a child. Grow up, Giselle. Just grow up," she shouted in front of their old friend.

Rage became her mother's shield after Papa left. It never changed anything. He was still gone. And Mother was still a tyrant.

Words kept silent too long spilled out. "I know why Papa left. It was you. It was *your* fault."

A sharp slap. Hand to skin so hard that her head jerked to one side. Even though the bruise healed, the imprint of the blow stayed, festering like an open wound. She closed her heart that day to the woman she called Mother.

As often as she vowed to do better, to be better, love still left on a camel train and never returned. Nothing about her was enough to make it stay. She'd always end up like her mother – alone and abandoned.

The knife pressed against her thigh as a reminder of Leonore's gift. Her hands were tied in front of her. She could reach into the baggy trousers and cut the bonds. Except for the surly guards who watched over her like she was some kind of prize. She heard the last threat from Anton. "Guard her with your lives."

A young mother with her baby sat nearby. The little one wiggled and cried a pitiful little mew at her mother's breast. She made slurping sounds as she finally quieted enough to eat.

The baby sat up in her mother's arms and stared at Giselle. She gurgled and held out her arms to Giselle.

Should she pretend she didn't notice a small child who acted like she knew her?

"No. Elise. That's not her." The young mother pulled the baby back into her arms. "Sorry. She thinks you're my cousin. You look so much like her. My name is Lucy. Yours?"

The girl looked barely old enough to have a child. Her clothing in hues of green hung in shreds around grimy, bruised feet protected by once delicate slippers. Her figure was lithe, and her skin was like Erik's, fair and ravaged by desert sun. Giselle had only seen a forest in one of the books Louis read to her on summer nights. This young one belonged there, in the shade of lush trees and filtered sun.

"I'm Giselle. How did you end up here?" She sucked in a breath as soon as the question spilled out. It wasn't her business to invade what had stolen the woman's freedom. Still, it was the reality they shared.

Lucy didn't seem offended. "We were captured outside our home, early one morning."

"Where were your people? Why were you and the baby unprotected?"

The young mother wrapped her arms tighter around the baby. "The attack came at dawn. The birds cried out in warning, but we were open targets. There was burning, so much burning. Our homes, our trees. The Nayeli destroyed them all." Her voice was as breathless as if she still fled with a baby in her arms. "My husband died defending us."

"Nayeli?"

Lucy nodded. "An ancient enemy. How were you taken?"

Surely, her facts were wrong. It couldn't have been a Nayeli attack. Her people only used defensive strategies. They never pillaged land and innocent people. "I'm from a city called Darras and was captured by runaway slaves."

"Darras." Lucy peered at Giselle intently. "The

center of Gad El Glas and it's worship."

Giselle fidgeted. This conversation had taken a strange turn. True, she'd never been outside Darras, and the rest of the world was a mystery. Lucy was an unexpected window into a universe she'd never known and wasn't sure she trusted anymore. "I don't know. I guess. My mother and I run an inn. Or at least, we did. We've always been too busy to worship anywhere."

Tears hurried down the young woman's cheeks. When the little one caught her ear and pulled, she unhooked pudgy fingers one by one and pulled her from her breast. She kissed the baby's forehead. "I believed that the universe would save us from our adversary. We'd been safe for such a long time. The enemy still came."

"I'm sorry." Empty words were all she had. "There are walls around our city and a gatekeeper. No one comes in or out without notice. Well, except for me. I climbed out of my bedroom window at night, planning to take a passage on the next camel train. I was captured, instead." She expected Lucy to snort with ridicule.

Instead, a tiny grin played on the girl's face. "Walls are too confining for thoughts that need to run free. Our mountain home is made of stone, but my favorite place is outside with the trees."

Another one enslaved and hauled away through the desert. She thought of Erik with a pang of grief. Even though he betrayed her, his friends, Ferdinand and Carnation, would be lost without him.

The door behind them swung open. Lucy scooted next to Giselle, so close that she smelled the urine of the child's diaper and wondered how she'd cared for her daughter with so little. Giselle draped her arm around them and held them close.

One of the guards yanked Lucy up to her feet as Elise squalled in the other arm.

Giselle leaped up, ready to use her knife, until Anton appeared before her, surrounded by priestly attendants. These men weren't soldiers of Apamea. They belonged to the company of the high priest, Ramaz. Two of them positioned themselves on each side, tightly gripping her arms. They led her away from the platform to the back of the crowd.

Anton already owned her. The fact that they hadn't left the area meant he had other slaves to purchase. Temple slaves were common, although the camel trains hand-delivered captives from throughout the region to Darras all the time. Why was this low-level priest in Apamea, and why had he murdered Erik? Worse, he stood, eyes scanning Lucy and Elise, as if they, too, were goods meant for the taking.

A gilded litter, carried by four slaves, appeared on one side of the platform. It was the same one that waited nearby when Anton murdered Erik. The fragrance of oud drifted on a slight breeze. Whoever sat inside was not only wealthy enough to afford the costly perfume but also oversaw that entire bloody exchange. Did it carry some unseen person waiting to buy slaves?

Giselle stood with Anton in front of the platform, waiting for the right time to cut the rope that bound her hands. As much as she distrusted Leonore, she thanked her over and over for the gift of the knife. Her hands were bound in front. It was only a matter of time before she freed herself and found a way to liberate Lucy and her baby.

A crowd grew and filled the area around the

platform with buyers ready to purchase human cargo. Lucy's body trembled, and she comforted Elise with kisses as she stood on the platform, alone except for the slave merchant who led the sale.

A woman stood with hands on her hips, looking them both up and down. Another shoved her way in, glaring at the other.

"Oi. The missus needs a scullery maid. Shove off."

"They be too pricey fer yer household. Royalty, don't you know."

The slave trader yelled over their argument. "Shaddup. Off limits to both of you."

She peered over at Lucy and the baby. They didn't look any more special than she did. They weren't dressed in fine robes. They wore no jewelry or, for that matter, any other evidence of wealth and influence.

A lanky young man dressed in a dark hood and pants stood at the edge of the mob. His height and stance reminded her of the one who threw obstacles in her pursuers' path the day before she ended up here as a slave.

The man fumbled through a bag of coins and sorted through them again and again. His gaze seemed tormented. Did he know Lucy and the baby? That was unlikely. Her home was so far from here. Maybe he was struck by the tragedy of a young woman and her child for sale. The Nayeli crowd didn't notice. Slaves were often separated from their families.

The slave merchant strode to the center of the platform. "Bidding on these fine slaves shall begin." He waved in the direction of Lucy and Elise. "Here be a young lass, with child in tow. Perfect for many years of faithful service and royal to boot."

"She don't look like any princess I've seen," a woman shouted.

The merchant snarled in response. "It don't matter what you thinks, do it?"

Anton took a step forward and raised his hand. "$200 drachmas."

The crowd sucked in a collective gasp. It was an outrageous price, especially for a woman with a child.

"200 drachmas for the woman and her little one." The merchant paused for a moment. "Other bids?"

Anton raised his voice. "Not the child. Only the woman."

Lucy clutched the child and peered down at Giselle with wild eyes. "No," she whispered.

A woman cried out in the back. "That ain't right, now."

The merchant pulled a dingy vest over his belly. "Ye said only the woman?"

As if to make up for any resistance from those who sympathized with a woman ripped from her child, Anton spoke again. "Make that 250 drachmas."

The agitated man on the outer edge of the crowd suddenly dashed forward and threw back his hood. It took seconds for her mind to sort out reality from the impossible.

It was Louis.

She needed to let him know she was there.

His eyes weren't on her, though. They were on Lucy and Elise. He leaped in one bound to the platform and lifted his voice in part plea and part command. "Wait! I'm here with valuable information. It regards the unauthorized sale of a woman." Louis spread his arms and shouted over the people who swarmed the platform's base. "Not just any woman. One who carries a key to untold wealth."

Untold wealth? The merchant signaled his soldiers, who rushed to surround Louis. "Let 'im speak."

Giselle searched the crowd for anyone who stood out. Looked like a typical motley crew of Nayeli tradespeople and merchants, with the priestly element thrown in.

Suddenly, people whirled in her direction and eyed her with new interest. Louis was pointing at her. "She's the one. She's the prize you desire."

He was selling her to the highest bidder.

Anton growled a low command to his men. "Stop him."

Out of the chaos, a stand-off between slave merchant guards and soldiers of the priest formed below the platform. Both groups had weapons. Both were willing to use them.

Louis cried out to the slave merchant. "She'll line your pockets with riches. Believe me."

A priest's authority meant nothing to the slave merchant who heard the sound of money and lots of it. "Trouble brewing, heh? Not on my watch." He held up one hand. In response, his burly men formed a barrier against the priestly guards.

This was a better show than the crowd bargained for. Not only a noteworthy sale, but also great fisticuffs along the way. They bumped elbows and hands, shouting "I wanna see. Outa me way," as they pressed in for a closer look.

Her heart twisted first in disbelief and then in despair.

Louis marketed her like a choice side of meat. He

was as intent on her sale as Anton. She opened her heart to a cook, a hired hand at the Gemini who was grateful for the opportunity to gain his fortune. Maybe he never loved them, never served at the Gemini because he wanted to. Maybe he always looked for a way to escape.

Like her.

Louis paused for dramatic effect. He waited for the crowd to quiet, lowering his tone until everyone gathered closer. Lifting his hands into the sky, he fanned them out with a whoosh toward Giselle. "She carries a sign from the gods."

"What kind of sign?" A merchant in brocaded robes heckled.

The priest gripped her tighter and snarled at a guard who pushed his way through the people. "Take him. Now, you idiot."

The slave merchant wasn't one to be pushed around. Not when cash was on the line. He addressed the priest's guard in no uncertain terms. "Stay offa me platform. We'll hear what the man has to say." His men snapped into a tighter line, blocking the way.

The usual slouch in Louis's stance was gone. He stood like a general, ordering his troops. He had the people's attention and knew it. His voice rose, loud and masterful, as he pointed at Anton. "This man claims ownership. Where is his deed of sale?"

The slave merchant perked up. "Ah. An illegal transaction, it is." He rubbed his hands with pleasure. He'd profit from this sale fair and square.

Louis continued his spiel. "What about this woman is so valuable that he takes her for himself? What does she carry that he is unwilling to share?"

Morning sun shifted into a bright, unwavering heat.

Louis brushed aside sweat that rolled down his face. "Surely, you've heard the prophecy. True, it is an ancient one. Only those educated in Nayeli history would know. 'The breaker, who opens a way through the gate, bursts through doors of bronze and bars of iron.'"

He threw out his arms toward Giselle again, in case anyone forgot his target. "Do you face an impossible obstacle? Wait no longer. This woman's gift will make a way."

Their friendship was a lie from the beginning. He hadn't come to her rescue. He waited for just the right time to offer her as a common slave. She refused to cry. Instead, she shot him a glare, wishing it was a dagger.

He returned her gaze. Then he lifted his hand, crossing the first two fingers.

It was their sign.

That signal was either the highest form of betrayal or proof of a plan that made no sense.

When Anton's attention turned to slaves carrying the opulent litter through the crowd, she pulled the knife from her pocket and sawed the rope binding her hands. In minutes, her hands were free.

The crowd surged against her as she ran toward the platform. She wanted to escape far, far away, except for the friends who were stood waiting for her.

She ducked hands that grabbed on every side and pressed through. Finally, the platform appeared. With one giant shove, she lurched up the stairs. The next minute she stood beside Louis and a flabbergasted merchant who whirled this way and that, trying to figure out what was going on with his slave market.

Lucy jumped up and down with Elise in her arms. "Elise. It's our friend."

Louis crinkled a happy grin her way as he pulled her to his side. "Nice to see you, stranger."

The slave merchant backed up for a moment. He wanted cash without outright war. "Err. Does we have a bid on this woman? Quick as a whip, she is." He scanned her up and down, looking for any value hiding in her stinky presence.

Louis nudged her and pointed to a man with golden slippers who exited the litter. The crowd hushed, then fell to the ground as the high priest, Ramaz, bowed ceremoniously. He scanned the people, as if to make sure each one showed proper reverence.

It was true that the center of Gad El Glas worship was in Darras, but every Nayeli citizen served without question a god who wielded supreme authority no matter where they lived in the kingdom.

The high priest's entrance into this chaos was perfect timing. He'd remember her from the inn and intervene for her freedom. Anton was in trouble now. She waited for his signal that allowed them to rise. "Sir. Sir! It's me, Giselle."

Those slippers. The ornate litter positioned near Anton right before he murdered Erik. The distinctive aroma of oud. It was the same fragrance Ramaz wore when he first visited the Gemini.

The high priest searched the crowd and found her. The look on his face was far from the smile she'd seen at the Gemini. His god-like serenity was gone. He was a totally uncomposed Highly Esteemed One who shook his fist in her direction and yowled. "Take her, take her now."

Betrayed again.

In the minute it took to respond, the ground beneath

the platform became an impassable barrier. Slave merchant guards sparred with priestly guards. Everywhere, there was chaos.

Ramaz strode through the crowd to the wooden stairs of the platform. If he caught her, it was the end. No one had the power to defy him.

A padlocked metal door leading to the warehouse stood before her. Louis spoke like a commander: "Open the door, Giselle. Now."

She looked at her hands. No tingle. Nothing.

An overpowering stink of rotten flesh filled the air as Ramaz rushed forward, his golden slippers taking ground with her, as prey, in sight.

Not if she could help it.

Louis grabbed Lucy and Elise and formed a barrier behind her. When her hand touched the latch, nothing happened.

She leaned against it and whispered. "Please."

The lock didn't budge.

"Now, I say. Open!"

The latch released, and the door flew open with the weight of Louis, Lucy, and her pressing against it.

Angry cries sounded from behind. She grasped the door and slammed it shut, lowering a metal bar against it. The commotion quieted into a hushed murmur.

A group of young women looked up in surprise from the floor.

This was no time for doubt. If she had the power to unlock doors, she had a knife to do the rest.

Slaves were divided into groups as if they were goats and cattle, instead of people. With Louis, Lucy, and Elise at her side, she dashed up and down the aisles, slashing ropes, and yelling, "You're free. Run!

Laurel Thomas

Louis pulled layers of Leonore's fabrics out of his cloak. "Put these on. Let's get out of here."

The door to the slave platform quivered with blows. Money, lots and lots of money disappeared behind that door. No one was willing to let it go without hot pursuit.

Louis held Lucy's hand as Lucy clutched Elise. He led the way as they zigzagged through the confusion to a door at the other end of the warehouse.

Giselle followed behind in time to face one last blocked exit that led to the city outside. Metal bars crisscrossed the towering doors. She didn't have time to beg, plead, or cry. She only had one word, and it had to work.

"Open!"

They jumped back as metal clattered to the ground. Heavy oaken doors creaked once and then hurtled wide.

"Follow me. I know a way out of the city." Louis led them to a narrow corridor between rows of stucco houses as a tumult rumbled just behind them.

How did Louis know the way?

This was no time for questions.

This was the time to follow.

Chapter 8

They ran that day until the sun drifted in the west and the coolness of night brushed their sweaty, exhausted bodies with relief. It was a race fueled with all the strength Giselle had as she gripped Lucy's arm and Lucy held tight to Elise. How they made it out, she'd never know.

Louis led them away from Apamea, far from slave traders, and from the priestly retinue. Their cook, who'd lived in Darras for years, navigated them through a Nayeli kingdom he didn't even know.

Hours later, they arrived at a tiny oasis. Lucy was so tired and Elise so hungry that Louis practically carried them both as they limped into the shelter of a leafy grove. They drank from a small pool and ate flatbread that Louis pulled from his pack. Lucy nursed Elise until both fell sound asleep, collapsing together in a small huddle.

She and Louis sat with their backs against a palm tree, aware that any pursuers could be close behind.

Fatigue took her whole being and sat on her like a lead weight. Worn out and still panting for air, she was as ragged as the new tunic, now stained and smelly. She went from slave, to free, to slave and now free again. Being dragged behind a racing camel couldn't feel any worse.

Like Erik, her heart was crushed when she believed Louis betrayed her. And Ramaz, too, for that matter.

Sitting with Louis at the end of the day brought a rush of emotions that tumbled out in question after question. "I don't know where to begin. Back there – what were you doing? What were you talking about?"

"It worked, didn't it?"

"I don't know what to say. Worked? You tried to get me sold."

"Of course. That's what I do with my friends – get the highest price for them on a slave platform. Who do you think I am, anyway?"

She ignored that question and moved on to her own. "Why were you in Apamea, anyway?"

"I followed you."

"From Darras?"

"I looked all over town after I got back to the inn that night. One of the guards saw you pay for passage on a camel train. I took the next one. It wasn't headed in the same direction, but at least I got a start. It didn't take long to get close enough to follow you. The stars we watched over the Gemini at night? They helped."

Memories of home flooded in, all mixed up with happy and sad. "Wait. Was Mother arrested that night?

"No. Why?"

"I saw her outside the palace. She was hiding the Magi infiltrator."

"Oh. So, that's what you call it." His forehead crinkled, and he looked away. "No. I left soon after you did. There weren't any soldiers around the inn or sign of an arrest, though."

She hiccupped with relief that rose in a gush. Then almost shouted in frustration before remembering to stuff it. "Why didn't you let me know you were following us? I was terrified."

"You were in – well, a compromising situation. I wasn't armed. At least, not enough to take down the whole crew. Besides, you were doing a good job of defending yourself. By the time you ended up in Apamea, you were a free woman. No theatrics necessary." He paused with a tender grin. "Well. Except for later. On the slave platform."

"Drama. You were pretty good at announcing my virtues to that whole mob. Every treasure hunter in the region will be after me."

"This would be the time to ask why you left home without a goodbye."

When she thought no one cared, he followed her. She needed to say thanks, something, except for the jumble of unanswered mysteries that crowded out her words. "What was all that about my gift? Papa used to speak those words over me at night before bed."

"You still don't understand?"

"That's a mean thing to say. I only…I heard those words. Then Papa left. Okay. I never understood. It wasn't my fault." Time to get back to the real question. "I thought you came to rescue me. You came for Lucy and Elise, instead."

"I came for you first, muttonhead. I just didn't know that Lucy and Elise had been taken as slaves. When I left them, they were safe at home. At least Lucy was. That was long before she was married. I counted on you to understand our signal. I expected you to get away during my little speech, uhm, distraction."

"You knew Lucy when she was little? Wait. What if your plan hadn't worked?"

"One question at a time. Listen. I followed you from Darras. I camped out with no shelter, got stung by a scorpion, and survived a sandstorm. It might be okay to trust me." He leveled a flat surface with one hand and laid out his cloak. "Time for sleep."

"You can't. I'm not done. Where will we go?"

"I'm too tired to answer. Except that I'm taking Lucy and Elise home."

"I…I need…I have to find Papa. I heard that the Magi might hold him."

"That's why you left without asking for help?"

"I. I had to go. It was time."

"You settled for a glance behind, instead of a real farewell to me, your friend."

"Would you have tried to stop me?"

"Probably." Louis shrugged and stretched his shoulders. "Lucy and Elise live in the mountains, many days from here. Come with us. Maybe you'll find out more about your Papa from our people."

"Our people?"

"Lucy is my sister." He snuggled down into the cloak and closed his eyes.

He was rescuing his family. That's why he panicked and jumped into action. A dim sadness stirred inside. "Wait. I have more questions."

With one last burrow into the woven cloak, he was sound asleep. She was left staring into the night sky and wondering what to do with all the unknowns behind and ahead of this journey.

Ramaz was behind her capture all along. He was the one in the ornamental litter, surrounded by temple guards. According to Anton, he'd followed her to Apamea, too. Somehow, he met Erik, who was willing to sell her for a bag of gold. That hadn't ended well for Erik. Or for her.

She'd been lied to so many times it was easy to imagine Louis had the same motives. That thought created such a spin in her heart that she took a deep breath, wrapped herself in Papa's cloak, and fell asleep.

She woke up the next morning to the aroma of fresh bread baking.

It was only a dream. Her stomach was empty and complaining about it. She dozed off again until a baby's voice chortled a stream of syllables.

Lucy sat by Louis who held Elise, jiggling her up and down on his lap, while breakfast cooked on a nearby fire. Longing overwhelmed her heart.

They were family, though not one she was a part of. Or ever would be.

"Time to eat." Louis invited them to a small picnic of hot tea, fresh bread, dates, soft cheese, and more water. How like him to prepare a feast even in this desolate place.

She fingered the tiny key on the necklace he placed around her neck in what felt like a lifetime ago. Louis couldn't have known how much she'd need the tiny constant of Papa nearby. He settled beside her as Lucy dressed Elise and rocked her to sleep for a quick nap.

"When were you last at home?"

"A long time ago. Since I came to work at the Gemini."

"Why did you leave?"

"I was on a mission."

"Like what kind? Saving us?"

"You needed saving."

"You're so irritating. Tell me the truth."

"Not now. Today, I'm heading home – for the first time in many years.

"Do you know the way?"

"The way home is etched in my heart, as surely as it is in the sky. I know every coordinate, every quadrant, every shift of the constellations by their season. I know each star that stays hidden unless studied by looking away." He gazed down at her as if he could say more but didn't. "Yes. I know the way home."

She remembered the stars overhead at home in Darras and in the desert as a would-be slave. She'd seen them darkened by a sandstorm and yearned for their sight as she was held captive with countless others in a barren warehouse.

They were the same stars. The heavens hadn't changed.

But she had.

She was no longer a naive girl longing for adventure. This journey took Papa's loss and confirmed that the world was way bigger than she imagined. It looked thrilling from inside her room, but that's where the excitement stopped, and the terror began.

She wasn't the Giselle she'd planned to be.

She still had plenty of wishful thinking, like about a future with the handsome Crown Prince, Makir. His eyes invited her with such promise. She imagined him sitting beside her now. He'd know what to do and how to get them out of this adventure turned nightmare. He'd make this crazy world right again.

If only she hadn't left so quickly. If only she stayed.

Maybe Mother told him how she left without a word. Maybe his soldiers searched for her. More likely, Makir thought she didn't care, didn't believe in a future together – however wonderful that looked.

Was there an unseen plan, an invisible thread that

coursed through life, leading to something that made sense and might even bring happiness?

Not that she'd ever known.

Today, she headed to a new place, hoping the journey would lead her to Papa.

The terrain didn't change day after day. When Giselle was convinced their walk would last forever, Lucy pointed out a huge cloud bank. "Home! Those are our mountains!"

Mountain peaks that filled the western sky looked like great, shadowy elephants she'd seen once. The enormous animals lumbered through the sand dunes, loaded with baggage, as they trudged to the nearest oasis. The mountains ahead were muted by an enormous cloud bank and so blue they didn't look real.

Lucy jiggled Elise as Louis spun them around in joy. She, on the other hand, wasn't sure what she felt.

They climbed a towering ridge of stone and sand, then plopped down in shock and fatigue. A stone wall loomed before them, encircling the desert as far as her eyes could see. It was the one the camel driver talked about, the one that stretched around the Nayeli kingdom.

It was too high to climb. They'd spent whole nights trudging through desert sands, then falling asleep on the ground. Each night, Papa's cloak enfolded her with its warmth, with its promise. When the mountains finally beckoned ahead, this wall was set to stop their flight.

"Can you see that?" Lucy pointed to a black form that soared far in the distance, swooping in and out of the sheer walls of a mesa.

Louis sucked in a deep breath. "It doesn't want you to escape."

"It? Who is it?"

"Gad El Glas."

Chapter 9

The creature in flight appeared to ascend on a wind current and then disappeared into the clouds. Too far away to know, it was probably only a large eagle. "Look. It left."

Lucy rose and stood beside Louis. "Not for long." She carried Elise all this time, although they traded off whenever Elise allowed a switch of arms. She was a young woman, but this journey was hard. Fatigue lined her sunburned face. "It lies in wait."

"Who is it expecting?"

"Us, of course."

Giselle turned to Louis. "You said it's Gad El Glas. I've never seen this god, even though it supposedly rules our people. I mean. Really. It's only this fearsome thing authorities concocted to keep people under control.

"That concoction is parading itself as a dragon right now."

Giselle scoffed. "Dragons are the stuff of old magic lore, made up to scare small children. No one, even you, has ever seen one." She remembered the shadow flying over the sandstorm. It was only her imagination.

"Who said I've never seen a dragon?" Louis stroked his chin as he sized up the wall.

"You never told me." She felt like a little kid with all her whys. Then again, Louis knew a lot of things she never expected. "Why would a mythical beast care about us?"

"We live where it dwells, Giselle."

"That's crazy. Darras has been my home all my life. Not once have I seen a fire-breathing serpent."

Louis shrugged. He rechecked the horizon. "You saw the effects of its tyranny. How many markets actively sell slaves, day and night, throughout Darras? What kind of smoke rises from the spire of the temple? You lived with evidence of its villainy all your life and never recognized it."

"I have no idea what you're talking about."

"Sadly, that's true."

"I guess you see all kinds of things no one else notices. What about this wall? It's built of individual stones, but there's no mortar."

"Master masons built it. They were Magi, enslaved just for that purpose. They're the only ones with the knowledge and skill to build a structure like this."

Giselle rolled her eyes. "Not only do you know everything, now you're intent on making us, the Nayeli, villains in your drama against the so-called Magi." She fingered the silver filigree necklace. Leonore had called it Magi-crafted.

It affirmed her link to Papa when nothing else survived the questions and passage of time. It didn't change the fact that Magi were demons in human form who pillaged their homes and villages. They were the enemy. They stole Papa.

Louis spoke with an appeal in his voice. "Try to listen. Reserve your prejudice and everything you've been taught for just a minute."

"It isn't prejudice. It's true."

"Evidence?"

"What about those invasions threatened? What about Papa? They took him away from us. They…"

"You have no proof there's ever been a threat of conquest by the Magi. You can't be sure they robbed you of your father. For that matter, although you distrust this fact as surely as you distrust all Magi, I am your friend." He paused and looked back into the sky. "And I am Magi."

She couldn't do this. Not now. Not when everything inside her faded to a dim weariness. Slowly, she backed away. Away from the three people she'd grown to love over days and days of grueling travel.

"Lucy and I were raised in those mountains beyond this wall. We have siblings and parents who love us. Have you ever known me to be dangerous?"

"No. Except maybe you were plotting against us all along."

"Of course. Perfect logic. I'll tell you a story my mother told me when I was little." He took a deep breath and blew it out slowly. "Generations ago, Magi were unsuspecting. Their innocence and unusual gifting made them an open target for the dragon's lust."

Giselle narrowed her eyes with doubtful scorn.

"Whether you believe it or not, our people were captured by emissaries of the dragon. Our extraordinary, loving people were put to work in the quarries of the western regions.

"It was the cruelest kind of slavery. hard, back-breaking work in the desert sun for a people at home in the forested mountains. Worse, the dragon knew that Magi wouldn't attack their own friends and family.

"They watched, powerless, as Magi built a wall to separate the Nayeli from us. It was an evil scheme to conceal that life as the Nayeli knew it was only a prison. It was a fortress controlled by an evil hidden with lies and subterfuge."

"A wall is a protection."

"This wall is a prison."

Giselle studied the stones carefully fashioned to fight tightly without mortar. They were connected so seamlessly that a piece of paper couldn't fit between them. "I lived inside the walls of Darras and never saw anything like this construction."

"The lighter stones were dragged over natural soil beds. The heavier boulders were transported on timber sleds by Magi horses, known for their strength. Workers pounded the porous stone until the final shape was perfect. It took years."

"How do you know this?"

"I had a life before the Gemini."

"Add this to everything you never told me."

"I told you what I could. At least, what you were willing to believe." He peered back at the wall. "Enough of that. We need a plan."

"Magi built the wall. We can find the hidden place." Lucy's voice was calm and confident. She took her place beside them as Elise played with a tiny lizard that kept escaping her grasp.

Giselle harumphed as loudly as she could. It wasn't that hard to figure out what to do. "We don't need a plan. We'll climb over it." She positioned her foot against one of the lower stones.

"No." Louis stood in front of the wall to block her. "Gad El Glas set its sorcery in place. Mortals can't scale this wall."

"That's ridiculous." She skirted Louis and

clambered up a large boulder. Then slid off and landed on her behind in the sand. She attacked the wall again. And again. Finally, she pulled out the knife and wedged it in one of the hairline cracks between the stones for a bit of traction.

The crack suddenly widened. A pair of eyes met hers.

Horns appeared on a triangular head from an impossibly narrow space, as if it was only a vapor, instead of a very real horned viper.

It felt the vibration of her movement and tasted her scent with its tongue, which jabbed in and out of its serpent mouth. She leaped back and fell to the ground.

Louis was at her side the next instant, pulling her to her feet as the serpent wound through the sand toward them. "Lucy. You and Elise go. You, too, Giselle."

Giselle pulled out her knife. Together, she and Louis stood against the snake, which paused and resumed its slow, calculated, winding pursuit.

"A horned viper isn't usually active now."

"This is no ordinary viper."

She brought this danger to all of them by her arrogance and stubbornness.

Lucy stood on the rise of a sand dune and called in a clear, commanding voice that intercepted terror with sudden, unexplained peace. Her words were a command from a woman no bigger than a child. "You. Sent from the dark realm of Gad El Glas."

The snake paused in its pursuit. Clearly, it knew exactly what it was and that it only paraded in disguise.

"Come no further." She stood with her feet planted like a petite general expecting to be obeyed.

A snake obeyed words?

Water trickled from where the snake emerged from the wall, joining streams from other rocks.

Another crack, another trickle until the entire wall looked as though it wept.

As Louis and Giselle backed away, a gully formed at their feet, becoming a shallow trench. Soon, water rushed from the wall for as far as they could see in both directions.

"Cross now." Louis waited for Lucy and Elise to join them. Together, they ran through sludge toward the wall like a water-filled valley. The snake floated on the surface, then disappeared in tumbling mud, water and sandy debris.

As they walked, first their shins, then their waists were submerged. They had to scale the towering wall, impossible only minutes before, and hope there were no more serpent visitors.

"Hang on to me," yelled Louis.

Hand in hand, they clambered up one rock, then another and another. With one foot positioned here, another here, the wall received them like a friend. Elise, tied to Lucy's back, giggled with joy.

Giselle followed Louis, grateful for his quiet support as they scaled higher and higher. Streams became rivers that paved their own trail amid a barren desert and rushed beneath them.

They stood at the top and marveled at a world that suddenly beckoned beyond the wall. Green grass, hills, trees were just beyond a ribbon of sand. It was as if desert stopped on the other side and life bloomed in its place. They clambered down the other side of the wall on hands and knees, until finally, they jumped into green grass.

The air was cool. A forest stood ahead, beckoning

them in hues of green and gold, shimmering in bright sunlight.

They were safe.

They toppled together, laughing, surprised, and grateful all at once. They were so tumbled up, so tossed that they weren't sure what had happened.

"Wait a minute. How did that happen? Where did the water come from?"

"Lucy didn't tell you about her gift?"

Giselle stared at him blankly.

"I'll explain later. Follow me." Louis took Lucy's hand, and Giselle trailed behind. They zigzagged through the dense woods toward the sound of an enormous rush that shook the ground under their feet.

What was it?

A river spilled from the top of a cliff. Not just any river. It crept to the edge of a precipice, and suddenly, free fell in a vaporous curtain that spilled unhindered, falling, falling, falling, until it smashed to a chaotic pool below.

Time suspended, even as the sun rose high over clear mountain air.

It was a waterfall.

Papa told her about raging rivers that fell to a forested floor from towering cliffs far above.

She hadn't believed him.

In the desert, date palm trees, tamarisk, and desert thyme waved over grassy knolls in what looked like random places. It wasn't haphazard at all. Life only thrived when there were water sources hidden deep below barren sands. Camel drivers and anyone who dared to journey through its desolation gauged each trip by how much water was available and how long it took to get there.

When water meant life or death, prosperity or famine, it had walls to protect it. Conduits ran throughout Darras, flowing from three springs tucked away in hills just inside their walls. The gatekeeper's job meant protecting access. Cutting off the springs by enemy hands meant death for the city.

She stood, transfixed by the wonder of billowing water. This was so much more. Like the sky opened to flood the earth in a beautiful, free, and abundant gale, it leaped and dashed with such force it muffled any other sound. The spray at its base soaked their hot, ravaged bodies.

It felt like paradise.

Louis grabbed her hand and pulled her away, as Lucy and Elise ducked out of sight into dense undergrowth.

"Wait. Just a little longer. Can't we stay here and rest?"

Louis's face tightened into a grimace. He nodded toward the river at their feet. "Look downstream."

An ebony serpent hovered over a canopy of trees. Its talons dangled like scythes under black, shimmering armor on its body.

It was a real-life version of the serpent on the Nayeli flag.

It couldn't be. Surely, it was only an image, a jagged scar against the forest's beauty, except for the stink of sulfur that drifted upstream. Its eyes combed the forest as puffs of smoke rolled out of its nostrils.

Forest surrounded them on both sides. The mountains they'd seen were too far away to reach. The waterfall that captured her heart with such awe blocked their flight.

Louis whispered. "Follow me." He led them to the falls that roared louder with every step closer. The spray of pounding water that captivated her only moments before was terrifying.

Closer and closer, soon they'd drown in the plummeting rapids. She was a desert girl. She had no idea how to swim. Not that swimming mattered in water that churned at her feet.

Louis held out his hand.

A narrow path ran along one side of the waterfall. Lucy and Elise disappeared in plumes of mist. Louis stood alone, with his hand extended.

Suddenly, the dragon lifted leathery wings and launched itself with a roar. Fire poured out of its mouth, swallowing the stream with its heat. "Mine. You're mine!"

Death by drowning. Death by fire.

She was no fool.

She'd take the waterfall.

She grabbed his hand, and they ran, weaving with the trail, until raging torrents swallowed them whole.

Chapter 10

Tumbling onto cool granite, she heaved for breath as the waterfall rushed like a gossamer curtain behind them. A giant steam plume rose behind the falls, and the pool beneath them boiled like a cauldron.

She scrambled forward and cried out. "Louis. Where are you?"

He was at her side the next moment, helping her to her feet. He led her deeper into a massive cave where Lucy and Elise already stood, looking strangely unafraid.

A banquet table, scorched as though pulled from fire, glimmered in cool light on one side of the room. A bowl of fresh grapes and a pitcher of fresh water with cups sat in the middle.

Real fruit. Real water.

Was it a trap?

Louis stood, catching his breath. "It's our table." His fingers lightly grazed its surface. "From the chateau."

Elise grabbed a bunch of grapes and crammed one in Lucy's mouth, then wiggled out of her mother's arms to explore. Lucy stroked its long bench. "I sat right here. When Aless let me."

"Who's Aless? Are you sure this is safe?"

Louis guzzled a cup of water and stuffed grapes into his mouth.

They finished off the grapes and water, peering around the immense quiet of the cave. It didn't matter that the dragon raged outside. They were safe here and out of reach.

The quiet brush of footsteps approached. Giselle stood, ready to run, knowing there was nowhere to go. She reached for Louis's hand and tried to gather Lucy and Elise close. They weren't cooperating.

Instead, they ran forward with happy leaps when two men, dressed in wintergreen and gold, appeared from an ornate door at the back of the room.

They were majestic.

At least one of them. The other looked like an aged skunk. He took a long look at her and scowled.

The men appeared to be human. After their battle with the viper, she wasn't sure anymore what was flesh and blood and what was a demon in disguise.

"Clarion! Brocagni!" shouted Louis and Lucy in unison. They rushed forward with many bows and almost hugs.

Clarion was tall and slender, like an elm that reached the peak of its beauty. He approached them with quiet grace. Surely, he was king of some mysterious kingdom.

A permanent frown etched into the other man's aged face covered in a random spray of silver whiskers. A white streak of hair stood straight up and ran down the middle of his head. Definitely part skunk.

"Welcome, friends. We've been expecting you."

Clarion was the spokesman. That was good, since Brocagni looked like he'd bitten into a pickled egg.

"Where is everyone?" Louis asked, fairly jumping up and down.

The two men led them through another door, then another. Each step led them deeper into the mountain, where chamber after chamber led them into a large open space.

The air around them cooled, and the pounding waterfall muffled as they entered a room lit by torches on each wall. On another long table, a meal of meats, cheeses, and breads beckoned.

Giselle drew back, unsure if hunger should outrun caution.

With Elise in tow, Louis and Lucy raced to meet people of all ages who flooded the room. There were cries of greeting and so much hugging, so many tears that they melded into one big puddle. Everyone talked at the same time, raising the noise to a chaotic din. They hugged again, laughed, and wiped away tears. Mostly, they laughed.

No one noticed that she stood alone, an awkward spectator.

"Marcella! You're all grown up – no more leaves in your hair." Louis embraced a young woman dressed in the same green that Lucy wore. "You always beat me when we climbed that sycamore."

She'd never seen joy like this in Louis. It started from some unknown place and spread out like the river they'd escaped behind the wall.

Louis and Lucy were having the time of their lives – to say nothing of Elise, who traveled from one set of arms to another with oohs and ahhs. Her tiny fingers grasped curls and yanked, as she chortled with lots to say about these strangers who showed up in a cave.

Never had Giselle felt so alone.

Louis talked back and forth in comfortable banter that echoed in the stone walls. He was totally at ease in the middle of what appeared to be loving relatives. A life he never mentioned.

Face to face with family that wasn't hers, she was surrounded by happiness she'd never known.

Why did it hurt so much?

Louis came to her side in one leap. "Alessandra. Everyone. This is my friend, Giselle Basir."

Brocagni took center stage unannounced. "She looks Nayeli." He spat a blob of spittle on the pristine granite.

"Shame, Brocagni." A woman walked forward, holding out her hand in welcome.

Giselle took a step back.

The woman smiled, as if she understood.

Her chestnut curls stood out in wild abandon. The woman carried herself with iron in her very bones. It was like looking into a long mirror. "I believe we're related. My name is Alessandra. We welcome you, Giselle, in the name of all that is brave and true. We honor your parents and their sacrifice for our people."

Looking at Alessandra propelled her into a past she never knew but recognized. Was she talking about Papa and Mother?

"Ahoy, buckos! Shiver me timbers and off the plank, ye go!" Laughing sounded from the back of the room, where a small horde of children wrestled with gales of giggles around an older man.

"Hey, it's my turn," clamored one. "Move outa the way." The kids tumbled like puppies on every side. He leapt to his feet, scattering children when he saw Louis. "Oi, off the galley for lemonade!" He dashed like a camel driver in a hurry for breakfast to Louis. He held him tight and wept without shame.

Then, as if he'd just noticed her presence, he turned and stared at Giselle.

She returned the stare. He was tall and gangly, much like Louis. Crow's feet etched around eyes that were blue starbursts. It was a face that smiled a lot over many years, if his scene with the little ones was any proof.

Those blue eyes filled with tears.

What had she done?

"Rory, this is Giselle."

Rory's face crinkled in an expression she couldn't read. He took his place beside Alessandra, who draped her arm over his shoulders.

She was the uninvited guest, unsure of how to explain why she was there. "I work with Louis at our inn, the Gemini."

A single tear coursed down Rory's cheek. "Oi. We're pleased to meet you." He almost choked on the last word. "Giselle."

Suddenly, he turned and left the room.

That was fast. She did or said something to offend him. Louis studied his hands as if they held something interesting.

"You didn't do anything wrong." Aless answered her confusion. "My husband's heart is his greatest gift. He treasures your presence with us."

Why? These people were Magi. She was Nayeli. Enough said.

"Maura!" Louis cried out. "Aiden?" An aged couple rushed forward, as if they'd waited their turn to greet them.

Thin etching lined Maura's face like an heirloom painting. She had the same starburst eyes she saw in Rory. Aiden's hair was a faded red mop. His parchment skin bore the marks of many sunburns. Freckles spread over his face, down his neck, and over his arms. He carried a faint aroma of leather, as if he arrived by horseback.

Louis scanned the room. "Where's Suzette? She must be all grown up and married, with her own children. When can I see her?" He twirled around the room with Elise, whose slobbery fingers encircled his neck. "Fearless. That's what she is. I'll never forget her charging down that hill, past the gnarly warriors. Dragon or not, she had a mission. Rory was going to be okay."

No one spoke. The once vibrant people settled into a hush.

Alessandra draped an arm around Lucy, who stood beside her. "She was killed in the last attack on the chateau."

Louis froze in place. "No."

One at a time, they approached until a small army formed a circle around him.

Bucket after bucket of love overturned on his trembling form. Until, finally, he stared at the ground, wavering like a slender tree in a strong wind.

He was going down. She knew it.

So did everyone else.

They caught him before he crumbled on the floor.

They were a potent force, this family. Far from stoic, they cried freely and loved with an unnerving abandon.

They did that now, each one patting Louis, and then Lucy, whispering a memory or word of comfort. The outpouring wasn't like dumping hot water on ice, but a gradual flow of warmth that finally overtook the cold grief.

Louis melted into a lake of tears.

It was the terrible, unrelenting sorrow she knew.

What if she and Mother had comforted each other

like this? Would they have had the constant arguments, the simmering rage that came out at the worst possible times?

Giselle looked around for a hiding place but nowhere made her feel less welcome. It was impossible to hide. She stood for the enemy who plundered them. Shame washed over her heart. They'd never invite her into their hearts. Not after this blow.

A prism of blue light danced against a stone wall at the back of the massive room.

Alessandra caught her eye. "Follow me. I'll show you."

Chapter 11

Instead of colder and darker, blue light multiplied as if it welcomed their approach. Oaken double doors stood before them like a giant barrier – or entrance, depending on what hid behind it.

She was tired and wet. Her tunic clung to her clammy legs, and she only wanted a bath. This woman was a stranger, even though she looked as familiar as a glance in a mirror.

She gripped one side of her wet tunic into a tight wad.

Alessandra didn't look ferocious. She carried herself more like a special guide or even protector in a weathered kind of way. Maybe she spent her days on horseback, chasing bad guys. Like a female militia of one. Something about the woman both terrified and drew her.

She could refuse to go in. The woman was taller than she was, though not big enough to drag her where she didn't want to go. Besides, she wasn't a child. She didn't need anyone to lead her by the hand.

Alessandra waited, proving she offered an invitation instead of a command. Who knew what she really wanted? What behind that door was so important to see, anyway?

The door stretched from the floor to the ceiling, more like a wall than an entrance. Symbols of an ancient language were carved into its surface. One design grabbed her attention. Just like the one in her window, a six-point star stood out in relief like a giant beacon in the center.

Time suspended like the massive door that loomed before her. Alessandra stood quietly, still waiting.

Maybe she was supposed to be quiet like the eerie Nayeli worship that offered no room for requests. All she had were questions. Silence was no help when she was lost and surrounded by Magi – a people she despised all her life.

She owed this place and this woman no reverence. She was Nayeli, not Magi. She had questions, she'd ask them. Or at least start with a simple observation. "I have a star like that in my bedroom window."

Papa never told her why he fashioned the ornament out of straw and hung it there. When it caught whatever breeze found its way through her window, it was like Papa whispering in a breath of desert wind.

Alessandra nodded, as if that was to be expected. "It's a sign of refuge."

She always believed Papa existed to make her own world sweeter. It was hard to imagine that he placed the ornament for anyone but her. Still, her window faced outside the city walls. Any traveler who needed a safe haven saw it.

Alessandra brushed the star with her fingers. "Magi carved this door from the oak tree that sheltered me when a dragon raged."

Another dragon? These people attracted ancient fiends she barely knew existed. The story around it didn't matter. It was only a door crafted by human hands from a tree.

"Not just any door." Alessandra answered Giselle's thoughts. "Rory took the fire of the serpent meant for me. He would've died, except for a little one with a healing gift who wasn't afraid to offer it."

The woman was speaking another language for all Giselle knew. Besides, there was a glaring problem with this supposedly extraordinary door. "There's no handle. How do you open it?"

Alessandra's voice was low and certain. "This door responds to the heart. It opens to those who are willing to see and to hear."

Proving her words, the door swung open on hinges hidden on each side. With a whoosh of fresh air, a brightly lit room stood before them.

There were no chandeliers or torches ensconced on the walls, yet light chased away shadows inside the towering granite walls. Instead of a ceiling, sunlight shone from the open sky above and filled the chamber.

Two ordinary stones stood on an altar. Luminescent as alabaster, they glowed in the center of the room as if lit from within. Peace tiptoed near her heart like a gentle visitor. Giselle steeled herself against its presence.

She didn't intend to be seduced into another snare. She trusted Erik and was wrong. Even Ramaz, the holiest man among all the Nayeli, turned traitor. She wouldn't be so naïve again. "Why isn't there a ceiling?"

"The builders knew we needed a reminder to look up." Alessandra studied her so closely that Giselle squirmed. "The blueprint of your life is bigger than you think."

She didn't know what to say. Her life was a mishmash of loss and more loss. The adventure in Apamea became a war over a gift unknown to her but coveted by others. Even Louis deceived her with allegiance to a people and family he'd never mentioned.

Alessandra bowed slightly, turned, and walked back to the entrance.

"Don't leave me."

Alessandra spoke like she was assuring a small child. "My purpose was only to lead you here. You aren't a captive. Stay long enough to see what you've never seen."

When the door closed, panic rushed into the space Alessandra left. She pounded on enormous oak until her knuckles were raw. She wouldn't stay. She couldn't.

How stupid to trust these people.

It didn't matter how kind they appeared. Like Erik, they only led her to a trap. The rumble of pounding water hummed through her body. It didn't take long to come to the end of any fight. She stopped struggling and pillowed her head in her arms.

She was done. She tried her best to escape every sorrow, every snare, every betrayal and failure. She was held as a slave by Ramaz, set free by Louis and chased across the desert, only to face an impenetrable wall, with its own personal dragon. They barely made it to this mysterious place under a pounding waterfall.

Nothing made sense anymore.

In moments, a scene unfolded before her eyes so real, she wondered if somehow, she was blasted back in time.

She was a little girl. Lightning slashed the night sky, and the smell of rain was in the air. Strange excitement stirred all around her. Papa was leaving on another journey.

"I'm afraid," she murmured into Mother's thick

hair.

"Hush, now. Papa has a mighty friend, a guardian who soars overhead. Their mission calls and they can't delay. We must watch the gate for him."

"What if he forgets us?"

Mama brushed her cheek with a kiss. "Silly girl. How could he forget the ones he loves most?"

The vision shifted to her mother alone in her room, crying.

What about her mother had she never known? Papa's disappearance was a silent thief that had taken Mother, too. She tossed blame back and forth for years, hoping it landed square on her mother's shoulders. It wasn't exactly comfort, although it quieted torment that raged, "It was you. All you."

The door opened in a quiet swoosh. Louis appeared, framed in light and unmoving, wondering if he was invited.

She'd missed her constant friend, his silly jokes, his wrinkled brow when he was lost in thought. In a hundred ways she missed him as if he'd been gone for years instead of minutes. Scrambling from the floor, she threw herself into his arms. "We need to stay, Louis. Bring in as many loved ones as we can. They'll be protected here."

Louis pressed his forehead against hers, smelling of evergreen and hope. "It's special, right?" He pulled away and brushed a stray curl from her eyes. "This is more than a sanctuary. It's a place of fresh vision."

"I can see just fine."

"It's what you can't see that threatens."

"You're speaking in riddles again. I did notice a dragon breathing down our necks."

Laurel Thomas

Louis grinned. "Hard to miss. Do you remember when we stargazed on the roof?

Giselle flushed with the memory of their arms brushing as they lay on their backs on the tiled roof. She loved the stillness of a cool summer evening with him at the end of a long day. Louis mimicked the most obnoxious customers until she rolled with laughter. "Of course. How could I forget your imitation of Sir Krackenberry?"

"One of my finest." Louis pointed a finger to the sky. "Do you remember Pleiades, the star cluster? How it only came into sight when we shifted our eyes to one side?"

"Yes. Something about your long-winded explanation of cones and rods, or whatever."

"Exactly. Proof that some things are hidden until we look in a new way. That's why this room was built. To help us see what we haven't understood before."

"Like how?

Louis started slowly. "Like knowing that your parents were here one day. That they stood on the same stone floor."

"In this cave? Why?"

"They lived in our community, Giselle."

"That can't be true. We're Nayeli. We've always been. The Magi are our...enemy." That didn't make much sense anymore. She couldn't forget her mother defending the stranger at the inn against Sir Damien's accusations. She watched her outside the palace masquerade, hooded and creeping through the darkness as she hid the man from Darras authorities.

Her last argument grew weaker by the moment. "They would've told me if they were Magi." Anger bubbled up out of hiding. Her words came out in a gush of frustration. "Wait. No. That means they hid the truth about themselves and about me. Why?"

He held up his hands in surrender. "Slow down. Can I explain before you leap into mad? This refuge inside the mountain has been here for many years. It was built because a real dragon raged against us." He breathed a deep sigh before speaking again. "Your parents were here, in this room, when a vision appeared. They saw a city where the dragon lived. And a people who needed them."

"Why would an unknown town need my parents?"

"They came as light in the darkness. Because Darras is the home of Gad El Glas."

"Light, you say? They kept me blind. On purpose."

"They had to protect you. You were inside the hub of the enemy's territory. They planned to tell you when you turned sixteen. By then – well, your father was gone, and your mother lost her vision." Louis studied his hands and then shrugged. "She was broken, Giselle. Her faith wavered. It happens."

Giselle sorted through a crush of emotions and tried to pick out one. She couldn't. "Do I have family here? Anyone?"

"Yes."

One word. One affirmation that somewhere, somehow, she belonged to a family outside of Papa and Mother. "Where are they? Why haven't I known this? How cruel to hide something so precious." She jerked away from Louis's embrace when Rory, Alessandra, and Maura entered the room. They were intruders into a moment that was hers alone. "What are they doing here?"

"I invited them. To prove that you do have a history. With us."

"This is none of their business." Giselle slashed the air with her hand. "I have nothing in common with any of them."

"You're very mistaken." Louis's words were calm. "They are your family."

"How can that be?" She whirled to face the three Magi. "Besides, what could have been mine, but wasn't doesn't count." Affection that could have grounded her, that could have comforted and helped her bear a load, hadn't been there. Not in any way she needed.

Alessandra's voice was strong. "It was too dangerous. Your parents couldn't leave. We couldn't visit. They accepted a mission that separated us forever."

"I. Don't. Understand. Who are you, anyway?"

Alessandra spoke up in her warrior-woman fashion. "Your mother, Ursula, is our daughter. Rory and I are your grandparents." She pointed to an oil painting on an easel in one corner of the room. "Maybe this picture will help."

A young woman with flowing raven hair, dark eyes, and ivory skin stood and peered down at a little girl at her side. The tilt of the woman's chin and the way she carried her shoulders were just like Mother's.

"Who is this?"

"My mother. Her name was Lilith. She died when I was very young."

"She looks like my mother." She took a breath. "Look, I don't mean to offend you. There's no way you could be my mother's mother."

Alessandra's laughter filled the room. "True. We couldn't have been more different. Yet, here I am, looking much like you. You're my evidence, granddaughter, that I didn't come out from under some rock."

The woman with wild brown curls was her grandmother. Mother always said she carried herself as if the world passed too quickly and she had to leap in to enter. Alessandra walked the same way. Her voice even lifted at the end of each sentence, waiting for an answer.

Giselle's mind spun in confusion. She remembered Rory's tears. "Rory is my grandfather."

Rory grinned and bowed slightly to Giselle. "You don't know me, dear. You look so much like your grandmother. It took me a bit of getting used to." He dashed away a stray tear.

Giselle walked forward and took his hand. When she did, a wave of love surged into her like a wave. She fell to her knees.

He lifted her up. "My brave one. You're not as unlike your mother as you think."

They stood, peering at one another, neither of them knowing what to say. He motioned to a couch and chairs under the picture of Lilith. "Come. Sit. I have a story about your mama when she was little."

She didn't know any stories. She wasn't sure Mother even had a childhood. "Yes, please."

"She had this old dog. Name was Rufus. He wasn't high on smarts, that mutt. Plus, he was ugly as all get out. She loved him, though."

He was a storyteller from long ago. She was as entranced as the children who hung around his knees.

"We lived in these mountains, in a chateau right next to a meadow. It was late fall. Grizzlies were looking for last minute snacks before they hibernated. This sow had

Rufus in its clutches and intended to haul him off for her personal lunch.

"Your mama was every bit of five years old. She charged that bear, hurled rocks, hollered and carried on until it dropped Rufus and ambled back into the woods. It gave up on a fight that wasn't worth a scrawny mongrel." Rory tilted his head, as if to get a better look at her. "You're like that, too. You go after what threatens the ones you love."

"Well." She thought about all the ways she'd sabotaged relationships with the most important people in her life – like Mother and Louis.

"Well, nothing. Your heart may be a tad shredded, but your instincts are good. Strong and compassionate – just like your mother and grandmother."

It was a priceless moment. For all the ways her gift was supposedly so great, for all the ways it was supposed to bring wealth and release freedom, she really only wanted one thing.

A family.

"I wish I'd known you all along."

Rory spoke as if she were a long-lost, much-loved child. "Your mama came to her mother and me when she was about your age. She was in love. Couldn't talk enough about that man. Said he had a mission, and it was one that called her, too. She was determined to go, wherever it took them. In this case, it was to Darras."

"How did you feel about that?"

"I didn't like it. The last place I wanted for our daughter. Wasn't sure I trusted your Papa, or anyone else, for that matter with my girl. Like her mother, though, she was fearless. And stubborn. No pleas on our part changed her mind. Nothing mattered except that man and his vision."

He sighed and looked away. The past drifted a little too close.

Alessandra patted his shoulder. "He's still not so sure."

Rory was a dad who let his daughter go, knowing he might never see her again. "Were you mad at Papa?"

Rory grinned. "Of course."

"Did she have a sister or brother?"

"No. She was our only child."

"Did she know how hard it was on you?" She felt herself already jumping to her grandfather's defense.

"Probably not. Young people, at least your mother and father, were full of bravery and big plans. Made daddy look dim in comparison." His wry, crooked grin made the sweetest dimple in one cheek.

"I bet she never forgot." Sadness swept over her heart. "Why wouldn't she tell me about you?"

Alessandra answered. "Perhaps it buried the pain. Easier not to speak of someone precious, yet so far away."

Maura hadn't said a word in all this. When she put her hand on Giselle's shoulder, peace came along with her. Without explanation, torment faded, and her heart settled. Why was that? "Who are you, Maura O'Donnell?"

Louis laughed softly. "Yes. Tell us."

Giselle felt like the brunt of a joke. "Don't make fun of me."

A bit of mischief lit Maura's starburst eyes as she pulled her chair closer to Giselle. "We weren't making fun of you. I was an orphaned outcast. An enemy cloaked in the garb of a family member lusted for my gift. She's the one who told me the truth about seeing the unseen. For the first time, I saw the value of a treasure I carried through an enemy's eyes. You might be like me in that way."

Giselle leaned back in her seat. "In my city, terrible things happen in a temple that I've heard about but never seen. Nor do I ever want to. Seeing the hidden would reveal things too awful to bear." She hesitated. Maybe she said too much. Then again, there was more. "The dragon's presence didn't seem to rile you up. Why is that?"

"Ask my husband if I ever get unraveled." She offered a tender look. "Evil seeks to hide itself. Seeing wickedness isn't enough. Full vision is discovering what overcomes it and then acting on it."

As delightful as this moment was, this was still nothing more than a fairy tale that supposedly connected her to a life and people she never knew. "I can't. I'm not. I hated the Magi. I hated my mother." If she could only toss the past aside and run far, far away.

Without warning, Alessandra took one hand, and Maura took the other. They stood under the open ceiling and lifted hands in a triangle.

"The breaker, who opens a way through the gate, bursts through doors of bronze and bars of iron."

She should try to wrest herself out of this odd scenario. Somehow, she didn't want to. Because peace flooded in, along with gladness that bubbled up without reason. A drop of water plopped on Giselle's arm.

Only it wasn't rain.

Liquid crystals descended from a clear, cloudless sky above.

Another and another raindrop fell. The rain didn't

peck her head and arms. Instead, it was warm against her skin and released a fragrance of rose and jasmine, her mother's favorite scent.

What looked like diamonds sprinkled, then filled the air around them. Each one burst into light and illumined the room with such brightness, Giselle expected to squint. She looked on, wide-eyed, as light expanded, and the crystals became drenching rain. The three women stood together in a radiant waterfall that saturated them with its fragrance.

Maura and Alessandra spoke in unison. "A three-fold cord is not easily broken."

She didn't understand. It didn't matter.

Minutes later, or maybe it had been hours, the rain was gone, the light dimmed, but the fragrance remained. Maura and Alessandra's hands lowered, and they stood as a sunlit trio.

Louis was there, his face full of delight she'd never seen in the years she knew him.

"This was the plan all along." Giselle looked for anger inside but couldn't find it. She searched her heart for the familiar fear. It was gone, too.

He held out his arms and she ran into them. They spun around in a dance as Maura, Rory and Alessandra looked on, laughing so hard, they doubled over. This was a party that spilled out goodness like an unexpected summer rain.

Until Louis stopped, midspin. He grabbed and held her tight, in a protective embrace.

"What are you doing? What's wrong?"

The stink of sulfur filtered as a noxious wave, a serpent seeking prey in a rose garden. Terror rose into her throat.

In her mind's eye, she was a child again. She was alone outside the city gates. Chestnut curls scattered like dust in scorching wind and her face burned. A dragon roared a thunderous taunt, teeth bared, and head waving from its scaley serpent neck.

The same gravelly voice broke into the sweetness of this moment. It hissed with certain triumph.

"Hello, again, Giselle. Your mother has five days to live. Wouldn't you like to say goodbye?"

Chapter 12

The stench lifted when the dragon's voice vanished as quickly as it arrived. Above, blue sky glittered with full-day sun, as if it hadn't noticed a beast hovering under its light. Without a word, Alessandra and Maura opened their hands to include Louis and Rory in a circle. The four of them stood, hands clasped and heads down.

Well, except for Giselle. Only Louis on one side and Maura on the other kept her legs from buckling.

Were they praying? Now, when she only had five days to return to Mother?

Five days to make it from the mountains over the wall, a river, and across the desert to Darras.

What kind of prayer worked for that?

She interrupted the silence. "I'm leaving. Now."

Alessandra's eyes were like tranquil pools, unruffled by a rogue wind. "We'll help. Our resources are yours." Her fingers grazed Giselle's shoulder. "Remember what happened here. The taunt of the evil one is designed to make you forget. Don't."

Giselle rested her head against Louis's chest. An image grew with the serpent's words. "I saw that dragon when I was little."

Maura and Alessandra retreated as Louis held her close. His fragrance was like something green. This was his home. His skin released the scent of evergreen, a tree that remained unchanged, no matter what the season.

Shame washed over her. Louis had unspeakable memories of the dragon. All she could remember were flashes of light and a nagging pain in her gut, long buried.

The warmth of Louis, and the strength of his arms were his only response.

She was no longer alone. Except no less guilty. "I should have run back inside the city walls. I should have…" She spoke from another time, another world. "It made me pay. It took Papa. Now Mother." She shook her head, longing to erase the torment, but knowing she couldn't. "I hated her for so many years. What if I can't save her?"

Louis steadied her quaking limbs with his embrace. He wiped a tear that dribbled down the side of her nose. "Don't do this to yourself. Not now. Not ever."

Another light flashed, this time with a surge of heat that traveled throughout her body. "I think. Because. I wouldn't let it in."

"Look at me." Louis gently tugged her chin upward and waited until their eyes met. "You were a child. You couldn't know that. Some memories are so terrible all we can do is bury them."

How many loved ones had he lost? His kindness hadn't wavered. There was no way she could ask him to follow where she had to go. "I have to leave for Darras. Now."

His answer came with the next breath. "I'm going with you."

His presence healed a wound she didn't know she had. She couldn't lose him. "Miles of desert stand between us and Darras. It's impossible, even if we could find a camel train."

"We'll find a way."

She'd never noticed Louis's rare heart hid amid angles and bones of his narrow frame. "This is a journey for me, alone. I'm a target now. Doors open to untold riches? It doesn't matter how many miles span the desert. News of our journey will draw treasure hunters from every direction." Memories of the pouch filled with gold, Erik's betrayal, and the bolted door unlocking by her hands flooded her mind.

Louis stood, looking into the sky that continued to shine despite the serpent's vile threat. "The dragon fears you."

"Nothing in me scares that beast."

"You have a Magi gift. That changes everything."

"Stop." She sighed, exasperated with all this spiritual talk she had no grid for. She stood at the brink of the universe. One more push and she'd be hurtled into its vast unknown. "My parents didn't tell me. You never told me. I've been ignorant of something that could've changed everything I know and love."

"I wish you grew up knowing the truth. Every pain, every loss contended for a gift already inside you. Its power worked when you weren't aware. Now that you do know, the gift becomes stronger." His fingers lightly grazed the key around her neck.

Warmth flooded her cheeks. "How do you understand all this? What makes you…" She couldn't finish the question. It was too big. Louis was a mystery unveiling before her eyes.

"I know because I… Never mind. Your brush with the dragon as a child proved that it knew what you carried. How did that end, anyway?"

Her head whirled with a wave of dizziness. This was

too much to take in. "I've tried to remember. I can't. Why is that?"

"Whether or not you remember doesn't matter. You thwarted some kind of destruction the dragon plotted."

Giselle didn't have the heart to consider anything outside of what had to be done but was impossible. "I have to find Mother. Right away."

There was no way. She already knew that. "A camel train takes weeks. I don't have that time. What if she's already..."

Maura appeared with Alessandra at her side. Where had they been? They were so quiet. Were they respecting this holy moment? Maura lifted her hand, as if to shift directions. "I know a way to get you home."

"There's nothing fast about traveling through the desert. No matter how I go."

"Wait! I know." Louis clapped his hands and uttered a single word. "Tobias."

"Who is Tobias and how can he get me back to Darras?"

"I'm going with her." Louis planted his feet. She knew that look. He wasn't changing his mind, even if the dragon itself showed up and offered safe passage.

"You can't," Maura insisted. "Tobias is the only one who can get her safely back to Darras. He can take to the skies where no obstacles hinder her travel."

"None except a dragon that shares the skies," Louis muttered in grim frustration.

They kept talking, as if she wasn't there.

"Tobias was created to guard treasure. He'll do that. Even if..." She took a deep breath as tears welled in her eyes. "He can be trusted. Even to the death."

"How can we reach him?"

"We go to the meadow."

"You're talking back and forth around me like I'm some luggage to be hauled back to Darras. I'll…Maybe we can bring Mother here." She needed to figure it all out, to find a way to get her mother back to this wonderful place. They could live out their days here, in safety with the Magi.

No longer pilgrims locked in a city surrounded by desert, they'd be here with a long-awaited family. "Besides, how do we know the dragon isn't waiting to turn us into cinders outside this sanctuary?"

Maura's voice was as serene as though they discussed a leisurely walk. "Our scouts have already gone ahead to secure the area. We've met Tobias in the meadow many times before. It has shelter, as well as an open area for the breadth of his wings. The others want to see him. And, of course, they want to say good-bye."

Good-bye? Every bit of courage Giselle drummed up made a sudden exit.

Louis took her hand. "Don't be afraid. Tobias is a friend."

What did friendship have to do with anything? Once again, these Magi operated in ways that defied explanation.

Mid-day sun dwindled into late afternoon. Alessandra showed her a spring-fed pool, tucked away in the rock. After she bathed and changed into fresh clothes, Lucy and Elise, then Louis took their turns.

Leafy shadows of towering oak and sycamore played along the rocky shore as they picked their way toward the chateau. Ahead, splotches of color dotted all kinds of flowering trees and bushes positioned like guardians before its lofty stone walls

"This was our home. Before the dragon." Louis pointed at a black, burnt-out structure just beyond the sprawling lawn.

The former grandeur of a chateau was charred ruins. Walls were broken, and the roof dangled over open spaces. A scorched door frame listed like a broken soldier. Ashes fed green grass around it.

A scout went before them and beckoned with one arm.

Unlike her, the Magi lived with the reality of a dragon for generations. Of course, they had scouts. Maura and Louis were careful, but not frantic as they walked through the fragrance of cherry and apple blossoms. Giselle reached out to touch the blossom of a mountain laurel, just to be sure it was real.

The meadow was hidden by a stand of aspen that circled an open pasture dotted with wildflowers. The blackened trunk of a towering oak lay on one side, as a token of the dragon's flames. Rory tucked Alessandra under one arm and kissed her forehead.

Maura turned her face to the sky and lifted her hands as if with a prayer.

The whoosh of massive wings appeared in the sky over the waterfall. In minutes, an eagle with a lion's body soared above the meadow. It was impossible that those wings, as huge as they were, supported the weight of a kingly lion.

Tobias was a griffin.

Papa talked about griffins, weaving them into his stories as if they belonged to all that was brave and good. They were guardians of treasure and lived among the cliffs where stores of gold lay hidden. He never mentioned how terrifying they were.

At least this one.

With precise aim, Tobias settled massive haunches with cat-like grace in front of Maura, dwarfing her with sheer weight and power. Without a word, he spread out the wingspan three times as wide as any eagle and bowed to the ground before her. "My queen."

Giselle took note. The majestic creature singled out this quiet woman with honor and allegiance. When everyone else bowed before Tobias, Giselle fell to the damp ground and did the same. With her head up so that she wouldn't miss anything.

She hadn't seen a griffin before, but if she had, she would've run for cover. He had the ferocity of a lion, and the sharp gaze of an eagle.

He didn't look happy. His bead-like eyes scanned her from head to toe and came up with a scowl. A visible scar ran down his chest, evidence of some mortal battle.

He knelt before Maura as though no one else was there.

Maura lightly stroked the broad, bare slash on his lion's chest, then leaned her head against his shoulder. "Dragon's fire."

"Suzette healed me. Before she died." The griffin's voice was like low thunder. He turned his gaze from Maura to Giselle. His eagle eyes were as intent as if he were the hunter and she were the prey.

Maura appeared at Giselle's side and bowed slightly to Tobias. "Her name is Giselle."

"She looks Nayeli." The griffin obviously shared Brocagni's opinion.

Once again, they spoke as if she wasn't there. She might have been offended; except she was glad not to be the focus of the griffin's attention.

"Giselle is one of us, even though she doesn't look like it," Maura began. "She's Ursula's daughter and must return to Darras quickly. Her mother is in trouble."

One of them? How long would it take for her to truly believe she was more than a bystander to this mysterious people?

A crowd gathered around them. Lucy, carrying Elise, wiggled their way through the throng of Magi. Elise reached for Giselle with her little face screwed up into a pucker.

"She wants a kiss," Lucy reminded her. She handed Elise to Giselle and unloaded a pile of bread, cheese, dried meat, and water skins. There was even a flint with a small mound of moss for starting a fire. She pointed to a bundle of fabric. "You'll need these. Leonore said to be sure they went with you – no matter where adventure called. Don't forget your knife."

The knife Leonore had given her – the one she tried to reject – freed her at the slave market in Apamea. As well as a whole warehouse of other slaves. Even the fabrics she gave them offered refuge in a way she never expected.

"One more thing." Lucy pulled out a tiny earthen pot with a battered lid. "This is a gift from my sister, Suzette. It's her healing ointment. Just in case."

Louis's face crumpled in sadness for a moment, then he nodded. "Suzette would be happy to share with Giselle."

It was a treasure that should give her fresh courage. Instead, when the mighty griffin stalked closer, Giselle almost ran away in terror. In any minute she'd be whisked away to a faraway eyrie full of sticks and thorns.

Instead of devouring her, Tobias knelt at her side.

"He's offering himself, Giselle," Maura said. "Few mortals have been carried on his strong wings."

What was she to do?

She might as well be carrying a sign, *I'm Nayeli*. She was a woman born and raised in the enemy's camp. A journey to Darras from this mountain kingdom carried no promises. The griffin was massive, but the dragon was even more enormous and had a fire in his gut.

According to Louis, their destination led them into its lair. Not only that, the griffin obviously didn't like her looks. He, like Brocagni, knew her as part of a culture that was sworn enemy.

He offered himself for Maura alone.

Just when she was closer to finding Papa, her mother needed her. A dragon held the woman whose domineering ways drove her away. Now, she was supposed to hop on the back of a mythical beast that looked at her like an unappetizing but necessary meal. The strangest mix of longing and resentment boiled inside her.

Louis helped her wrap a long length of Leonore's fabric around her and Tobias. "Watch. Learn this knot."

"Or what? I'll go flying?" The sweetness she felt behind the waterfall disappeared as terror took its place. She remembered what she'd always known.

Family was great.

Until they left.

Her heart felt sick. Anger was so much safer than the always lingering sorrow.

She worked up steam as he tied her securely to the back of the griffin. Or at least by what looked like a fixed knot. She traveled by foot through the desert, climbed an impenetrable wall that released a venomous snake, then escaped over said wall to the back of a towering waterfall. "You're sending me to my death with my mother as an excuse. How convenient. One Nayeli down, another one out of harm's way."

His real heart showed up on that slave platform in Apamea. He intervened to save Lucy and Elise. She only came along for the ride. She spit out words, hoping they cut as deep a gash as the fear she felt. "You're only pretending to care."

Louis stood without saying a word. She recognized his hurt. She searched out the vulnerable place in his heart and stabbed it with her sharpest words.

"Don't give me that look." She glared at Tobias, then back to Louis. "There has to be another way. You're trying to get rid of me. You just don't have the courage to do the job."

Louis slumped for a moment, then straightened. Hardness covered his face. He retreated. He was gone. Almost.

"Brilliant planning. Because I brought you safely here, to my relatives. To your own family. Loved ones who shared their most cherished gifts. You're too blind to even notice." He turned away, then whirled around to face her again. "I wondered why you could never say a simple thank you.

"Now I know. You expect people to hurt you, then cut them off before they get a chance." His voice was icy. "You blame your mother for everything. If you think she was a bully, go look in the mirror. You're far worse." He strode through the crowd of Magi into the forest.

And with that, the good-byes were over. Giselle's belly lurched as Tobias launched his mighty lion legs, muscles surging against her.

The Magi waved and shouted their blessings.
Louis wasn't there.

Chapter 13

Giselle shifted from terror of certain death to a queasy stomach threatening to give up its lunch as Tobias ascended through a gap of towering pines.

Shades of green wavered and brushed her legs until, finally, an expanse of blue appeared from hundreds of trees below. The same sky that blasted whirling sand in the desert, spread like endless blue linen before her.

Until a few days ago, she'd never seen mountains, or even a decent hill other than a sand dune. Unlike Papa's sundial that tethered her to Earth, this flight soared through time and space that stretched as far as she could see.

The mountains were like a muted cloud bank. They were disappearing as surely as Louis had. Why couldn't she just say it?

She was scared spitless.

Louis claimed she was a bully.

A lie, a bald-faced lie.

Well.

Her words were a blade, wielded on purpose.

She had a good reason. He was Magi. And now, she was supposed to fly through the sky on the back of a mythical beast as if that made any sense.

Besides, the Louis she thought she knew – the one who belonged to her and Mother and the inn, was far from the one she'd seen surrounded by siblings, loved by parents and grandparents.

It wasn't fair.

Rory was the grandfather she always wanted. She would've loved him from the beginning. Alessandra, her grandmother, was full of spunk. Her likeness was proof that she belonged not only somewhere, but in a real family. A peculiar one, but still, a family.

Even though she was alone on the back of a griffin who treated her like so much baggage, it was crazy to believe that the people she'd met, and the Louis she trusted, plotted to be rid of her forever.

Except for the fact that they were Magi.

It was late afternoon. The sun was really hot. She was miserable. When a stray wind current hit them like a stony roadblock, she hurled herself against his eagle's neck and screamed. "What if I fall off?"

"Hang on." Tobias growled, as if he shushed a wailing child.

"Nice. That helps." Had she expected a friendly chat along the way? There would be no answers to questions that nagged her, much less relief for the fear that never left. A good camel was a better transport than this arrogant beast.

Five days. They had five days to cross a hostile desert, brave its searing heat and arrive in time to somehow protect Mother from a dragon. Her legs rested around his lion's chest that moved from coarse fur to eagle feathers. She was tired and tempted to rest her head. Then again, flying didn't make her stupid. Only incredibly naïve.

Tobias glided, his eyes on the skies without distraction, sometimes soaring on a wind current and other times beating his mighty wings against an opposing gale.

Her legs cramped with giant clenches. No one consulted her on this mission. No one cared that she wasn't used to flying for hours without a break. She ducked her head as an eagle whooshed nearby, then plummeted to nab a rabbit or some animal hidden below.

Tobias headed toward a grove of acacia trees. A large pool sprang from an opening in a small rise hidden by vegetation. She was reminded of the waterfall. She never got over the comfort of seeing water rise out of nowhere in desert wasteland.

This gathering of date palms and acacia was smaller than most. She was surprised they were the only ones there. Even a small oasis like this would be marked on the maps of camel drivers from throughout the region as they carried their loads of salt one way, then returned with loads of goods for city markets.

Tobias landed with a bump beside a pool of water, then crouched silently as she untied the mangled knot and plopped to the ground. She scurried to stretch her legs, relieve her bladder, and fill the water skins.

Sweat dripped into her eyes and stung as she gathered dates from the ground and stashed them into her pack. Every few minutes, she studied Tobias from a safe distance.

His golden eyes constantly scanned around them and above. Clearly, he was too important for such petty tasks like gathering dates and more water for their journey.

A plump sandgrouse rustled through the brush as a calm breeze tousled her hair. When Tobias's haunches suddenly tightened, as if ready to spring into flight, she searched outside the oasis for an approaching caravan or camel train. Nothing. "It was just a bird. We're safe here."

"Cover yourself with the fabric." His voice sounded like gravel rattling in a metal pan. What had she expected him to sound like? A teddy bear?

"Look." She gathered steam. This griffin might be huge and intimidating, except he was not in charge. Besides, he could barely hide his contempt. "You haven't lowered yourself to speak this many words to me since we left. Why should I rush to obey now – just because you command it?"

No response. Only those eyes that studied her without blinking.

The sky around them was no less blue, the air no less fresh. It was a spring day in the desert, like one of many she'd known in Darras.

Enough of this. She trounced to the edge of the oasis and examined land and sky for any predator. Nothing but a dust devil whipped across the sand. She finally sat down at a safe distance from the griffin who gazed at a line of ragged cliffs far from them. "Nothing. Anywhere."

"The dragon watches from the mesa."

She sucked in a breath. Did she think the dragon would suddenly disappear? Could she trust Tobias? Maybe he'd swoop low and toss her to the ground when things got bad. He flew faster without her, for sure.

Then again, he appeared to have this code of honor.

She just wasn't sure she was included in it.

She got as close to him as she could without caving in to fear. Griffin on one side, dragon on another. She was in a bad way.

She strained her eyes but only saw red rock and

sand. Tobias was being overly cautious. "Why is it that I never saw a dragon until I met the Magi?"

His words were a matter of fact. "They've always existed. They just don't appear in an area they already possess."

"What does that mean?" This griffin was as much a puzzle as the Magi.

His eagle head turned to give her a sufficient glare. "Why contend for something that is already yours? Magi, on the other hand, represent treasure the dragon has never been able to steal. Very frustrating for a beast accustomed to seizing whatever it wants."

"All I see are a bunch of red rocks on a cliff."

"This dragon is a shapeshifter. It takes whatever shape it needs to lure its prey."

"Like what kind? The one that chased us behind the waterfall had a crimson spot on its throat. What other shape could it take?" This was probably more information than she wanted.

The otherwise taciturn griffin kept talking with his eyes focused on the mesa. "It takes human form or even the body of a serpent. It reveals its true nature only when its seduction fails. Like a venomous spider, it weaves a web to snare, wrapping its quarry in shrouds of flattery and deception before it devours."

She sat in silence for as long as she could hold her tongue. Which wasn't long. "This one seems far away." She remembered how it appeared without notice after they'd entered the forest. "Can it tell that we're here?"

"We can only hope it's too far away to pick up our scent." Tobias stirred, then rose to his full height, his wings tucked at his side and his lion's chest heaving.

Suddenly, a dragon stretched its long neck out of the

cliffs, as if it woke up from a long nap inside the rocks. It yawned, almost ceremoniously. An eerie stillness descended.

"Get on." Tobias growled. "Now."

This was no time for protocol. She made an extra knot in the fabric around her waist and ran to Tobias. She tied herself to his chest just before he launched with such force, her eyelids peeled back with the gusty wind.

In minutes, a dragon's voice, just as gravelly and many times louder than Tobias closed the distance between them. "I smell lion in the sky. Are you alone, Tobias?"

It was the same fiend that chased them into the Magi sanctuary. The same voice that slipped in through the waterfall and curdled her heart with fear.

It knew the griffin's name. There was history here and not the good kind.

Tobias stiffened. He muttered a low command, "Hang on."

"I'm already hanging on for dear life. What more do you want?"

Without warning, the dragon roared across the plains, spewing fire.

Tobias plummeted to the desert floor. Grit sprayed her mouth and nose as she pressed her eyes shut. By the time he climbed back into the air, flames smoldered at the tip of one of his wings. With each rise and each fall, wind blew embers into a small blaze. A stench of burning feathers, flesh and bone rushed into her nostrils.

His body flinched.

Still, he flew.

She untied Papa's cloak from around her waist and tried to smother the fire without hindering the griffin's flight.

The dragon dived, and Tobias shot upward.

The cloak flew out of her hand. It drifted through the air like a stork riding the wind currents. She couldn't reach for it, couldn't do anything but hang on for all she was worth.

The cloak carried away the constant reminder of Papa's presence and left behind more grief. No time to mourn, though. Air pressure shifted, then shifted again. Her insides lurched, then rolled. No time to be sick. She ducked her head into the feathery neck as he propelled them into a thick patch of clouds.

Cool mist arrived like an unexpected refuge. All was damp and hushed around them. The dragon thundered from below, but they were out or reach, at least for now.

"I can't see," she whispered.

"You don't need to." Tobias took off again, racing through the thick mist, just missing a soggy blast that was extinguished before it reached them. Without warning, he dove out of the shelter of the clouds, took a sharp turn, and headed straight toward a range of cliffs that overlooked a river.

The dragon pursued them with a scream.

Waves of dizziness and nausea rolled through her body. She couldn't hold on much longer.

Tobias hurtled toward the river. In minutes, water rushed against her legs and drenched her body. With the dragon on their heels, Tobias flew straight up like a funnel cloud. He aimed at what looked like a small crevice in the face of the granite cliff.

There was no way they could fit. They'd be crushed together and end this chase with exactly what the dragon wanted.

Tobias's voice was urgent. "Trust me."

She scrunched as low as she could as sandstone walls hurtled toward them. Only they were the ones hurtling. The cliffs weren't going anywhere. Their stony surface wouldn't give a centimeter to receive their bodies.

This was a suicide mission, with her on the back of the very one determined to die. She waited to hear the crunch of Tobias's wings.

Instead, Tobias became a flying cylinder with her squashed against him. The rush of wind stopped abruptly as they entered the crevasse, skimming the top, sides, and bottom of the opening, like sausage filling its casing.

They were stuck, entombed in stone, until suddenly, Tobias landed with a splat on the floor of a cave.

Giselle slumped against Tobias, heaving deep breaths, willing herself not to scream in relief.

Tobias unfurled wings that stretched from one side of the cave to the other. Charred feathers exposed raw wounds and bare cartilage on one wing. Their flight had cost him.

He took her through an inferno and brought her safely here. She wasn't afraid of him anymore.

She dug through her bag until she found Suzette's ointment and gently applied it to the griffin's wing.

Together, they pressed against the back of the cave as Giselle whooshed Leonore's fabric over them and held it tight. They huddled under the fabric, exhausted.

The flames stopped, but terror remained. The dragon was there, its shadow obscuring light at the opening of the tunnel.

It reasoned, as if wooing a timid child. "Tobias. Old friend and former captive. You escaped me once again.

At least for a while." He tilted his head back in a low chuckle. "Good news. You brought me the treasure I've sought without success. Hand delivery – so thoughtful."

Tobias said nothing.

"I have a place of service for you, my friend. Only release the girl. You carry Nayeli blood on your back, for she aligns herself with me." The dragon repeated the prophecy. "The breaker, who opens a way through the gate, bursts through doors of bronze and bars of iron." He spoke like a kindly uncle. "Who would've thought she came in the wrapping of the enemy."

"She is Magi," said Tobias.

What? Wait a minute.

Magi were like a special race of people. Erik had told her about them when they'd trudged through the desert on their way out of Darras. Did being a daughter of two Magi make her one? Weren't there some special qualifications? Like bravery?

There had to be more than a gift that flowed through a blood line. There had to be at least some knowledge that she was a part of a race she once hated. She was a long way from Magi, no matter what she'd heard in that wonderful space behind the waterfall.

"Ah. You speak." The dragon mocked. "Really. She's a mutant, a misfit. Has been all along."

The dragon heard her thoughts. Not only was it fire-breathing, it was also a diviner of her heart.

Tobias spoke simply and with authority. "She was raised Nayeli, but her calling is proof of her lineage." Tobias shifted once, as if in pain. "You know that what she carries is untouchable."

"A gift cloaked in human form is easily sifted. These humans are feeble, driven by a thousand things that don't matter. Not to worry. She'll hand over that treasure with barely a sigh."

Not true. The dragon obviously didn't know her.

"Not when she understands its power."

"When I destroy what she loves, she'll yield her power to me. She'll go weak in the legs, her heart will fail, etc., etc." The dragon snorted in disdain. "Her resolve will melt into a tiny puddle at my feet."

Destroy what she loved? She was caught in a whirlwind with no escape.

Tobias ducked his head and whispered to Giselle. "Wrap the fabric around us. Tighter."

A stream of fire sucked oxygen out of the cave. The walls glowed as if they became molten.

"Still willing to be cooked in your very own oven? I can be patient until you appear like roasted birds ready to be devoured."

The griffin's response wavered first, then became strong. "You want Giselle alive."

"True. I could save my breath, so to speak. After all, I've controlled her for years."

Giselle jerked so hard that Tobias wrapped a wing around her.

"She knows that now. I feel it." The dragon's voice turned to musing. "I prepared for this very day. I took her beloved father and in doing so, stole her mother, too." It paused, as if for emphasis, as if it savored how each word stabbed her heart. "Loss defines her, limits her, and skews her heart. She won't stand against me."

The dragon had been behind it all. A trace of a memory dislodged from a forgotten place. She struggled free from Tobias and shouted. "I did once."

The dragon's laugh filled the cave, the skies, and

terrified every living thing into stillness. "You won't this time." The flap of giant wings sounded, then suddenly, it was gone.

"What did it mean? When were you the dragon's captive?"

The griffin shuddered and he was silent for a moment. "Long before you were born. For many years."

Tobias unfurled his wings, but she pressed near his heart, unwilling to leave his shelter. She watched with alarm as he slumped over and curled his eagle head on the lion's paws.

Was he dead? She pressed her ear against his back, desperate to hear the thump, thump of his enormous heart.

Soon his breathing became deep, even.

He was asleep.

She stayed as near as she could. Her heart pounded, even as the stone walls around them cooled.

Stillness arrived like a witness. At least for now, they were safe.

She missed Papa's cloak. In a day pursued and almost overtaken by a dragon, it should have felt like a tiny loss. Instead, she ached with another layer of sorrow. Finally, leaning against Tobias, she slept.

Daylight filtered through the long tunnel hours later. She was cold, surrounded by scorched granite. She stood and spun around, trying to remember why she'd awakened in a charred tomb. Alone.

It was the second day.

Tobias was gone.

Crawling to the edge of the crevasse, she peered into the sky and then to the ground far below. Sheer cliffs ended at a raging river so far away that it looked like a babbling spring.

The walls around her were a stony prison, with an opening only to the impossible. There was no way to escape without wings.

And the wings had abandoned her.

Chapter 14

Mother's soup. It was a random memory that stirred her empty stomach. Mother hadn't been much for comfort, unless she was sick. Then, she arrived with a bowl of soup on a tray with warm flatbread. Warmth filled her heart with every spoonful as she'd peered up at her mother who sat, not stood, at her bedside.

Regrets rose like an army. It was the second day of her race back to Darras. Four more days, still too short, to save Mother.

What terror and what delay would this day bring?

If only she stayed at the inn, waited for her mother's return, and demanded answers. The adventure she longed for became a stream of calamities. Even now, she sat suspended on a ledge, hoping that Tobias, who obviously despised her, might find it in his griffin heart to rescue her.

A mother Ibex tripped down the cliffs, eyeing the stream of water hundreds of feet below. Two kids navigated behind her, scattering loose rocks as they leaped, found their footing, and then leaped again.

Unlike them, she wasn't going anywhere.

Life never listened or cooperated. Like a curse that never got tired of repeating itself, she was stuck and alone.

A speck of brown soared in the distance, swooping up and down on wind currents. It was Tobias, having the time of his life, totally unconcerned about her certain peril. He only taunted her on his way to another destination.

In what felt like hours later, he landed lightly on the ledge beside her, with perfect aim. His wing was bald in places and pink but healed. "Let's go."

"No, hello. No, how are you? I'm not crouched on this cliff for fun." She bit her tongue. After all, Tobias might decide she could find another way down. "Don't. Go." She wrapped the sash around herself and the griffin, then sucked in a breath.

There was no way to prepare for what took her breath away every time. It was the launch into nothingness, the rush of air as Tobias dipped then rose on the wind. He flew in wide arcs, lower and lower until they landed at a quiet pool that bubbled from a rock platform, surrounded by palms and desert brush.

Giselle untied and scrambled off his back. She planted her feet on land she could run through, skip around, and not worry about hurtling over. Never had the sandy ground felt so good. An outcropping of water-smoothed stones jutted out. She leaped from it into the water like a little kid who discovered a puddle in the middle of summer heat.

Was it magic water?

Maybe. Whatever it was, fear, filth and smoke washed away with every dip, and every stroke. She flipped over and around, lost in yet another atmosphere that didn't tether her to earth.

When Tobias stood overhead with a wriggling fish in his mouth, she gave a war whoop. She used Lucy's flint to ignite a wad of dried grass and blew until a flame appeared. Before long, not one, but several fish sizzled over a fire. She ate and ate as Tobias took his fish right from the river.

They didn't have much to say. For one thing, they were hungry.

For another, their eyes were on the sky.

The little she knew about dragons confirmed at least one fact. It didn't give up its prey easily.

The dragon's taunt in the Magi sanctuary was real. At least as true as anything a dragon uttered.

It captured Mother.

That knowledge made her heart pound. She learned more about her mother after time with the Magi than she ever knew before. It was only a skeleton shape, although more than she imagined. "Do we have a plan?"

"Get to Darras."

"Right." It didn't matter that her legs ached like she rode ten camels all the way to Darras. Tobias was pompous and overbearing, but he'd laid down his life to get them this far. She wouldn't chicken out now.

With a giant stride and launch, Tobias took off on the last leg of their journey. His mighty wings surged up and down until he found and caught a warm air current that kept them aloft. He scanned every direction as he soared over open desert.

There were few hiding places. Only sand dunes shifted and moaned their plaintive cry. A band of ostrich ran below, legs outstretched and wings floating, unafraid of predators.

A shapeshifter. This one seemed partial to fire-breathing serpent, alias dragon that looked suspiciously like the one outside the waterfall. Worse, it knew her. That was weirdly impossible, even as it hissed an evil vendetta into their hiding place, tucked away in the cliffs.

Papa told her hair-raising stories about thieving, murderous beasts with impossibly hard armor before Mother interrupted him. The only image she remembered was on their flag.

This dragon morphed out of stony mesas and supposedly inhabited other beings. She remembered the searing heat of the cave, its taunting voice, and the fear that drowned her courage. Everything inside screamed, "Run." Good thing for her, the cave offered no escape outside of Tobias's wings.

Tobias soared above wispy clouds, far above the searing heat below. Hopefully, out of the dragon's view. Once, she thought she saw it prowling around a line of cliffs in the distance. Even though she struggled to breathe in the thin air when the griffin soared higher, she was thankful to be out of sight.

After a sudden detour around a curious vulture, she double-checked the knot that bound her to Tobias. The one Louis taught her to tie.

Louis. Her friend.

At least he used to be a friend. Right now, he was tucked away with his family, as far from Darras and her as he could get. He wouldn't come back. She made sure of that. She swallowed a bitter taste of regret.

An image of the Crown Prince returned, and with it, a daydream of the glorious man clad in angel wings swooping down and rescuing her from the fiery dragon. She imagined him commanding an army across the desert to rescue her. What seemed so close and so good vanished as quickly as it appeared. And with it, any army sent to deliver.

She sabotaged what might have been.

Makir was… Well. Incredibly handsome. Like a lot

handsome. Heat rose from a fire inside and traveled to the roots of her hair in his presence. She sucked in random breaths like a silly goat, trying not to crumble into a disheveled blob. A wistful, unmet longing rose from memories of the masquerade.

It didn't matter anymore.

The prince returned to his mountain kingdom by now, along with his scary mother.

Was it love? Who really knew?

She and Tobias flew over open desert hour after hour. She was thirsty, tired, and hungry. Her belly already forgot the fish she had for breakfast.

Tobias interrupted the silence. "Loosen your grip. I can't breathe."

A reminder that she was merely along for a ride.

She prepared for the customary lurch as they landed beside a stand of date palms in a small oasis. After untying the knot that bound them together, she scrambled to forage and refill her water skin. Finally, she spread Leonore's fabric near one of the largest palms and lay on her back, her body secured on land. At least for a moment.

Tobias spread out like a giant cat over a bed of cool sand.

A question nagged her since the dragon's attack. Maybe he'd answer. Maybe not. She'd try. "That shapeshifting monster knew you. How?"

The griffin took so long to respond, she thought he was asleep. At a closer look, his eagle eyes scanned the perimeter of the oasis. "I was young. An envoy from Gad El Glas, the demon that fuels the dragon, surrounded me as I hunted. They cast an enchanted web over me." He took a breath, as if the words sucked life out of him.

"There was no escape."

She tried to imagine the griffin bound and unable to fly. The image of the brave and mighty creature struggling against impossible chains was too hard to bear.

"Black arts bound me in human form. My loved ones searched." His voice became clipped and hard. "They never found me."

Giselle remembered his massive wings pumping, even as fire ravaged one and threatened the other, pressing through terrible pain. He'd rather go down in flames than be captured again.

His voice grew tender. "Years later, Maura O'Donnell appeared in Sanctuary. Somehow, she knew me. Then, set me free." He rose to stretch like a cat before a cozy fire. "I've been her sworn protector since."

This was as much as Tobias had spoken to her. She barely breathed, hoping that he wasn't done talking.

"I almost missed the attack that took Suzette," he offered slowly. "The Magi were cautious because they knew you were on the way. Still, the dragon was stealthy."

"What do you mean? They couldn't have known I was coming."

"They were waiting for you."

She jerked to attention. "That couldn't be. I've been in Darras all my life until I was kidnapped. How could they know I was coming?"

"A mystery."

"More like a flood of bad luck," Giselle snorted.

"The dragon we see stands for a demon we can't see. Its name is Gad El Glas, although it takes many forms. Darras is the center of its worship." Tobias stared at her with golden, unblinking eyes for a long moment.

"You're waiting for me to get mad. Just say it."

Tobias scanned the distant skies. Did he still long for home? Surely, he'd been able to return by now. Finally, he asked his own question. "Ever wonder why you hated the Magi?"

"Because. I believed they were..." Old adjectives didn't work anymore. She couldn't remember when she changed her mind about the Magi. She blamed them for taking Papa. She was wrong. And now, her search was no longer for him, but for Mother. It felt like new grief piled on old loss.

"Gad El Glas knows how to manipulate," Tobias continued. "Especially the ones who worship it."

Giselle stuffed her irritation. She had to understand, even though his words blasted a hole in the city she loved. Tobias wasn't a liar. That she knew. "No one I know has seen Gad El Glas, even though the Nayeli worship around that name. It has no identity, except to control its people by fear."

Tobias spoke simply. "You've met the demon before."

"Okay, yes. I was a little girl when I *thought* I saw a dragon. It never said it was Gad El Glas. Maybe it was only a bad dream, or I made it up."

"Like your gift to unlock doors?"

She rose to defend herself, to carefully refuse a gift she wasn't sure existed. Then, settled back into a slump.

"Your father had the same gift."

"You knew him?"

"He was my best friend."

"No." She followed him everywhere, tripping along, hurrying to stay in pace with his giant stride. Sometimes his bluster turned to temper, like an unexpected cloudburst. Then, as quickly as the storm appeared, sunshine returned. "He would've told me."

Wouldn't he?

They sat together, side by side. It was the second time she hadn't kept her distance, at least other than when she was tied onto his massive frame and had no choice. Her body relaxed in the stillness of the oasis beside the brave griffin who knew her father.

"We were bound together for life. Odd for most people, but not for Magi. They love the griffins." A low growl escaped its body. "Your father hated to see anything held captive. He freed birds from their snares, rabbits from their traps. He couldn't help himself."

"Was he ever imprisoned?"

"Not that I knew. Compassion drove him." He paused for a minute, as memories crowded in. "We went on excursions day after day, each time flying farther and farther from home. Our parents warned us about Gad El Glas. We were too young and arrogant to be afraid." He turned his eagle eyes to study the desert around them. "One day, as we rested near an oasis, a metal net descended from nowhere. Your father rolled away just in time. I was snared.

"He tore his hands, clawing at the net. He couldn't free me. Black arts were in motion. He traveled outside our region, into the dragon's territory, determined to find me." A sigh heaved his lion's chest. "He never forgot. Never recovered from the grief of not saving me. He searched for years, but of course, I was hidden from sight.

"He vowed to make the dragon pay by releasing his most cherished victims – the gifted Magi. Magi set apart for as long as anyone can remember. Counselors of kings, carriers of gifts that defeat darkness, who release the light of freedom. Gifts as varied as themselves."

"Freeing the Magi became your father's lifetime vendetta. When he met your mother, he loved her. She loved him. She knew what their lives would be like and chose him, anyway."

"That's what brought them to Darras."

"They went to set captives free. Although, in truth, your father taunted the dragon in his very lair. Your mother went to be with him."

"We reunited after Maura set me free, although he never allowed me to come too close to Darras. He rode at night with a captive, sometimes two in tow. We met at appointed places so that I could return them to their families."

"He was the gatekeeper. How did he do that job and travel so often?"

"He and your mother were a team from the beginning, side by side in the purpose that drove your father's heart. We had our own personal rescue team. Until one night."

"What happened?" Giselle held her breath. This was knowledge she'd longed for since Papa disappeared.

"He was driven to mock the dragon. He took more risks. Somehow an emissary of the dragon apprehended him."

"That's how you knew how to find Darras. Why didn't my parents tell me any of this?"

"You were too little. They were protecting you."

"So, it wasn't the Magi who took him." One terrible thought rose that she couldn't silence any longer. "Is he…?"

Tobias answered quickly. "I believe he is alive. He is too great a prize." He gazed into her eyes, searching. "Did you ever hear about Maura's battle against Gad El Glas?

"A little. Our time together was short."

"Every battle comes down to this truth. Once the power behind the dark arts is destroyed, captives are freed. I am proof of that. I returned to my true form after years of captivity when Maura faced down Gad El Glas in her territory."

"You speak the language of a world I don't know."

"A new age has risen – one that you represent. As Magi." He looked at her with those unblinking amber eyes.

She backed up inside. The memory of the waterfall was dim. She recalled Alessandra's words, listened even to Maura. What was so certain then became only a fleeting memory. "I'm not Magi. I…I don't have anything to defeat a dragon."

"Whether you believe it or not, your gift defines you as Magi. It is a calling that isn't yours alone. It belongs to captives who cry out in the bondage of their chains. It belongs to the generations."

"I don't know how to begin. It's too much."

"You're going to Darras to find your mother. Gad El Glas sought to destroy the cord between you. Your love restores a relationship you must have in place to defeat it forever."

Defeat the dragon forever? She sounded weak and petty. So be it. "I never asked to face down a demon."

"Nor did I."

They were heading right where she didn't want to go. Tobias was brave. So were the Magi.

She wasn't. "I never told you. I should have been there. I told Papa I'd meet him at the sundial. On the morning of the winter solstice…"

"It wasn't your fault that he didn't come home."

She sucked in a jagged breath. Her griffin friend was right. Believing that she could have done something, been something more, still haunted her. That kind of despair didn't have to make sense. It just was.

The western sky smoldered like dying flames, in shades of crimson and gold, behind it when the fortified walls of Darras appeared below. Sand dunes wavered in peaks and valleys in the sand. It was the city she'd known all her life and dreamed of leaving.

Everything had changed.

Mother was there. Somewhere. Was she in pain? Had she lost her, like Papa, with no goodbye?

Ramaz waited for her there.

Her escape was a disgrace to his high office, if nothing else. Others lay in wait for a gift that supposedly made its possessor infinitely powerful and wealthy. What other betrayals lurked in this city called home?

Mother sheltered her in more ways than she understood.

So had Louis.

Now, she was alone in the middle of the familiar with danger at every turn.

One thing she understood. The closer they came to Darras, the nearer Tobias came to being captured again. Because of her.

That couldn't happen.

He was on a mission for Maura and bound by friendship with Papa. His courage was unyielding. He'd fulfill the assignment or die trying.

She had to go alone. She had to find a way to make him leave.

A deep sigh escaped without permission. She had nothing to change a mind and heart like his. Nothing inside her was enough to shift a loyalty so binding that she was ashamed of every time she cut and run.

Maybe she could convince him she wasn't worth the risk.

Kicking the sand like a two-year-old, she whirled to face the mighty griffin. "Magi mythology? I am Nayeli through and through."

Tobias sat, crouched at rest in the desert sand. His gaze didn't waver. "You can't make me leave. You may not see me in Darras, but I'll be nearby. Watch for me."

Had she ever bound herself to a person in a way that she'd die, rather than leave them? She fell to his feet, undone. She had no more energy for a façade neither of them believed. Bowing her head, she whispered, "Go back. I'm not worth the promise you made."

Tobias's words were more command than response. "You are the gatekeeper. Rise to the calling you were born for."

The griffin was wise, but he didn't know her. She couldn't lift her eyes to his. "What if I can't?"

Tobias stood like a monument against the desert, a kingly griffin, his wings tucked, eyes burning like bright embers. "What if you won't?"

This wasn't about a gift.

It was about a decision.

Because none of it mattered if her heart failed.

She turned to face the city walls. Pillars of smoke rose from the temple in the distance from fires that consumed for so many years without notice. Perhaps the dragon's breath drifted from its lair in delight over yet another sacrifice.

Five days. Two down and three to go. Was there hope for Mother?

She couldn't know.

This journey didn't require hope.

Only one step toward those city gates.

A steady wind blew, constantly shaping the dunes and releasing their song. Tobias stood as a mythical warrior.

She kept walking toward the gates.

Maybe hope would show up along the way.

Chapter 15

Silence met her at the towering gates that opened to Darras. She looked back for one more comforting glimpse of Tobias. He was gone, or at least, out of sight.

Turning her gaze toward the city, she faced the entrance she knew. This wasn't like any other day she entered the city after a morning visit to the sundial. Darras held a dragon that knew she returned to its lair.

Like ensigns of the fiery serpent itself, guards dressed in smoldering black from head to toe stood, positioned on the rampart. Their faces were hidden by hooded tunics that obscured everything except dark eyes.

A shadow crept through the gates and dashed behind her. It disappeared before she could decide if she really saw it.

"Chronos! Is that you?"

The gates were closed in the middle of the day. Nothing stirred outside an entrance usually full of braying of ill-tempered camels. Empty wooden enclosures trembled in the breeze. No drivers loitered nearby, resting before a nighttime journey.

"Where are you? It's me, Giselle."

Chronos was notoriously deaf to anything he didn't want to hear. Even if he was off duty, someone had to be around. She tugged at the gates. They were bolted from the inside.

She studied her hands, the ones that had unlocked

doors in Apamea.

If only her hands tingled to prove they were indeed special. Instead, they were the same hands, now crusty with sand and grime. She yanked back her sleeve to find her birthmark scarlet and throbbing like it had when she'd first met Ramaz. Was it some kind of sign?

Longing to run into her mother's arms washed over her. If there wasn't a way through the gates, she'd make one. Banging on the metal with all the determination of a weary camel driver, she shouted, "Open! Open now!"

Suddenly, a rush of cold and substance that could be seen, but not grasped, whirled around her like dense smoke. As she kept pounding, each shadow became a black-clad warrior with glittering yellow eyes.

She dropped her hands and turned to face the ghouls.

Faceless, malevolent eyes searched and probed her own. Her insides jumped and then stayed where they leaped.

Mother needed her. She had to get inside.

They were terrifying, yes.

They had no fire. Only those eyes.

They wouldn't keep her out of this city. Not if she could help it. "My name is…"

An icy blast pressed against her chest, making it hard to breathe, much less speak. "I live here. In Darras."

Only a gust of shifting crosswinds answered.

"I must get through. My mother and I…"

The warriors were as immovable as the gates.

This was Darras.

But it wasn't home.

A man's voice shouted from inside the city gates. "Make way. Make way."

The ghostly militia evaporated like vapor as the

gates opened, clanging against their stone enclosure. Familiar, crimson-garbed palace guards appeared with the sound of bugles.

This was a lot of fanfare for a simple entry into Darras. Blond hair strayed from an embellished helmet. It was Aaron, the knight in shining armor, who invited her to the masquerade.

"Aaron! It's me. Giselle."

He stared at a point beyond her and shouted a command. "Giselle Basir. You're summoned by the king."

"Why do I need a summons to a place I've freely visited? I'm going to the Gemini, to my home."

Aaron already turned to lead the contingent to the palace. She could ignore his curt order, except for the well-armed contingent of guards he led. They surrounded her so thoroughly that she couldn't escape without bursting through human barriers armed with swords.

The palace. Memories of the masquerade and Makir, the Crown Prince, flooded her mind. As kind and attentive as he seemed, Makir hadn't sent anyone to find her. Then again, he couldn't know that she was captured and hauled away.

Ramaz, on the other hand, proved that it hadn't been difficult to find her. According to his underling priest, her gift had come of age. Whatever that meant.

One thing she knew. A target was on her back, and Darras was more like a trap than the city she once knew and loved.

The muscular arm of a guard bumped against her, and she almost tumbled to the ground. At least these men were flesh and blood. One of them had to recognize her.

Off-duty palace soldiers often ate at their tables and joked as she handed out food trays.

The Gemini stood before them, locked, windows boarded, and deserted.

"Wait. I need to go inside. I…"

No one stopped walking or diverted from the path. Aaron continued, leading the battalion past the inn and toward the palace.

"Can you hear me? I'm…My name is Giselle Basir. This is our inn."

Still, no response.

Bypassing walls she longed to enter, Aaron forged a way through corridors of neighbor's homes and into the marketplace. Soldiers stood at attention on every corner and every thoroughfare, grasping weapons tightly at their sides.

There were no children at play, no barking dogs. No sign of life.

Even the bustling market was deserted. No one beckoned from the booths, offering their wares. It looked like an unruly giant rushed through, overturning carts, and randomly smashing what had once been there.

No cries of 'Jameela! Here!' greeted her. No one thrust a swatch of fabric or bundle of spices into her hands. Surely, local businesses weren't included in the ban. The vendors had families to feed.

Midday sun beat on her uncovered head. Leonore's scarf was in a pack she carried at her side, except soldiers pressed so closely she was afraid to take it out. She feared doing anything other than marching forward.

They came to a residential area just beyond the marketplace when a dark-haired little boy dashed out of a flat-roofed home after a mongrel pup. A company of smoky-garbed warriors rushed from a back alley as the mother ran after her child.

The woman cried out in terror. "He's a child." Grabbing the little boy, she scurried back into the house. The pup wandered around the doorstep, whimpering.

She heard about lockdowns when an enemy threatened or surrounded the massive city walls. Food supplies became scarce and access to the springs outside the city was cut off. Hunger. Thirst. Far from anything she ever experienced.

No enemy encroached on the city's boundaries, though. There was no reason for martial law that paralyzed citizens and kept them prisoners in their homes. The only adversaries were the ones she met at the city gates and those positioned at every intersection.

As they approached the palace, soldiers stationed themselves in an unyielding line at the palace's marble entrance.

Aaron pushed Giselle behind him. "Don't speak," he whispered. "Keep your head down."

The guards drew their weapons. Tension shivered in her gut until she recognized one of the centurions as he strode toward them. The man, whose face crinkled in a grin whenever he greeted her at the Gemini, stared as if he didn't recognize her.

A battalion of soldiers marched toward them from a narrow lane from the gardens. They snapped into an impenetrable line, blocking the palace entrance.

Aaron bowed to the centurion. "Here are my orders, sir." When the officer nodded, Aaron's calloused hand grasped her elbow.

They walked through the splendid entry as soldiers parted a narrow way. Aaron's steps were measured and unfaltering. His grip on her elbow hurt. When Giselle slowed to take a better look, he growled. "Straight ahead. Don't stop."

King Abusari never summoned her before. As a leading merchant of a bustling inn on the city wall, it was Mother who commanded his attention. Surely, he knew where she was and would explain what was going on in the city.

Massive doors opened silently where a servant dressed in a simple white tunic waited.

Aaron led her through a maze of rooms. Glimpses through open doors revealed a courtyard full of lemon trees and plumeria. Finally, they turned into a room at the end of a corridor that appeared sealed off from the outside, except for a window into the courtyard.

She wanted to rush away in panic. There was no reason to be escorted to a room instead of an audience with King Abusari. She was treated more like a captive than an adult citizen of Darras. "Please. Don't go."

Aaron turned without a word and walked away.

The room was decorated in hues of purple and gold, from the downy comforter to heavy brocade curtains that almost concealed windows open to the manicured courtyard. A gilded birdcage stood in one corner, where a tiny bunting perched, its feathers bright blue against the stucco walls. The bunting's beauty far outweighed the golden cage. When it began to sing, the servant covered the cage with fabric and proceeded to lay clothing on the bed.

"What are these for? I've only come to see King Abusari."

The young woman curtsied and kept her eyes on the floor. "My orders were to prepare you for your audience with the king. Here's water to bathe and fresh clothing."

Giselle looked down at the tunic that barely survived a journey across the desert on the back of a griffin, to say nothing of a dragon attack. Yes. She needed a bath and clean gown.

It was strange, but then again, she didn't want to knock King Abusari off his throne with her unbathed, unkempt self.

The bath was a low, sunken tub adorned with ceramic tiles. Flower petals dotted the water. The servant poured a vial of aromatic oil into the water.

Giselle felt invaded by a woman she didn't know. "You may go."

The servant bowed and backed away.

The water felt like a dip in the pool at Apamea. Before everything turned upside down. She didn't have time to linger in the cool water. Okay, maybe she did. Buoyed by the fragrant water, she finally had time to think.

King Abusari was an oddly bumbling royal with a bulbous nose and wrinkled neck who Mother considered a friend. He was foppish and not much of a terror to anyone unless you stood in the way of a table of food. Still, he was king. He had authority over the soldiers and whoever else would try to stop her quest.

With one more long dunk under water and swish of her hair, she forced herself out of the tub and toweled herself dry. The flowers were smashed, and the water was brown by the time she climbed out. Who knew what collected in her hair since her last swim in the desert pool?

A nearby comb finally untangled knots in her curls, and she looked good enough. A crimson dress embroidered with golden thread lay on the bed. It was a gown meant for royalty – or at least for one meeting a king. A lot of fuss just to meet the portly regent.

Crown Prince Makir, not King Abusari, waited alone at the entrance of a covered portico with flowering trees and a garden, looking like the Greek god she first met.

He wore no mask to conceal the symmetry of that dark face and eyes that sought her out. She was embarrassed. She hadn't spent enough time on her hair or make-up. It didn't matter for King Abusari.

Makir, on the other hand, was as enchanting as she remembered. She took a deep breath and let it out slowly, determined not to melt into a puddle of infatuation.

His royal bearing disappeared as he hurried to her. "I was so worried. Why did you leave us?" He took a step closer until they almost touched. His fragrance, mixed with cardamon, was uniquely him. Fatigue disappeared instantly, and she was glad she was clean, at least.

His presence made her far too giddy. She planted her feet, refusing to totter into his arms. Not yet, anyway. "Runaway slaves kidnaped me."

A dangerous look appeared in his eyes. "They will pay."

She shivered and kept her head bowed. "I'm safe now." How would he react knowing she journeyed here on the back of a griffin? What did he know about the dragon? She had more questions than answers.

"I never forgot that night at the masquerade. I thought you left the city when I couldn't find you the next day." His eyes caught hers and held them. "Because you didn't care."

He was handsome. Wonderful. All the things. Still, she couldn't be diverted. Not now. "Where is the king? Why is the city locked down?"

"Magi infiltrators poisoned King Abusari. We wouldn't need these measures if there wasn't a significant threat. I promise, this is only temporary."

On one side of the room, an oil painting of Makir, seated on an ivory throne, extended from floor to ceiling. His mother stood, imperious, on his right side. What an odd addition to a palace that didn't belong to either of them. She took a breath and rushed in. "I'm here to find my mother. She wouldn't have left the Gemini. Not for any reason."

Makir's concern turned to sympathy. "All businesses are closed until we can secure the city."

"The inn is my home."

He spoke in a low voice with an appeal. "This isn't the Darras you left. I fear for your safety with the inn so close to city gates. Please. Stay at the palace until our security is restored." He leaned closer. "In the meantime, I promise to help find your mother."

She didn't know she'd been holding her breath until it came out in a big huff. Help was here all along. Why had she left?

"Come. Sit."

Attendants served a feast prepared just for the two of them. A bite of a delicate pastry filled with dates reminded her of the masquerade. And how that evening felt like life in another universe. There was a question she had to ask. "The warriors who met me at the gates were mere shadows. Then they weren't. I feel their presence around this palace. What does that mean?"

"These are matters to discuss with Ramaz."

"Is he the one in charge?"

"What makes you ask?"

She hesitated only for a moment. "I need the one who wields real power. That person will help me find Mother."

"You believe she's here, in Darras? I don't remember meeting her at the masquerade."

"She is… innkeeper of the Gemini. She often visited the palace. King Abusari loved our baked goods. He…they were friends." She smiled ruefully. "Unlike Mother and me." The comment spilled out of an unexpected place, far too soon to share with a man she barely knew.

Instead of building a wall, he nodded, as if he understood. Just maybe there was more between them than a chance meeting at the masquerade. She felt her heart lean in.

"My father was king of our mountain domain. His power and authority were unequaled. He was a good king, kind and generous. He welcomed Magi into his counsel." He peered into the garden outside. His shoulders lifted and then fell. "That decision became his death sentence. They murdered him in his sleep."

A brittle look crept over his face, then vanished with a shake of his head. "I grew up without him. When I was trained to come into a place of power, I vowed that none of my subjects would suffer the loss I had. Never again would we be seduced by those who appeared so wise, so knowledgeable. Even now, my goal remains certain. We must cleanse our territories of their vile presence for all time."

Like the blast she felt at the city gates, a chill rushed over her being.

Makir's hate made bitterness against her mom feel like a hangnail. The young prince lost his father, like she had. He understood the vacuum his absence left in her life. A moment changed everything for him, too.

There was something else hard to define. Something unspoken dashed across his eyes, like a current hiding in the depths of a river.

He bowed his head and studied a decorative tile at his feet. "My mother rose to power. She groomed me to take his place. We came to Darras for an alliance between Nayeli kingdoms – to increase our expanse."

Was it fear she saw before she was sure it was there? "King Abusari was killed. What does that mean for you?"

"In the terms of our alliance, I took my place as king here, too."

"Won't you miss your home?"

His forehead creased as if she'd asked him to solve a riddle. "My home was the place of rigorous training since I was a child. There was only one plan for my life – to rule an ever-expanding kingdom."

"Is that what you wanted?"

"What an odd question. What about you? What do you want, Giselle?"

No wonder Makir was so gracious and attentive. They shared a sorrow that few understood.

Then again, she didn't know the young king well enough to bare her soul. She'd open her heart. Carefully. "I wanted to leave Darras, never to return. After being kidnapped, I discovered a world I didn't know existed." She left out the part about the Magi. Instead, she blurted a question. "Have you ever seen a dragon?"

"Yes. I have."

"What? I've never seen one in Darras. At least not since…Are there more? The one I met wanted me captive or dead. Either seemed fine. I don't understand why I suddenly encountered that fiend not once, but several times."

"Perhaps it knew you were on a path of learning who you are."

"What a strange reason for a dragon to appear."

"Not unusual, considering its nature. A dragon is a collector of all things precious. It hides in its lair until a glittering treasure beckons. Then it arises in the fullness of its terror and might to steal it."

"Forgive me. It seems odd that you know so much about them."

"Gold and diamonds hide in our mountain kingdom. It wasn't unusual to see a dragon prowling at night, gills crimson with fire, warding off would-be thieves and protecting its riches."

She shivered in the warm air as a memory rose. "The high priest, Ramaz, pursued and then captured me in Apamea. One of his emissaries enslaved me because of a gift I supposedly carry." She paused. "That sounds most dragon-like."

A vein throbbed in Makir's temple. "Ramaz was unauthorized. I can't speak for his plot, other than to say, I apologize. Enslaving a Nayeli is punishable by death."

"I got away, then met the dragon. Or it met me. It threatened my mother's life and said that if I didn't return to Darras, I'd never see her again."

"The dragon has many faces."

This was the strangest leap in what was becoming an even more bizarre conversation. Makir seemed as unfazed as he would be discussing the weather that day.

"You don't think it's odd that a dragon talked to me? What kind of world are you from?" She studied his eyes to see if he was making fun of her. "The only face I saw streamed fire to reduce everything to ashes."

"There are more fearsome things than a dragon."

"Name one."

"The one that fuels its fire."

She remembered smoke rising from the temple as she stood outside the city. "Who is that?"

"The Nayeli culture is full of secrets. You share that world with me, even though I came from another part of the kingdom. You didn't know there was a bigger world. You tasted its freedom only to return to a place that called you back."

The room was unnaturally quiet. She searched for guards, or anyone who might use what she said against her. "I came to find my mother who, according to the dragon, is in trouble. What use is a gift if it doesn't help me in what matters most? I tried to enter the inn when I first arrived, but palace soldiers refused to let me go inside."

"You were summoned at the gate because I heard you had arrived. You need the protection of the palace."

She did need the king's defense. "How did you know I was there?"

"I'd be a terrible excuse for a ruler if I didn't keep my eyes on the primary entrance to the city." His lips grazed her fingers. "You're free to go home, if that's what you desire. Please stay tonight, though. Darkness is a perilous time. I'll send a contingent of palace guards to escort you tomorrow morning."

Relief flooded her heart. "Thank you." She curtsied deeply. "Your kindness is a balm to my heart."

Chapter 16

The room was quiet, except for a stirring inside the gilded cage. When she removed the cover, the tiny bird began to sing.

A bunting often perched nearby as she stood at the sundial, searching for Papa. Generations before, Nayeli warriors wore bunting charms when they went into battle. They were small but resilient. Instinct told them when to stand still and when to take swift action. Warfare essentials.

The bird sang and sang as if it looked forward to her return as she changed into her own tunic and sandals. Its melody cleared tension there so long that she forgot its presence. For the first time in many days, she was encouraged.

Finding Mother was in sight. Makir pledged his help, and the palace provided refuge until she returned to Gemini.

Words drifted into her consciousness from long ago as the bird trilled. She'd drifted off to sleep to the same lullaby night after night. Words rose from a place tucked away in her heart.

Lift up your heads, O' gates, open, O' ancient doors.
The gatekeeper must come, and she will not fail.

She never thought about the lyrics. Now, they flowed out of her as she sang along with the bird's melody. With every word, anticipation sprouted and bloomed into courage. She'd been a cage of her own for so long.

She always believed those chains were attached to Mother.

Maybe not.

The bunting pecked at the latch again and again. Clearly, the bird didn't belong in captivity. It was meant to be outside, not stashed away in a room, no matter how lavish.

She pulled gently, and the door creaked open slowly, inch by inch. Instantly, the bird darted past her with such speed that it brushed her hair with a small whoosh and flitted around the room. Ignoring the open window to the courtyard, it flew back and forth from her to the bedroom door.

"What? I thought you wanted freedom."

The bird perched on the top of the door frame and cocked its head. For whatever reason, it wanted to leave the room. Why choose a tour of the palace instead of escaping outdoors, though?

Her mind ticked through possibilities.

It was a crazy thought.

What if the bird was a tiny guide?

If there was a chance Mother was hidden away in the palace, she needed to know. After all, Makir wasn't the only one who wielded power. Ramaz had influence far beyond the palace. He may have imprisoned Mother right here.

A flash of indigo feathers rushed out as the door opened to a dimly lit corridor with a staircase at the end. The bird flew down the hallway without waiting to see if she followed.

An occasional torch smoldered stone walls, and the

air smelled like a sour cloth left out in the kitchen. She regretted her decision at once.

The bird returned and flit around her, as if to say, "Come on." The next moment, it became a flash of blue yards ahead.

Otherwise, all was quiet.

Of course, everything around was silent. No one ventured into this cold darkness on purpose. Her calves burned, and her toes gripped her sandals, as she descended a granite staircase. Alone, with only the tiny bunting as her guide, fear hammered in a thousand voices. "Go back."

If the bird hadn't dodged back and forth to encourage her, she would've hiked up her tunic and run in blind fear back to the refuge of her room. She needed the bunting's melody to remember why she'd come.

Papa told her once that a bird sang every morning to remind the world that a new day, and therefore, hope, was on the horizon. A bird didn't have human understanding or intelligence, only instinct. Yet this one was intent on guiding her through eerie shadows to some unknown destination.

When a stone wall loomed before her, with a narrow entrance on one side, a man's voice called, "Giselle."

It was the voice she heard the last morning at the inn. When her world was intact. When Mother was in charge. When Louis still liked her.

It was the high priest, Ramaz. The man turned betrayer.

She stood, frozen in terror.

"I know it's you. Come closer. I can't hurt you anymore."

The bird flitted through the crevice, then dashed

back as if it didn't like what it saw.

She had to face him. She shuddered, remembering the moment she realized he was the one behind Erik's murder and her capture. What was the most powerful man in the kingdom doing in a dungeon? She couldn't bear to think that he held Mother here, only to bait her.

Ramaz stood behind towering bars, his pale face etched in a rueful smirk.

He was alone, with a crude bed in one corner. Far from the lavish fragrance of oud that had defined his presence, this cell reeked of raw sewage.

His stance was still arrogant. He spread his arms as if to show off his new dwelling. "You look appalled. My circumstances have changed since we last met." His voice sounded like the dragon's words that taunted her and Tobias inside the cliff.

She refused to show fear. "You bought me, a Nayeli citizen, as your property."

"Ah. A thwarted mission. Heavy-handed, to be sure."

"What was your plot? Other than to betray and enslave me?"

"That I cannot reveal. However, it landed me here."

"You're the high priest. No one is more powerful."

"You're wondering how the Highly Esteemed One found himself imprisoned. That is understandable. In truth, a power greater than mine turned against me. My position of favor vanished as surely as a shadow warrior."

The hellish soldiers at the gate had a name, after all.

"Yes. You met them at the entrance of Darras. They're new, of course, and of a world that I no longer command." Ramaz bowed low with a flourish. "But you

– your hands. They can open this door and loose my chains. If only you will…"

She sucked in a deep breath. "Tell me plainly. Why are you here?"

"I could say that I'm falsely accused. Actually, the power that usurped mine judged me insufficient, and lacking. Worse, it perceived me as a threat to its preeminence."

His words were like the maze outside the palace walls, twisting, turning and designed as a trap. "You would've taken me as your slave if I hadn't escaped."

"True, although if you free me, I'll return the favor."

"I'm no captive."

Ramaz's teeth appeared in a mirthless smile.

Giselle struggled to be composed. She felt the same ooze of seduction when the court jester mocked her at the masquerade. "You were the jester. I remember your vile presence, your innuendos. Were you spying? Or merely tormenting me?"

"Oh. Indeed. Both, I'm afraid." The man shrugged his thin shoulders, clothed in a dingy linen tunic instead of the elaborate robes of his former glory. "Shame is a mighty force, carried on the wings of simple words. At least for you, it didn't require any basis. It was easy to convince you of guilt that wasn't yours. Not that I wasn't happy to keep you in my sights."

She hated to react or to agree with the evil man in any way. He was right, though. "I hadn't done anything wrong."

"Exactly. Take that as a lesson from your high priest. Beware an enemy so familiar that you no longer recognize it."

"You speak in riddles."

"Puzzles are all around you, dear one. You must solve them. Remember your gift."

"The gift that makes me valuable enough to steal me away, to use for your purposes?"

"I am not alone in what I sought."

A faint stink of sulfur traveled down the stairs. She recognized the icy chill that threatened to take her breath away. In the darkness, a noxious train of smoke crept along the stone floor.

Ramaz stiffened. "Leave me. Now."

In seconds, frigid air rushed like a sudden storm through her body as if she was made of mere air.

The cold was an entity of shadows and smoke. It crept along the stone floor and into the prison cell.

Ramaz backed further and further into the cell, holding his hands against it, to ward off a shadowy river of ice.

Ashen tentacles shot around the priest's feet. It encompassed his arms and torso, speeding upward like a ghastly rope. He grabbed his throat and pulled. A smoldering cord tightened like a vice until he could only gasp. "Go!"

Unrelenting tendrils of smoke bound Ramaz in an ever-thickening shroud. He no longer spoke, only writhed like a large cobra, shifting to the tune of its master.

The cell filled with inky blackness, so dark that she no longer saw Ramaz, but heard strangled moans. She stood, in shock, as his cries faded and became a ghastly silence.

The tentacles changed their course and traveled to her.

She watched, unmoving, in terrified submission at

their advance.

Out of nowhere, the bunting zoomed so close that Giselle dashed it away like a buzzing fly. It dove again. This time it pecked her hard against the cheek. Again and again, it nose-dived until Giselle batted it away like a crazy woman fighting off a pesky wasp.

The shadows were almost at her feet.

Zoom. Another attack of the bunting. This one, more determined.

A spell broke with one last dive bomb onto her head. She ripped away what felt like smoldering cords and sped around the dividing wall toward the granite staircase.

She raced, hair flailing behind her, as she scaled the granite stairs. The bird was a tiny arrow propelled by its bow. When her strength threatened to give way, it flew upward like a beacon, proving that escape was possible.

Light shone from a window at the top of the stairs. In one giant hoist, she opened the window. The bird flew away as she plummeted out of the window to the ground below.

Cool grass felt like a blanket. Time suspended in the dungeon as night arrived in a moonless sky. The bird disappeared into the maze of hedges, then appeared, dodging this way and that, as if to figure out a way through its hopeless tangle.

It didn't take long to get totally lost. Like Ramaz and his words, she was caught in a trap. Soon, the shadowy demon guard would arrive unhindered by any barriers. Her end would be just like the high priest's.

A woman in gauzy white drifted through the maze ahead. The edge of her gown shimmered, then disappeared. Shadows lengthened, then wavered in a gentle breeze. It was hard to keep sight of the tiny bird in the darkness. She could breathe, though. Warmth flooded through her body, replacing the oozing chill. Familiar landmarks proved the inn was just ahead.

An animal growled from behind her.

The bird swooped low, then rushed forward.

Another low snarl sounded.

She couldn't help herself. She had to look.

The light of a random torch placed against a neighbor's home revealed a burly mastiff that crept from an alley behind her.

She was close to the inn.

Not close enough to escape a dog running full-tilt.

A pebble, then another, scattered in the distance. A voice whispered from branches that dangled over a stucco wall. "Hurry. I'll keep it away."

Giselle wondered about the identity of her treetop friend only long enough to take a breath and run faster.

The dog was diverted for a moment.

Whoever was in the tree dropped to the ground and hurled another object in the opposite direction.

The animal's snuffling growl moved away.

She lifted her tunic and raced toward the inn.

In minutes, the dog ignored distractions and howled as it charged closer. It homed in on its target as Giselle bolted down an alley. She hurled a stray rock and shouted. "Go. Now." Like that was going to help. She kept yelling anyway. Surely, a neighbor would open his doors and welcome her inside.

Candlelight appeared in the first one, then other windows. With all that noise, the race for her life wasn't hidden. Yet no one came to her defense. No one opened a door to usher her to safety as she skirted one obstacle, raced around another corner, and prayed that she didn't stumble.

The hound's pursuit didn't waver as it charged in and out of narrow turns and alleys.

Just ahead, the shadow of the Gemini Inn appeared in the gloom. No lights flickered a welcome through its latticed windows. The bird flew to the door and hovered there.

What if the doors were locked?

Her lungs burned and legs pumped as she sprinted down the last stretch. There were only seconds left. If the door was padlocked, the beast would catch her at the threshold. Grabbing the double doors in both hands, she yanked on the handle.

It didn't open.

She screamed, desperate for the place and the person she always knew as home. "Mama!"

The door opened with one more shove, and she tumbled inside. Then rushed to lock the door before she sprawled headlong on the floor.

The dog charged the entrance, pummeling the door, and yowling in frustration.

She lay on the floor, hardly daring to look up in the stillness.

She was alone.

No Mother.

No Louis.

No customers finishing their last brew for the night. Even the bird hadn't followed her inside. She scrambled to her feet, missing the presence of her little guide at once. Only ghosts of what used to be murmured in the ordinary creaks and groans as wind brushed against the windows.

She called her mother again, so afraid and so alone. "Where are you?"

Some merciful person helped her escape the mastiff. Somehow her hands had opened the doors.

She remembered Tobias and their conversation.

"What if I can't?"

"What if you won't?"

What did that matter now?

Chapter 17

It was the morning of the third day. Strangers plundered the Gemini. They scaled the stairs she skipped down since she was old enough to walk. Windows were boarded with scrap lumber and hammered willy-nilly into the walls. Bedrooms were pillaged. Rifled letters judged as trash littered the floor. Closet doors hung by their hinges like tottering fools. Gowns ripped off their hangers lay, lifeless, like the rest of the inn.

An overturned pot of fragrance filled the air with its sweetness. If only it washed away the stink of those who pillaged their home and laid it bare to prying eyes.

Grabbing a board over her bedroom window, she yanked. It wobbled, then dangled by one nail. Over and over, she ripped boards until her hands bled, and the window emerged free, open to the desert sky she loved.

By the time the timbers were stacked for firewood, her eyes burned with sweat, and her muscles ached. Her work wasn't complete. She had to find Mother. Today.

But now, she'd hang the six-point star in her window.

The same star was etched on the massive oaken door behind the waterfall. The door where she entered a world that was fresh and life-giving. One that offered sanctuary no matter what kind of monster raged around them.

The woven star dangled on a threadbare piece of yarn, a homespun sign that maybe the words of the Magi were true. Maybe her hands did open doors of freedom. Not that she understood how all that worked. The gift had a mind of its own. It acted with or without her permission in moments she couldn't contrive or manipulate.

Sunlight streamed through the windows to prove darkness retreated – at least for now. She ran her fingers through her mop of curls and dressed in a clean tunic tucked away at the back of her closet. It was time to search the inn for any clues Mother left behind.

The creak of her aching knees was the only sound as she ambled down the stairs. No one shouted orders in the stillness. No one commanded her presence. The cupboard doors were wide open in the deserted kitchen.

A creepy thought drifted in as she stood, looking around the place where she had spent so many years.

She wasn't alone.

Her knife was in the dirty tunic on the floor in her room. A broom would have to do. If nothing else, it would crack a head or two.

Raising the broom like a battle axe, she searched closets, behind doors, and under beds.

No one.

She returned to the kitchen, relieved and feeling silly. Her brain still recovered from the craziness of the last few days. The weeks since she first left Darras were a dream that propelled her through the incredible and back home via griffin wings. It was a journey as bizarre as a traveling gypsy show.

She searched for the tiny bunting outside the window.

Nothing.

There were no people, no marketplace vendors

bustling with morning business. What were their neighbors doing for food?

Untouched stores of grain were stacked from floor to ceiling in the pantry. She had to do something, anything to bring her mind and her heart back to a home she recognized.

One job always brought her heart back home.

She'd bake bread.

Comfort drifted into her battered soul as she gathered ingredients. The same wooden mixing bowl, the same dented measuring cup. Four cups of flour, a pinch of salt, and a dash of yeast. She emptied the last bit of water from a glass jar and reached for a second. She had to go to the spring for more.

Then again, how would she get out of an armed city for water? Because the inn was built into the walls of Darras, they used the spring outside the gates. That wasn't an option, anymore. Water that flowed from three springs tucked away in the hills still supplied most of the city. Their streams never failed and never would unless an enemy broke in and cut them off. Right now, food was scarce enough. No water was unthinkable.

An earthen vase held the olive oil. She mixed the ingredients with her hands, feeling her muscles flex and her heart relax.

She and Louis made bread every week.

Well. He made it. She helped.

The dough became art in his hands with a pinch of mystery. Something about the precise weight of his fingers, along with an exact amount of kneading and a perfect time of rest in between.

She watched him for so many years. Her bread was never as good.

In the past, she banged around on the dough, pounding it into submission. She was always in a hurry. The process couldn't take that long.

Louis, on the other hand, got lost in a kind of dance that ended in wonder. Warm out of the oven, the flatbread melted goat cheese perfectly and became one of the Gemini's calling cards.

She missed him.

Even though she did her best to chase him away. She treated the friend who followed her through the desert and then came to her rescue like dirt. Like less than dirt.

She'd think about that later.

She pulled wood from a pallet in one corner and fired the oven. As the dough rested, she puttered around, cleaning this and that, feeling like home was within grasp once again. Before long, it was time to section the dough into loaves, then place them into the oven.

When the first batch finished baking, its aroma filled the room like the promise of better days. Louis appeared in her memories right along with it.

One time he hid behind the pantry door. That wasn't unusual. He was full of pranks. This time, though, she held a wooden bowl in one hand. When he sprang out like a child's toy on a spring, she screamed and hit him over the head.

The bowl had been empty. It knocked him out, anyway.

She thought she murdered him.

She was sobbing by the time he fluttered those impossibly long eyelashes said, "How many loaves do we need today?"

She pulled him up and hugged him.

He hugged her back.

They sat on the floor, rocking back and forth.

"I thought. I killed you." She cried in torrents.

"No." He muttered, drifting in and out of consciousness. "Then I'd have to leave you."

It had been almost a declaration that she didn't know what to do with it. As quickly as the words popped out, he added. "Stop rocking me. I'm dizzy."

Some things never changed. She was the attacker. He was the comforter.

A noise rustled like a leafy branch in the dining room. It was her imagination. She stood by the door and listened.

When a chair scraped against stone, she grabbed the broom and stood behind the partially opened door.

A shadow moved against the wall and became a person in a hooded tunic, crouching on the floor.

She faced a dragon and rode across the desert on the back of a griffin. She even escaped the ghostly shadows. This was nothing a good broom couldn't handle. Charging out of the kitchen, she screamed. "Eeeeya!"

A man spun around and held his hands up. "Giselle. It's me."

"Louis!" She threw the broom aside and almost toppled him with her hug.

Actually, she hugged him a lot harder than he hugged her back. He seemed careful, as if she still carried the broom.

She hurried to fill up the awkward silence. "You're smelly. And skinny. Way skinnier than I've ever seen. When was the last time you ate? Come into the kitchen. I'm baking bread."

Louis loped in and practically fell onto the bench. He held the fresh bread in one hand, as if in reverence, then stuffed half of an entire round into his mouth. Then finished it in another bite.

"I don't have milk. Only some water."

He chugged one glass and kept drinking until the jar was empty.

"What are you doing here? I was ready to deck you with the broom."

"A fearsome weapon, to be sure. And after I saved you from that dog last night."

"That was you in the tree?"

Louis rested his chin on one hand, as if studying the thought. "Perched in a tree? Perhaps tree monkey or squirrel."

"When did you come back? How did you find a way into the city past those ghastly shadow warriors?" At least, that's what Ramaz had called them.

"Lots of questions. It was a long trip."

"All the way from the mountains?"

"Uhm. Yes." He kept his distance, even when she sat beside him on the bench and watched him eat.

"By yourself?"

"Mostly."

His one-word answers told her what she already knew. Her last words when she perched on the back of the griffin still stung. It was time to say what she'd been rehearsing for so many days. "Louis. I. I'm sorry. I was mean. And stupid."

He stopped chewing. "I'm not your enemy? I mean. That's what I heard in the mountains."

She'd tried the plain truth. "I was scared."

"I get that. It hurt, anyway."

She cleared her throat and took a deep breath. "I'm sorry."

He smiled a crooked grin and held out a battered hand. "Truce?"

She took it. They had an almost moment before he pulled away and dusted his hands on dingy trousers.

Her friend was back. He sat as if this was any other moment in thousands of meals at this table.

Giselle jumped in. "I have so much to tell you. King Abusari was poisoned. That's why the city is in lockdown. Makir is the new king."

"And you know this how?"

"I saw Makir. He promised to help find Mother."

"Convenient."

"How can you say that?" She was ticked. "Okay. You're still mad at me. But I traveled on the back of a griffin and survived another dragon attack to find Mother. I only have five days, according to the dragon. Why wouldn't I want the king's help?"

Louis didn't say anything. He stood by the pantry door and counted supplies, instead.

"Don't say anything, then. I'm going to the palace right now to see if there is any news."

"The last time I went by, it was heavily guarded."

"Yes. I'm allowed in, though. Makir is my friend."

"That gives you a free pass to what – everything?"

She wouldn't respond to that. He was jealous. Much better than standoffish former best friend, now turned interrogator. "You don't know the king like I do. He has the resources and authority we need. Besides, he promised to help find Mother."

"Favor of the new king. How nice."

"You're suspicious. You'll see. He can be trusted."

"Proof?"

"You're making fun of me. How do we find a way

to argue about everything?"

"We?"

"Yes, we. It takes two to argue."

"It takes one to speak truth – even when it isn't wanted."

"Truth? Makir is kind. He is…"

"Someone put martial law in effect. People are afraid, starving. Don't be blind to what is all around you."

"You're awful. I do see. Makir believes he's protecting the city."

"By starving it into submission?"

"Of course not. Give me time. I know better than anyone else that he thinks Magi are the enemy. Just like every Nayeli. How do you think the truth will come?" The loathing that brushed Makir's face earlier came to mind. It was such a fleeting moment. Probably she misread the look.

"You're trusting Makir will be moved by your wise words and pretty face."

"My face? Are you blind? No. If I have his favor, I'll use it to help him see. It's the third day. I'm bringing Mother home where she belongs."

Louis sighed and turned away. "May it be so. Go to your prince. Deliver your mother. I need sleep."

He was obstinate and overly guarded. When Mother was back home, she'd prove she was right.

For now, she needed another one of her mother's gowns. This time she didn't feel like a thief. She was an ambassador from the Gemini to appeal for her.

She pulled out a light, airy floral gown, more feminine than Mother's eclectic style usually allowed. A slip of stationery fell out of one of its sleeves. Her heart jumped when she recognized her flowing script.

Dearest one – Don't leave me. Not now when life darkens, and no light is in sight. I can no longer fly to the mountains in my dreams, nor can I remember why we came here, to the den of the adversary itself.

I've failed. Totally and completely. All hope is gone.

It was a message from a frightened, vulnerable mother. What else had been hidden – or that she refused to notice? There hadn't been any joy for such a long time. For the most part, they spent their energy turning simple statements into insults. Both swore an unspoken vendetta. "You must pay. Pay, for my broken heart."

Probably they looked for a way out of the war.

Just not at the same time.

She couldn't imagine what the dragon meant that it *had* her mother. She was convinced that the bird led her to Mother. Instead, it was Ramaz – the betrayer and would-be captor. It was horrifying to see the man overtaken by the black shadows, no matter how vile.

He was right about one thing. All of life had presented a puzzle.

Except now, she had the favor of the king.

Chapter 18

Makir met her without his normal retinue of guards, proving she was a special guest who didn't require usual protocol. There had to be official matters at hand, yet he waited as if time with her were more important. She straightened her shoulders and tried not to wobble on what felt like the brink of a waterfall.

He led them to a cool garden room where a hint of eucalyptus lingered in the air. "Are you hungry? Thirsty?" They sat on an elaborate Oriental couch near a table filled with dishes of meat and vegetables she'd never seen. His presence was like a shield that embraced her. Mother would be safe with him, too. It was the afternoon of the third day. As much as she enjoyed this time, her goal was to find Mother.

Makir leaned close. "You're safe here. Please don't run away. Danger surrounds us."

"I ran away because I was afraid. I found Ramaz. The warriors made of smoke and shadows murdered him. It was horrible."

Was it surprise that brushed his face? He shook his head and looked away. "He tried to enslave you, a Nayeli citizen. He knew the law."

Dread quivered inside. "Someone commanded those demons. Was it you?"

"When a decree is in place, retribution follows. Whether I command it or not."

"Who else would command it?" She ran through her mind, searching for Nayeli decrees she was supposed to know but didn't. They lived on the city's outskirts and so far from the temple, she wasn't sure what Gad El Glas required.

King Abusari was never feared. She hadn't witnessed what Makir referred to as retribution. "I was terrified. What are those ghouls called? They looked human, and then they weren't." She searched the young king's face, which appeared unguarded.

Makir shrugged. His answer was matter of fact. "The shadow guard is an effective deterrent. There are many mysteries in the Nayeli world. They are one of them."

"I've never seen or heard of them before."

"They protect the mountain kingdom where my mother and I rule. They've been active on our behalf for generations. I grew up knowing their presence and learned their power as I ruled as Crown Prince."

"You've experienced dragons and know the existence of black clouds that carry death. You're comfortable with a supernatural realm I never knew existed."

"Our world consists of layers. Layers of what we see and of what we cannot see." He grazed her hands lightly. "I knew you were special when I met you at the masquerade."

She wanted to ask him more about Ramaz, except he shifted the conversation as smoothly as if they were here to discuss her place in his heart.

"You stood at the masquerade, in the center of that madness and yet not a part of it. You had no idea of the presence you carried." He took a breath and pulled her closer. "Do you understand that I came here, to Darras, for you?"

Being near him was like being next to a fire in the chill of a desert night. Perspiration sprinkled her nose as he plucked a stray curl from her eyes.

He did care.

Then again, she fell headlong into trust with Erik, and even Ramaz. Was this declaration as without substance as the shadow guard? "You came for an alliance between kingdoms. You couldn't have known I'd be at the masquerade. I wasn't even sure until that day."

"My eyes see what might be. I expected to meet you there."

She hesitated. This was like a dream come true. Or as dangerous as the precipice she felt when she first arrived.

Makir answered as if he read her mind. "We don't know each other well. That doesn't change the fact that we were destined to meet that night. Even this moment in time is appointed."

"You're so. Handsome. And seem wonderful. I'm an innkeeper's daughter, accustomed to customers shouting demands. Please. Tell me the truth. This is the third day, and I must find my mother."

"I have a truth that is very good news." His regal bearing merged into a wide smile. "Your mother is here, waiting to see you. I'll take you to her."

Giselle grabbed him around the neck and hugged him. So much for caution. Kingly reserve melted as he spun her in his arms.

"Thank you. Thank you." She murmured over and over into the warmth of his muscular chest.

"Come." He laughed as he settled her curls that sprouted in every direction. Taking her hand in his, they walked down a stone hallway without any palace guards or fanfare.

Makir knocked, then opened the door to a lavish suite dressed in gold and green velvet. A servant attended a woman who reclined on a brocade couch. Raven hair hung on the woman's thin shoulders. Her dark eyes were deeply shadowed.

Giselle came closer. "Mother?"

The woman sprang upright and held out her hands with joy. "Giselle!"

She rushed into her arms and burst into tears. "You're here. I was so worried." Sharp angles of bones pressed against her own warmth. "Are you sick? You're so thin."

"Hush, child. All is well, now that you're here."

"She's safe here, for as long as she needs." Makir bowed. "I'll take my leave. Signal the guards when you're done."

She melted into her mother's arms.

Ursula whispered. "There are eyes upon us. Ears that listen."

Giselle didn't know what to say or do. "Let me take you back to the inn."

"Not yet. I'll tell you when it's time. Until then, remember the waterfall."

"How did you know? Where have you been all this time? A dragon said it captured you. I traveled here…so worried that I was too late." She took her mother's hand and found it cool. The hands that had run a busy inn day and night were limp. "Wait. Why can't I take you home?"

A tear escaped and dribbled down her mother's porcelain skin. She was a demolished version of her confident self. The picture of Lilith, Alessandra's mother, became flesh right in front of her. She longed to rush in with all she'd discovered in the Magi kingdom.

"King Abusari was murdered shortly after you left," she began. "I was delivering bread to the palace when the city closed." Her breath came in short stabs, and her words stilted as if she memorized a script. "When Makir became king, he was gracious to let me stay. I've been directing the palace kitchen."

Giselle was alarmed. "You're so weak. Come home with me. I'll take care of you."

Her mother barely had strength for a few sentences before she fell back onto the couch, with her hand still in Giselle's. "I can't. Not now. I'm helping – here at the palace."

"How can you help when you barely have strength to stand?"

Mother brushed aside her concern. "I'm fine. Please. Bring my slippers when you come back."

What an odd shift in conversation, following a long-awaited greeting. Something was wrong.

Mother had left the inn quickly and never returned to the Gemini? The inn wasn't only a place of business, it was home. Nothing would keep her away for long.

And her request was strange, to say the least.

Mother's bedroom was a private sanctuary that Giselle had rarely entered before the masquerade. As far as she knew, her proper mother didn't own, much less ever wear, a pair of slippers. She had countless embellished sandals, shoes with tiny, jeweled heels, and embroidered flats. There were shoes dyed in vibrant hues of magenta, and every color of the rainbow. Never slippers.

She reached over to hug her mother again and whispered. "Tell me that you're safe here."

Mother's body quaked against hers. "Go back to the inn – you'll know what to do."

She flew across the desert with Tobias, barely survived a dragon attack, and navigated a city under martial law. Now she was supposed to leave the mother she came to save? Besides, if she was in the palace all along, why hadn't Makir brought them together earlier? "I can't leave you. I won't. I'll stay here at the palace."

"No!" The answer pulled on the last bit of her mother's strength, "Don't be afraid. Go back to the Gemini. We need you there."

We? Louis was there, although Mother didn't know that. When the king didn't reappear, a small group of palace guards escorted her back through the marketplace. Soldiers waved them through checkpoints without stopping to search her. It was as if Makir sent instructions to protect her way back to the Gemini.

By the time she was safely back at the inn, the shadow of the mother she left continued to haunt her. Mother's bearing, so elegant and composed, slumped, as if her spine had been soaked in water.

The fact that she wouldn't return to the inn made no sense. Worse, her direct mother had used a code word, fearing someone overheard their conversation.

Yet, she found Mother with King Makir's help. She wasn't sure how he did that, but she was grateful. She'd bring her back home tomorrow, no matter what.

It was time to search again for whatever her mother meant when she said *slippers*. She pulled out shoe after shoe from the bedroom closet and even pried up the floorboards. Nothing, not even a scribbled note, appeared as a clue.

She plopped at the kitchen table to rest and gather her thoughts after the search. One thing was clear. Makir did exactly what he promised. He helped find Mother.

Her belly tingled with the possibility that she was really, truly adored by the young king. Not that she understood why. He was as layered and full of mystery as the Nayeli culture. Then again, one look into his ebony eyes made the most puzzling enigma seem perfectly natural.

Makir invited trust. And honestly, a longing ready to ignite with a random touch. Being in his presence was like standing in front of a floodgate that held back surging waters. She was excited and panicked at the same time.

She never had time for anything other than noticing an attractive customer and wondering what it was like to fall in love. If a customer got out of hand, she decked him, or Mother booted him off the property.

Louis stepped in once. It was the morning Ramaz arrived with his priestly contingent. An expression she'd never seen brushed his face when he saw the high priest. If she didn't know better, it looked like hate.

Only one conclusion made sense. Ramaz was behind the villainy in the palace. Makir, in whatever way, dealt that evil a fatal blow. If there was a power play, as Ramaz hinted, Makir won.

She allowed herself a glimmer of relief that even the dragon had been fueled by Ramaz. The scheme that lusted for her gift, and for her mother, dismantled when he died.

Tomorrow Mother would truly be free because of Makir's compassion.

Louis was in the kitchen, pulling out round after round of flatbread from a hot oven.

"What are you doing?"

"Baking bread."

"We have plenty."

"This is for the neighbors."

"Is that legal?"

"You aren't serious. Is it legal for people to starve because their king decides they're in too much danger to eat?"

"Of course, not. Makir said the lockdown is only temporary."

"How long does it take to get hungry? A day, three days, a week? It's not right. I'm going to find a way to get bread to them."

There was that gulf between them again.

He turned his back and muttered. "You can help or not. Oh, I forgot, the king is your friend. He might not approve."

"You're the most aggravating man."

Louis went back to kneading a circle of dough with careful punches. "I thought you were bringing your mother home."

"She. She wouldn't come home with me. I'll go back tomorrow."

"Let me go with you."

"No." Her answer came out with more heat than she expected. "Why?"

"Never mind. It was only a thought."

"I'll leave in the morning and return with Mother. In the meantime, scoot over. I'll help."

Chapter 19

It was the fourth day, and all was well. Makir thwarted the plot of the Ramaz, who obviously embodied the dragon. All she had to do now was get Mother back to the Gemini. With rest and care at the home she loved, it wouldn't take long to get her strength back.

She requested a formal audience with the king that morning, even though she didn't need one. She only affirmed her respect. Besides, he always appeared right away.

Minutes ticked away into a full hour as she paced and paced some more in the sumptuous entry of the palace. Guards, positioned at the entrance, stood silently with weapons at their side. She looked them over nervously.

She posed no threat to the king. He certainly was no menace to her. Still, soldiers were expected in the palace. They guarded the one who ruled their city.

When Makir finally arrived, he nodded slightly and stood apart, instead of hurrying toward her. "Giselle." He remained fully royal – and aloof. "We don't have much time. There's been a new development. I must speak truth, even though it's hard to hear."

She hadn't heard his serious, almost stern voice. At least not with her. She was immediately cautious. "What have you been speaking if it hasn't been truth?" No, that was rude. Makir was her friend. "What is it? You seem…distant."

The set of his jaw was like chiseled stone. Important things commanded his attention in the kingdom. Her timing was wrong. She had to get Mother home, though. Her weakened state was proof of that.

She studied the king's bearing and saw hardness.

This was worse than some unknown affair of state. The warmth they shared only yesterday chilled without explanation. "I'm afraid. Suddenly, I don't know you."

Makir took a breath and straightened his royal bearing to its full height. "We've discovered grave evidence. It's about your mother."

"What is it? She…she's sick. I came to take her home. Today."

"We believe her baked goods poisoned King Abusari."

She almost laughed. "Who is *we?* That's ridiculous."

The king's face was like a mask. "She's held under guard as the matter is investigated. Trust me when I say she is safe here."

"You mean she isn't in the same dungeon that held Ramaz? What exactly does safe mean? You accused her of murdering King Abusari."

"There is more here than you understand, Giselle. More at stake than you know."

"I can't imagine higher stakes than my mother held as a murderer. She baked for the palace as long as I remember. She and the king were friends. Why would she poison him?"

"She harbored Magi at the Gemini. For many years."

A warning shot through her veins, hot and insistent.

She had to be careful with her words. "I would've known. We served everyone who came through those city gates. How could she know if one was Magi?"

"Sir Damien."

The confrontation between Mother and Sir Damien scared her from the beginning. "What did he know? Those accusations were based only on rumor."

"You remember the incident."

"Any testimony against her is a lie. She's been a faithful citizen, a prosperous businesswoman whose inn welcomed the world – and its gold – into Darras. How could she be blamed for a random stranger who visited? You're receiving lies against an innocent woman." This was not going well. She had to move fast. "You have no right to treat her like a common criminal. I must see her. I insist."

Only days ago, a simple whim released Makir's favor. This king was unyielding. "Give me one week. Then, if she's proven innocent, you can take her home." He lifted a hand, and soldiers streamed into the inner chamber.

Mother wasn't working in the palace kitchen. She wasn't a palace visitor. She was a prisoner.

As Makir turned and walked away, crimson-clad soldiers surrounded her without a word and escorted her back to the Gemini.

"Louis! Where are you?" She rushed around the inn, panicked. Now that she needed him, he was nowhere in sight. The enemy wasn't Ramaz, after all. Whoever it was still lurked in the palace and held Mother.

She hurried to her mother's room, reminded of the random slippers. There had to be a note, something, somewhere. She ran her hand through the gowns, rustling each one, longing for another letter. She pillaged the vanity, pulling out make-up, stationery, pens, and brushes.

Nothing.

She plopped into the corner of the room, head in hands and defeated.

Memories raged here in Mother's room. Just not in the light she'd always known them. Her heart saw what it hadn't seen before.

She'd been dragon-like, herself.

She required Mother to bow to her pain, even above her own. She insisted that she made wrongs right, even when that was impossible. Most of all, she expected her mother to somehow take away the ache in her heart.

Or else.

Or else, she'd hold her broken mother captive in the stew of her own bitterness.

As the keeper of hurts, of wrongs, and of fabricated spins, she made her pay.

She left home without a good-bye.

Mother paid, all right. Soldiers hauled her away to the palace with no one to defend her. She could've done something, anything, to protect her. She could've kept her mother at home where she belonged.

Lots of ifs that made no difference now.

Because once more, she'd skipped like an unsuspecting child into a trap.

There was a name for that.

Stupid.

For one who considered herself so wise, she was a bumbling fool.

Beating herself up on the inside, only made her heart throb right along with aching muscles. The vanity was ransacked, emptied by her search. She could at least put things where they'd been.

Maybe she imagined Mother's clue. Maybe it meant nothing at all.

A crinkled piece of paper brushed her fingers at the back of the drawer. She pulled, careful not to tear it until it broke free into her hands. It was a picture with words scrawled and pocked with random ink on the back.

A young Rory with starburst eyes and Alessandra with untamed curls smiled back at her. They stood on one side of the plummeting waterfall.

She'd seen that towering flood. The backdrop for this picture was the mountains where she first met her Magi family. A raven-haired little girl with ivory skin and fire in her eyes perched on a black Mustang.

The child was her mother.

She looked for any similarities between Rory, Alessandra, and her mother. There were none. Only a striking resemblance to the picture of Alessandra's mother, Lilith, she saw in the granite refuge behind the falls.

The writing on the back was almost too smudged to be legible. She smoothed it out and struggled to read what appeared to be a hurried note.

Villainy is upon the palace. Praying that you find this, and that I live to see you return.

Villainy in the palace. Not the temple.

Mother lied about working at the palace. The only truth she told was a caution that an enemy listened to their conversation.

A gentle knock sounded on the door that opened to the marketplace.

Louis wouldn't knock on a door. He was family.

Maybe someone needed help.

Instead of a distressed neighbor, Makir stood with a personal attendant at his side. Instead of royal robes, he wore a simple linen tunic under the kingly medallion. He bowed and stood, as if he waited to be invited inside.

She held the door against his entrance. "Why are you here? What do you demand of me, King Makir?"

"I've come to apologize."

"You imprisoned my mother after telling me that I could bring her home."

"I bowed to pressure." he answered without fanfare. "Come back to the palace. You may see her. I give my word."

She studied his eyes, longing for some clue, some sign of Makir's heart. Louis was right. She'd been blind for too long. She trusted the wrong people, over and over. "Your promises waver like the wind. You forgot about our meeting this morning. You acted like you…didn't know me. Like you…"

"I do care."

When he stepped closer, she grasped the door, ready to slam it shut. "I can't imagine why. We had a chance meeting at a masquerade, wearing masks to cover who we really were. What you supposedly felt changed on a whim – or at least a fabricated accusation. I don't need promises based on a lie. Go."

He held his hand against the door and spoke quietly. "I'm king first. Always. Then friend. I believed the wrong people at the wrong time."

"Who convinced you of her guilt? Mother has no enemies in the city. No one would accuse her without some kind of evil motive."

"I lead the Nayeli people. When a credible

accusation comes to my attention, I must address it."

"I'm tired of betrayal. I have no idea who you really are."

"Let me prove my heart. Come back to the palace. '

"Now I understand. You need my gift. A door of impossibility is still locked to your desire. What would that be?" Her jaw hardened. "You could've asked. Instead, you're like every other swindler and cheat. You flatter until you have me in your grasp."

"You're the one who will gain." He extended his hands, as if in surrender. "You may take your mother home."

Her heart leaped despite herself. "How can I be sure you're telling me the truth?" She slapped her hand against the door, then rubbed it in pain. "Give me a clue " she said bitterly. "Like a shift in your eyes or a touch of your hand that proves your intention. Mother is weak and vulnerable. Certainly, no threat to the Nayeli kingdom. Should I trust a snake to release her to me?"

"I'm no serpent. I offer you an open door, back to the palace, and back to your mother."

She studied him. He'd given her no reason not to trust him until that morning. He was king, but he was also human. He might have listened to the wrong counsel. Perhaps now he spoke the truth.

Something about Makir made her toss every doubt into the sand and believe that what she hoped was true. There was only one way to find out. "I receive your offer. Not because I trust you. Only because I won't spend another day without my mother in this inn."

He bowed slightly. "I'll send my guards to escort you."

Dashing upstairs, she grabbed a gown with pockets

and dressed quickly. If she was going back to the palace, she'd go armed. She put the knife and Suzette's ointment in her pocket, then covered herself in Leonore's fabric as a shawl.

She left Louis a note in the kitchen. "At the palace. Mother and I will be back."

A small retinue of palace guards waited as she locked the door and slipped its key into her pocket. They escorted Giselle through the deserted marketplace where merchants usually began closing their shops and covering stalls for the night. Stillness descended along with the sun as it lowered against the horizon in shades of crimson and blue.

She saw through Louis's eyes as she walked through the quiet neighborhoods where friends hid inside their homes. Gardens here and there kept families alive, but that was about it. There was no way to get provisions into a city that was closed to traders.

Makir was nowhere in sight by the time she reached the palace. Something evil hovered in the atmosphere. Was it the shadow guard? A heavy fragrance of musk filled the air and made her dizzy. She whirled around, unsure of what to do and where to go.

A woman in a filmy white gown appeared from the garden atrium, where she and Makir ate together after her arrival in the city. Something about her looked like the ghostly figure from the maze the night she was chased home by a hound.

This woman was real. At least she thought so. She was Queen Naifa from the Eastern Mountains who presided over the masquerade with King Abusari. The one who summoned her son that night with one look.

The guards were unmoving, careful to silence even

the clink of bronze medallions. Fear shrouded the palace like a heavy tapestry flung over the atmosphere, dulling every sound, and dimming light.

"Giselle. Welcome to the palace." There was no melody in this imperious voice.

The soldiers surrounding her didn't have to bind her hands to tell her what she knew.

Makir's invitation was a trap.

Chapter 20

Palace guards led her past the tiled garden room and into one corridor after another. She was lured here and caught, just like an insect snared in a spider's web.

So much for tokens of affection and noble words about her calling. All his devoted attention was only a lovely shell for a plot he crafted all along. He was like a marionette at the market, jerked into motion by an unseen puppet master. Obviously, his mother ruled behind his façade of regal bearing. How weak was that?

A page stepped in front of massive double doors. "King Makir of the Nayeli kingdom."

There he was, face chiseled in ivory, dark curls wrapping his head like some god dropped to earth.

Holding her head high, she marched forward, shoulders back. "You lied to me. About everything."

Makir remained seated. He made no move to greet her.

His mother stood beside him with a languid hand on his shoulder. She must've taken some secret passageway to this interior throne room.

Her smile said it all. Makir belonged to her. He was merely a pawn for the queen's intrigues.

If this was a show of power, she refused to be intimidated.

She addressed Makir and ignored Queen Naifa. "King Makir. A dragon spoke to me in the mountains. I had five days to return to Darras, to save my mother. You promised to help me find her. You acted as if you had no idea where she was. Was that true?"

Makir fidgeted a bit.

The queen stepped in. "We are not on trial here."

"I was led to believe my mother was here by her own will. All this time, she was a captive. You, my king, promised that I could take her home today. Now, I, too, am a prisoner." She offered a small curtsey. "It appears that those who rule Darras are no different than Ramaz, who purchased me as a slave."

"You are no slave." Makir spoke firmly.

"You offered a royal summons to the palace. One that allowed me to take my mother home. Are you a friend or a betrayer?

"Enough of this impertinence," Queen Naifa nodded, and the nearest guard drew his sword.

"Stop." Makir lifted his hand. "Don't touch her."

The queen barely glanced at Makir, then began her interrogation. "Your mother harbored Magi infiltrators. You were a willing accomplice."

Where did this woman come from? She was totally cold, totally powerful.

"If you only knew. I was anything but willing. Now, I see the tragedy of that." She had to be very careful in this web. The woman sought weakness and misplaced words to use against her. And Mother.

"Are you saying you knew your mother broke the law and refused to cooperate with her?"

"You long to convict me with my words."

Queen Naifa was unrelenting. "Answer a simple question. Did you agree with your mother's actions?"

"I didn't know my mother's actions. Who appointed

you as interrogator and judge?"

The queen arched an eyebrow, and the guards rushed forward again.

Makir's voice rose. "I. Said. Don't touch her."

The woman was undeterred. Her eyes were direct, searching. "You're lying. You knew what your mother was doing."

She discovered a source of information other than Sir Damien. That knowledge was a trump card, waiting to be played at the right time.

"You've judged my mother and me, two Nayeli citizens, without trial."

Makir's words were an appeal. "We need the truth, Giselle."

"We? You haven't told me the truth. You led me to believe that you were my advocate."

"I *am* on your side."

"Prove that. Take me to my mother. Then set us free."

Queen Naifa stepped in. "Declare your true allegiance to the Nayeli people."

"Why would I be asked to declare what my life has proven? I respect our culture and our people. Sadly, I've become an enemy fit only for deception. I'll ask again. What do you really want?"

"Makir is your king. That is enough."

Makir stood abruptly, as if to halt his mother's words. "Stop." He took his place between the queen and Giselle. "Guards. Escort everyone except the woman and me from this room."

The queen looked long and hard. She had no intention of leaving.

Makir bowed his head and stood without speaking.

Suddenly, the woman turned with a graceful shift as though leaving had been her plan all along. She glanced back when she reached the door, jabbing her words like a sword. "We'll find the truth. No matter what it takes."

Giselle whirled to Makir as the queen left the room along with her thick, perfumed scent. Even her fragrance was a weapon. "No matter what it takes? Tell me. Will you carry out those threats? Or will she."

"Please. Let me speak my heart."

"What have you been speaking? Your mother's will?"

Makir flinched a little. "I want you here. I…I need you, Giselle."

Did he say he wanted her? Loved her? "Explain what that means."

"You bring me joy in many ways. Yet, regardless of what you think about Magi, I know differently. An invasion is imminent." His body tensed, and what looked like dread brushed over his face.

"I was outside the city gates only days ago. There was no one as far as the eye could see. The Magi are peace-loving people. What would they look for here?"

Makir despised the Magi, believing they killed his father. Just like she once believed about her own father. They shared a common grief, as well as a common lie. Given time, she hoped to convince the young king that the Magi were not the fiends he believed them to be.

How naïve she'd been.

"The Magi have been sworn enemies for generations. Darras controls the riches of an entire region. They lust after this city, which is a place of power and authority – as well as immense wealth."

"The Magi I met were kind. They're pursued

relentlessly by a dragon. They have…their own kind of wealth with gifts that make no sense in the natural world but are powerful for good."

"How do you know that?"

She was on dangerous ground. She could be hauled off and executed without warning. "I…spent time with them. They rescued me from Ramaz in Apamea."

Was she getting them in trouble? No doubt, the queen hovered nearby, leaning into every word.

Makir listened intently. "I'm grateful they protected you. Ramaz, of course, has been judged." His words were full of venom. "Magi are equally dangerous, regardless of their appearance. Our greatest treasure is our way of life. The Nayeli kingdom endures because of it. You're part of that culture. You're one of us. Have you forgotten?

This was hardly a declaration of love. "Of course not."

Just then, two attendants carried in a chaise lounge as if it weighed nothing. Her mother lay against it. She struggled to sit up when she saw Giselle.

She ran to her mother and held her against her chest, willing strength into her heartbeat that skipped and wavered. Her frailty was its own warning and time piece. She didn't have long to bring her home.

Who was the real enemy?

She had no idea.

"Please. I must take her home."

Makir came closer. "For now, believe me that you're both safer here." He reached for her hand. "Will you trust me?"

She studied those graceful fingers, untouched by callous or scars. His touch, no matter how tender, beckoned an almost flame. She backed away, refusing to take it. "That's the question, is it not?"

There was no reason to rail against Makir. Nothing she said or did changed his mind. It was time for another plan. As the guards carried her out of the room, she kissed her mother and vowed to see her again.

Anger and frustration threatened to mow her down. She took Mother's strength for granted all these years. Now, she had to find a way out for them both.

Security was tight as guards marched her back to the gorgeous room that had become her cell. The noxious presence of the demonic warriors remained stationed outside her locked door. Their shadows also hovered near her window to the courtyard.

Was betrayal a curse that followed her, built into the very cells of her body, as strong and certain as her gift to open doors? After all, it was a familiar enemy. She knew its sting far too well.

Makir, or whoever was in charge, held her under lock and key, for her protection.

Right.

Tomorrow was the fifth day.

Mother was getting weaker, not stronger.

It didn't matter what Makir believed. He was wrong. If he wasn't dangerous, his mother certainly was.

She was caught in a snare but not for long. If there was no escape, she'd make one.

For herself and for Mother.

It was hopeless, of course. She had to find and then carry her frail mother through locked doors and demonic shadow guard to the Gemini.

Resolve formed slowly in her mind. Maybe it came from her time behind the waterfall. Maybe it took time to know what became clear after this last deceit.

If wickedness wanted the power of her gift, she wanted it more.

She'd discover its strength for good. If her hands truly opened doors to wealth and freedom, they could also outsmart the wickedness that lusted for it.

It was up to her. Would she believe that, finally?

After all, it was her gift.

And if it was hers, it would work when it mattered.

She'd been seduced and caught in a net instead of saving her mother.

And yet, in the end, the gift belonged only to her.

She couldn't dash around, cutting bonds and shouting 'Run!' like she had at the slave market. She stared down at her hands. "What? What am I supposed to do?"

She remembered the crystal rain and the peace that washed over her heart as the prophecy was spoken. "The breaker, who opens a way through the gate, bursts through doors of bronze and bars of iron."

Truth had been shouting for a long time. This time, she was listening.

Chapter 21

The indigo bunting sang as though its heart broke. When she opened the cage, it rushed out and flew around the ceiling. Finally, it flitted onto her open hand for a moment before it circled the ceiling tiles again.

The shadow guard blocked the door. The windows were, too.

There was only one way of escape.

She pointed to the ceiling.

The bird darted around it and sang as if applauding.

Brass tiles glimmered like mirrors above. She had no tools, except for the three she needed, her knife, Suzette's ointment, and Leonore's fabric. She smeared Suzette's ointment on the base of the door and the window. Its fragrance disguised her absence and would trick the shadow guard into believing she was still in the room.

She pulled a small table under one of the ceiling tiles and patted the knife in her pocket. It would have to work.

Tottering on her perch, she reached up with the knife as far as she could. She finally reached the tile and pried once, twice, and then again, nicking her finger. When the tile popped into her hand, it almost clattered to the floor. She caught it, and herself, before they both crashed to the ground.

The space above the tile opened to a narrow passageway. Hoping they bore her weight, she grasped the surrounding tiles and hoisted herself up. She wiggled her body into the small opening until she landed on a wooden framework. As far as she could see in either direction, a labyrinth of timbers lined a narrow space above the ceiling tiles.

Which way should she go? She had no idea where to find Mother.

The bird didn't care that she was confused and afraid. It flew, knowing exactly where it was headed.

Glimmers of light peeked through the rooms' ceilings as she crawled on her hands and knees in the dark. She had to trust her tiny friend that her mother was not in the dungeon but held somewhere above ground.

Raw wood scrapped her knees. Timbers quaked and wavered with her weight. With no sense of distance or time, she followed the blue feathers that raced forward. The pathway became a dark tunnel, and her eyes strained to see flashes of the bunting ahead.

After what was minutes or hours, fresh air rose at her feet.

She knew where she was.

It was an alcove connecting the palace and temple. The whoosh of air stirred a memory. She was a little girl, gripping her mother's skirt as they approached the temple to celebrate the summer solstice.

Spires of the temple rose like swords, and the drone of a thousand wasps pressed against her young ears. She begged Mother to go home.

"Only for a bit. We'll have cake when we get home. I promise."

There had been no music, only a blazing red light that felt hot and sticky in an otherwise cold place. Ramaz stood, dressed in black and gold. His retinue of attendants formed a dark semi-circle behind him, bobbing up and down like ravens, searching for tidbits on the ground. Fawning over the high priest was somehow necessary.

Ramaz had extended his hands over the worshippers and crooned a sing-song decree. "You are Nayeli. Rise in this age against our enemy, the Magi. Touch nothing of theirs, reject every appearance of their filth. Plunder, enslave them for the sake of your children, in the name of El Glas."

Even now a hint of sulfur grew into a stench that made her eyes water and throat burn. Had the memory become so real that its stink filled her senses?

She whispered as if the bunting understood. Or stopped to listen. "It's too dark. I'm too afraid. I'm not going."

The bird continued to lead her forward. She inched on a wooden framework that became a downward slope. Lower and lower, she crept as the air grew hotter, swallowing the coolness of a desert evening.

The taste of salt burned as strong as the sulfur against her senses. Her throat constricted, each airway suddenly parched. The very air assaulted her lungs as tiny particles saturated every breath. A wave of dizziness almost took her out until she remembered Leonore's fabric and placed it over her mouth.

Thirsty. She was so, so thirsty. The atmosphere itself leached moisture from her body as heat from a mighty furnace rose below.

This was a descent into Hades.

She couldn't go any further.

This journey was too much. It was more than her body could endure. More than her soul imagined.

Louis wove tales of Greek mythology as they gazed into the night sky. The Princess Andromeda was there. So was Aquarius, the Water Bearer. Even the northern crown, Corona Borealis, worn by Princess Ariadne on her wedding day glittered like a promise.

The story of Hades chilled her heart and made her press closer to Louis's warmth. This ancient god was hidden not only in the stars but in creation itself. Hades stole the maiden Persephone and whisked her away to a living death in the underworld. As a result, the plants of Earth ceased to grow, and the human race faced extinction.

Persephone had a mother, though.

The goddess Demeter went right to the top of the Greek god chain. Finally, Zeus intervened and convinced Hades to release her daughter. When he did, springtime returned to Earth.

That was some kind of mother.

Demeter fought to save her daughter from an evil god in a way that caught Zeus's attention and returned life to a hurting world.

Persephone was a captive in the underworld with no hope of seeing sunlight again. She'd never taste the freshness of water, never feel it against her hot skin. She was separated from family and from all that made life good.

What was that like?

In her heart, she knew.

It smoldered below.

Mother was like Demeter, strong, courageous, determined. The world still needed her. She needed her.

The bunting dashed back and forth in front of her but made no sound.

Maybe she was a hopeless coward.

Then again, maybe courage would come.

One more inch.

Then one more.

Her hand met hot air instead of roof timbers. She stifled a scream, caught herself, and reeled back, almost losing balance.

By the time her breathing and resolve returned, she leaned her head over nothingness.

Except it wasn't emptiness.

She teetered at the brink of a wide expanse of white stone. Even in the gloom, a multitude of men, women, and children hacked away at the ground and walls. Their only light was a smoldering fire that wavered back and forth in the distance.

As the flames approached, she ducked out of sight, and a black, armored tail swished below.

Stone as pale as death lined the floor, the walls, and the ceiling. It wasn't a cavern, at least not like caves she heard about, tucked away in the rocky outcroppings of an oasis.

She knew what she didn't want to know.

This was a salt mine.

It was here all along, hidden beneath the stark spires of the temple.

Erik refused to go back to the salt mines, even if it meant selling her as a slave. She heard of them, of course. Not here, though. Not enslaving people under the very temple where they worshipped.

A man who looked like Erik, young and Nordic, swung a pickaxe over and over against a mountain of salt. An aged man and woman hacked a pillar with slow, deliberate movements as a young woman hushed her crying child.

No one saw her. She studied each countenance, noted the bent backs, and recognized the grace and dignity in each movement. These slaves were Magi, a royal race who counseled kings and released gifts in others.

Those who set others free were prisoners in a real-life Hades, crafted by a demon, yes, but enforced by man.

Makir knew about it. He had to. The man who seemed so kind aligned himself, on purpose, with a hellish venture. Maybe his motive was pure greed. Wealth poured into the Nayeli kingdom through this mine.

Then again, Magi slaves in a hidden salt mine satisfied his lust for vengeance. He lined his own purse with the captivity of those he despised. Any relationship with the handsome king meant she allied herself with wickedness that gashed the very earth with one vicious blow after another.

Magi, hidden in an underground hell, were the treasure the dragon hoarded. The mines were a lair, filled with riches, kept by and for the dragon itself.

This wealth didn't glitter like gold. These were priceless gems of human beings – meant for so much more, who slaved in the salt-saturated air, with oozing sores and parched lips.

The bird led her to a place she didn't want to see.

So that she finally understood what was at stake.

Did her parents know this mine was under the temple all this time? A rescue of one or two slaves would never be enough to empty it.

Papa was a gatekeeper. Couldn't he have opened these awful gates and emptied this pit of its plunder?

She looked at her hands. What about her?

What was she going to do?

The ground moaned under the burden of hundreds of slaves. She heard about work in the salt mines. They couldn't operate without an evil trading network of human beings. That explained Erik, Ferdinand, and Carnation.

These were the doors that must be unlocked.

But how?

She had to get Mother out of the palace tonight. Once they were home, she and Louis would decide what to do. She turned to crawl back and whispered to the indigo bunting. "Find Louis. Bring him to the window."

Her knees felt like scorched rubber. Hours later, the fragrance of rose and jasmine wafted up. It was Mother's scent and her voice singing the lullaby.

Lift up your heads, O gates, lift them up ancient doors.

The gatekeeper must come, and she will not fail.

She came too far to fail. Her mother was just below, waiting to be rescued. She pried open a ceiling tile with her knife. As it clattered to the floor, Mother jerked up from a reclining couch. She smiled and held out her arms as if to offer a fragile net.

She just faced hell itself.

This was only a leap.

Dropping her legs into the open space, she aimed for the cushioned bed that angled just out of the way. If she landed on the stone floor, her body would break. She'd be worthless for any rescue.

Still, it wasn't Hades below. It was Mother.

The bunting appeared at her legs. Nice, though not much help. It was time to launch and find courage later.

217

With a giant push that rattled wooden timbers where she hung on tired fingers, she jumped, then dropped into the center of a cushioned bed with a thump.

Straightening her tunic, she checked to make sure all her parts worked. The bed took a hit, but she was good. She crept over to Mother and knelt beside her with a tired grin. "I've come to take you home."

Suddenly, her mother pleaded, as if it was their last time together. "I was wrong not to tell you. I've been wrong about so many things. I shut you out. I was so… My heart betrayed me. And you."

Giselle remembered the despairing note she found. "Your heart wasn't the only one at fault." She reached to hug her mother one more time. "Let's go home."

"Wait. I have to do something."

"What? We need to leave. Now."

"Come closer."

Giselle bent into an unnatural coolness in her mother's embrace. Mother pressed against her daughter's hair and spoke in jagged puffs of breath. "I release who I am and what I carry."

Before she could protest, warmth flooded the center of her being, as if it knew its mark and didn't intend to miss. A sweet, aromatic oil crept through the pores of her skin. It was like salve for her battered, dirty skin that rose from the inside out.

The peace she felt in the mountain cave rolled over her being. It was real, after all, and not only bound only to that beautiful refuge. It showed up here through her mother to saturate a war-ravaged heart.

She couldn't speak. If she interrupted in any way, maybe this would go away. They needed to leave. What if…

"Rest for a moment. It won't leave you. I promise." Mother sighed, as if in deep, satisfied relief. They lay together on the couch, soaking in the beauty of this moment. "I love you, Giselle."

Tenderness engulfed her like the wave she felt with Rory, filling cracks and broken places. It seeped through her being like the fragrant oil that refreshed her senses. "Thank you, Mama. Thank you." She leaned in for a soft embrace and rested there. "I love you."

There was so much to say, so much to make right. Not now, though. This was a sanctuary on earth like none other. How it happened didn't matter now that it was here, healing two hearts.

Her mother's voice was a whisper. "I release my heart to you, beloved. I offer all that I am. Guard it well."

"But…"

"Please say it. Say I will."

The memory of her last conversation with Tobias outside the city gates rushed in. Those were his words. Her mother spoke to them with the same urgency, with the same resolve.

Thieves and predators hoped to steal the very gift she didn't understand. Even now, she didn't know everything at risk. Except it was her mother who asked.

Now it was time to trust. "I will, Mother. Whatever it is, I say yes."

Mother heaved another sigh and kissed her daughter's forehead.

It was hard to protest in the middle of the serenity that enfolded her entire being. Power surged in her legs and arms. Energy arrived as if she had a good meal and a night of sleep.

Mother lay back, spent.

Her own strength hadn't returned for nothing. She had plenty for Mother, too. "It's your turn. I'm getting you out of here."

"I can't stand."

She anointed her mother's head gently with Suzette's ointment.

"Magi oils. It's been so long."

Much of what she'd seen as Mother's control was really a protective shield. One that defended her from an enemy she didn't know existed. Ramaz was no stranger to her. She remembered the icy greeting her mother gave the high priest when he and his entourage visited the inn. And her hard words, commanding her to leave Darras that night.

No wonder. Mother knew the enemy and recognized when its sights were trained on her daughter.

"I didn't understand, Mother. I'm learning, though. We both have a lot of explaining. Right now, let's go home."

Suzette's ointment disguised her absence and covered Louis as he crept to the window of the palace courtyard. She pressed against the pane, praying for no creaks as it slid open. Kissing her on the forehead, she laid Mother into her friend's waiting arms.

The bunting flitted around them both like a tiny guardian. It became a flash of blue, leading them out of the courtyard and through a deserted expanse of road leading home.

This was too easy, and she knew it. Glancing behind, a tendril of smoke formed at the window they just escaped. Smoldering tentacles gathered like a garment and wound along the road like a serpent in pursuit.

Her lungs pulled in the fresh air as she ran. A taste of salt lingered with each breath as a reminder of the ones left behind. This was no time for her mortal body to fail.

Louis raced ahead, holding her frail mother like a child in his arms.

Reaching into her tunic pocket, her heart sank.

Nothing.

She bolted the doors before she left that afternoon. The key fell out in the palace somewhere.

They'd all be captured.

The queen would show no mercy.

Her mind raced through moments when the gift in her hands actually worked. It never bowed to her will, as if she were the owner.

Warehouse doors swung wide at the slave market. She also opened the door to a trap with Makir. Why didn't her gift work all the time? If it did, she'd stand by the entrance of that terrible mine and lead everyone out.

Into a city ruled by the same dragon that captured them in the first place.

A message propelled straight out of her heart, hoping it connected with her hands. "I receive you."

Peace filtered into the panic.

The gift of her hands unlocked doors to greater treasure than would-be robbers ever imagined. Like saving the mother she loved. She extended that gift on purpose. She was a steward of something good, something that set captives free.

By the time she arrived at the door, Louis stood, holding her mother. He wasn't afraid her gift wouldn't work. He never stopped believing. Even when she didn't.

She grasped the door latch.

For Mother.

For the Magi.

The door caught, then swung wide.

Long enough to embrace a prisoner set free.

The tiny bird flew away just before she locked the familiar oak and fell against it.

Embracing Louis and her mother, she knew.

A counterattack was already on the way.

Chapter 22

It was almost like any other morning in the kitchen. Other than her heart that finally settled after their wild escape from the palace. So many unfounded dreams and lies found their home in that glittering place. She went from trusting Makir completely, to being uncertain, and finally, to the acrid taste of his trap.

Makir never intended to release Mother.

He never cared for her. *Could-bes* and *maybes* were only pipe dreams. She'd seen yellow-skinned, ravaged opium users sprawled on tattered couches, tucked away from sight in the marketplace.

What kept them bound when life bustled all around them?

Maybe their dreams looked so much better than reality. Maybe they wanted flight from the ordinary waking up, working, going to sleep, then repeating the same over and over. In the end, perhaps, they sought escape from the heartache of never finding what they longed for.

Of course, some dreams were nightmares all along.

She wanted to believe that Makir was all she desired. In reality, what they shared was never love, only wishful thinking as unstable as shifting sand.

Water from the barrel trickled into Mother's cup until a single drip became no water. Someone cut off access to the upper springs. She knew exactly who it was.

She hadn't been outside the city since she arrived six days ago. It didn't matter how dangerous it was to go now. Mother had to have water.

The gate opened with a clack as she pushed her weight against it. No guards. That was strange. No sentinels glared down from the battlements above. The small pool that signaled the presence of water bubbling from underground was ahead, just beyond the olive tree.

All was peaceful. The tree's leafy branches beckoned and reminded her of the mornings she rested there. She could retreat there now. For a moment she'd escape the war-clad life that pressed from every side.

To prove no refuge existed, a swarm of black dust rushed toward the spring, surrounding, then veiling it totally in darkness. A slender ebony cloud drifted closer until Queen Naifa stood before her, clad in a flowing gown.

Fear rumbled inside and threatened to turn her limbs into mush. By now, terror was a familiar slave driver.

The queen wielded it as a strategic weapon. Seduction made it look lovely and inviting. Like the spider web, it was woven by demonic knowledge of what she yearned for.

Time to rip away those sticky tentacles.

"Good morning, Giselle." The queen's porcelain face was serene. Of course. Her power source was the same swirling terror that destroyed Ramaz.

"Tell me plainly. What do you want?"

"One thing. I want *you*."

"What a strange request. You had me in your grasp. Even now, you could apprehend me with your hateful thugs."

"Fulfill your calling. Forge an alliance between

Nayeli and Magi."

"An alliance? With the Magi you despise? Your lust hides under subterfuge. Identify it for me. What do you really want?"

"Marry my son. Or this city dies of thirst."

"You and your son promise only deception and captivity. I refuse your offer."

"I blocked the upper springs into the city. This one is still open. When it is cut off, the people of Darras will know their true enemy." She shrugged, as if lifting any responsibility from her own shoulders. "Such a simple choice. You say you love the Nayeli people. Prove it. I expect your answer tonight."

With a graceful pirouette, her body left its flesh and became a smoldering wind. An overpowering scent of sulfur lingered to foul the morning air.

Marriage? Makir never loved her. That she knew. His mother totally controlled him. There was more at stake than the queen revealed.

She had to find Louis. The sentinels were back on the wall, although no one appeared to stop her at the gate. It closed behind her without a sound as she hurried back into the Gemini.

Louis was in the courtyard, leaning over an enclosure of stones mortared together. A bend in that long back betrayed an exhausted man. He'd been in and out of the inn without a word to her about what he was doing. She missed him in more ways than she could count.

"I found the mines," she blurted out. "I saw the slaves."

Dark circles lined his eyes. Had he been working all night? "Where?"

"Before I got Mother free. Did you know all along?"

Louis mustered a deep sigh. "All that we've done has been less than a drop in a bucket. A captive released, here and there, from under the dragon's nose. It noticed, of course. Then made the other slaves pay."

"The queen commanded me to marry Makir. It makes no sense. Why marriage?"

Louis strangled a cough and glanced away.

"No. Really." She felt strangely free. Finally.

What she felt for Makir wavered like the shadow guard, luring her into a snare. Her desire amounted to nothing more than turning cartwheels to prove that she was loveable. To the wrong person.

Louis sat down with a plop. He rested his head in his hands long enough to take a breath. "The queen embodies the dragon's lust. She wants your gift. She can't have it legally. Not without marriage."

"She could've just grabbed me and taken me to the palace. Forced some kind of marriage ceremony."

"True. Except she knows Magi law."

"Which law is that?"

"Ask, and the gift is yours. Seek, and you'll discover. Knock, and the door will be opened."

"Which means…"

"The gift can't be stolen. It can only be offered." Louis lay a rock against the mortared stones and reached for another, as if he was too busy to talk. "Magi have frustrated the dragon for generations. It captures, even enslaves, but can't force their gifts to operate. The slaves you saw are like diamonds scattered on the floor of that smoldering mine."

"The dragon controls them."

"Only their bodies. Their gifts are locked away.

That's where the dragon hopes you come in." He stopped midair with brick in hand. His eyes held something she longed for but didn't have words for. "It wants you."

"I still don't get it."

"You're the key. Marriage to someone controlled by the dragon places that key into its hands. It wants to plunder untold wealth with you at its side."

She shivered in fear.

"Here. Try it out." He handed her a cup. Then lowered a bucket into a deep hole dug into the sand.

Water glistened at the bottom.

"Water? How did you do that?"

"We couldn't go to the spring. I brought it here."

She pulled up the bucket. There was silt at the bottom, but the water was clear and cool. Louis brought water into the Gemini from the spring when it was forbidden by the queen and surrounded by guards. He was working on the solution before the threat ever arrived.

Impossible. And yet, he did it. "How?"

He wiped his brow, then rubbed his hands, preparing for a longer explanation than she understood. "So, water flows from high pressure to low pressure. Sand is a perfect medium." He drew a series of intersecting lines in the sand. "A pump draws the groundwater. A screen at the bottom filters out the silt.

"Groundwater couldn't be so close."

"That's what I thought. It is, though."

"Can we get water to the people of Darras?"

"Yes. With a little help."

"You…you found a way around the queen's threat. The city won't die of thirst. What would they… I do without you?"

Would he move closer? Would he fill the gap she'd felt since he returned from the mountains?

If he didn't, she would.

Bolting into his arms, she pressed her body into his. Her heart pummeled as his fingers tightened around her waist. She melded into his quiet strength and rested. Until something else pounded, a longing so deep that words weren't enough.

His beard straggled here and there over a grin that was a long way from brotherly. He lowered his lips until they met hers in a kiss so sweet, so lingering, she whispered, "More."

He wrapped his arms around her, pulled her closer, and deepened his kiss.

Oh. This was good. This was wonderful.

This was her friend, her... Love was right here, holding her in his arms. Her face nestled under his chin. "More. So much more."

Louis kissed her one more time, this time his body hot against her own. They lost all sense of time and place. Well, not exactly. Somehow, they found themselves in the shade of the well, the coolness of the sand against them like a soft mattress.

With one more long kiss, he pulled himself away.

"Wait. Don't. Stop." She wasn't done kissing him. He was more than a shelter she didn't want to leave. So much more. He was joy. He was desire barely met that invited her to live right here forever.

If it wasn't for a dragon masquerading as a queen and her challenge. And the suffering of the Magi right under her nose all these years.

She shifted her tunic back where it belonged and took a deep breath to settle her rattled heart. "What can we do?"

He rested his head on one arm, grazing her cheek as if he didn't want to let go either. "An army is coming. We've been preparing."

"We? How can I help?"

"You need to talk to your mother."

"She's so weak."

"Talk to her."

He brushed her lips with first one kiss, then another that was far more. She reached out to draw him closer, but he wrenched himself away. "Not yet."

He held her at arm's length with a tired smile curving his lips. "Go. See your mother." Standing to his feet with a wince, he ambled back inside the inn.

Watching him walk away was like being cut off from the spring, from what she discovered had been there all along. It was frustrating. And confusing. And wonderful.

He was right. She needed answers to mysteries that only Mother knew.

Mother had slept for hour upon hour since they brought her home. Her eyes blinked a couple of times as Giselle held a glass of precious water to her lips.

She was back in the room where Mother had hidden away so often after Papa left. Back to the room that held many secrets.

A family she never knew.

A grieving mother her child's heart never recognized.

A calling that drew not only a dragon, but also a brave, legendary people who happened to be family.

Her proud, regal mother lay in bed. Her dark eyes were feverish, and shallow puffs of air barely moved her chest. She took another sip of water before her head fell back into the pillow.

Mother was home. Finally.

She should have been stronger by now. Searching her mother's eyes, she found only wavering light. A tremor of fear rattled her core.

Mother struggled to sit upright, then settled back into the pillow.

"You can sleep, Mother. I'll come back."

"No. Stay." Those eyes glimmered with fire she recognized. "I wanted to tell you. That night." A quiet wheeze sounded with her words. "I didn't want him to go. We had angry, hateful words."

Mother didn't have to tell her which night. Papa leaving was the moment that defined them both. "It's all forgiven."

Mother shook her head, sadly. "I came here with your father, the one I loved. We knew Gad El Glas. We understood its history. Together, we'd set people free."

She paused for such a long time that Giselle wasn't sure if she'd fallen asleep. When she spoke again, her voice faltered. "We never planned to have a family here."

She wasn't sure she wanted to hear this. "One more drink."

The woman refused the cup and clutched Giselle's wrist. "We planned to stay a few years. There were so many captives… so much work. Your papa despised being gatekeeper only in name."

"What do you mean, in name?"

"He was so brave. So passionate… for freedom. His gifting was immense."

"How could that be? Everyone knew him as

gatekeeper."

"The Nayeli people would never accept a woman. It was me, Giselle. I carried the mantle."

Giselle stifled a gasp, not daring to frighten her mother or stop her from talking.

"Like my mother, Alessandra."

"I met her. In the mountains. She looks like me." She wanted to rush in with the wonders of what she discovered in the Magi kingdom – and in their family.

A smile creased her mother's lips. "I should've told you. She returned to me every time I looked at you."

Did you love her? Why did you leave? She had so many questions, yet her mother was too weak to answer. She squeezed her hand lightly.

"My mother carried the Stones. She defeated Gad El Glas, just as her cousin Maura had. The Stones in her hands opened gates for those who lived in darkness." Her voice and grip strengthened. The commander was back. Not as strong, but still present. "The dragon fears you. As a third-generation gatekeeper, it was only a matter of time until you received your calling. Until you and your heart became a gate."

Giselle started to protest, but her mother held up her hand.

"I wanted to live my life the way I chose, not the path laid out for generations." She pulled in a rattling breath. "I wanted a new destiny by your father's side. I needed to prove…I didn't need them."

Ouch.

Her mother's tone faded again. "It was a hard road with your father driven to avenge Tobias. We couldn't tell you that we were Magi. One slip, and we would've lost you. Losing the mission was terrible. Losing you was unimaginable." Even her sigh was shallow in her lungs, which somehow refused to cooperate. "I was empty and stone cold. And you...were more." A smile traveled over her face and into her eyes. "More than I understood."

More. Like extra instead of not enough.

"We were so different. Know that I loved you. Always. And forever."

A place deep in Giselle's heart melted once again in the warmth of what she'd longed for and yet believed was forever out of reach. She went through the facts she knew but never put together, like a puzzle left in pieces. Mother was a prominent businesswoman who ran the largest trading post of the Nayeli kingdom. She had the favor of King Abusari. It was the perfect place to administrate rescues behind the scenes.

"Nayeli culture wouldn't receive a woman as gatekeeper, so I served alongside your Papa."

Giselle finally understood. "You were behind the rescues."

She waved her hand, as if brushing away a pesky gnat. "Your Papa pushed further and further into the enemy's territory, mocking an ancient fiend far stronger than us." Her eyes were frantic, even in the recalling. "When I warned him, he said, 'It was my friend it held. I'll die getting captives out of its lair.'"

She crumpled into a fresh batch of tears. She patted Giselle's hand with the softest touches. "He never understood. It was unfair. He was the leader. He should've been Gatekeeper."

Oh.

In her eyes, Papa was perfect. The father she loved was bold and courageous. He also insisted on his own mission, ignoring wisdom that could have kept him safe. Worse, he resented the one who carried a gift he believed should be his.

"I lost my will after he left. I couldn't lose you, too. I did, anyway." Her mother slumped into the pillow, exhausted. "My heart was a coffin, full of dead dreams and loss. I'm sorry. Very sorry."

Giselle blamed her mother for so much. She was a fool. "You didn't lose me. I'm here now." She reached over and kissed her mother's forehead. "I was wrong, too. I refused to understand how you grieved."

Her mom was fading but she had more to say. "Love me. Honor me by receiving my most precious gift." With a sigh, she fell into a deep sleep. The conversation was over.

By the time she found her way into the kitchen, Louis was there with an aged man at his side. "I found a friend of ours."

"Chronos!"

Chronos was so old and battered. Giselle gave him a tentative hug, then backed away.

Louis held a protective arm around his shoulder. "I found him. He was with his granddaughter."

"How did you get through the soldiers? It isn't safe for you to be here."

"I had to come," he protested. "I never told ye. Now be the time."

In faltering half-sentences, he described the end of the Darras they'd known. Queen Naifa, who directed the demonic guard, took over after King Abusari died. Sorcery rained like a flood season over the people of Darras.

Poison was the queen's most potent weapon. Top

officials died for no clear reason. Others disappeared, never to be seen again. If Makir knew, he did nothing to stop her.

"Poison." She shuddered. "That's why the dragon said five days. Mother would've died if…if we hadn't gotten her out yesterday. The queen kept her alive as bait, to draw me back to Darras."

"Ye faced that demon as a child."

"The dragon I met in the mountains?"

"Ye think the queen be human?" Chronos peered with rheumy eyes. He shook his head so hard his ear lobes flopped. "No, indeedy."

Chapter 23

Midday heat found its way into the quiet kitchen. Louis led Chronos to a chair and poured him a cup of water.

Chronos was a man with a mission. He ignored the water and thumped his hand against the table. "It were long ago when ye were a bitty child. It were the same devil. It were going to wipe out the city – everyone in it – man, woman and wee childrens."

Giselle drew in a shuddering breath. No wonder she sensed the dragon's presence in the queen. The shapeshifter took human form.

When Louis offered the piece of warm flatbread, Chronos pushed it away. "I won't be takin' that. Not when me family be starving." He began his saga again, as if he was rudely interrupted. "Yer parents would've whisked you away if they'd known. And been kilt. You stood, though. It mocked ye. Still, ye stood. Yelled in that babe's voice. 'Ye can't. Ye won't.'

"I remember it's laugh. T'was awful. If ye'd backed up an inch, it would've been the end of ye – of everyone." He paused and cleared his throat. "Ye didn't. It be your time, dontcha' know." He shook a trembling fist. "Ye gotta know."

Louis spoke quietly. "I arrived from the mountains after your Papa disappeared. Your mother's family missed her, begged her to come home. She wouldn't. The

Gemini was a refuge in the center of the dragon's lair. She couldn't lose it."

He paused for a long moment. "It's true that you met the dragon as a child. You averted something terrible. Queen Naifa gave herself to the same demon."

"You never knew me as a child."

"Magi know their own. We knew your calling before you were born."

History. Connection. What she always longed for and found right at his side.

"We may look like our people are isolated, although that's far from true. A network binds our hearts and minds like the trees."

"Lucy told me. Besides, she looked like a young sapling herself."

He smiled at the mention of Lucy's name. His expression changed the next moment. "The queen wants to turn Darras into a dragon's lair, filled with the most priceless treasure – human beings. Instead of a sanctuary, the Gemini will be the entrance of a prison. The salt mines thrive with Magi labor. When one dies, that person will be replaced by ten more."

Chronos held her chin in his gnarled hand. "It don't want ye to remember, Gatekeeper. Ye must remember. Ye must." A rattling cough overtook his aged body.

Louis held out a hand that Chronos received. Together, they disappeared into the pantry and exited through a door she'd never seen.

Network. Somehow, he'd created one between their neighbors. How had she been blind to the hero she'd known for years?

Trudging back upstairs to her mother's room, she decided. She'd wait for Louis to return, and together, they'd work out a strategy. They'd find a way to get water to the city. Somehow.

Sunset came and left. It had been dark for hours and he hadn't returned. She couldn't leave Mother long enough to scour the neighborhood. There was only one place she could still think, still breathe.

It was the rooftop.

Perched on cool tiles, she looked out over the desert and Darras under the same starry canopy. On one side, stretched miles and miles of sand. An entire city suffered in darkness on the other side of that towering city wall. Flickers of light were the only evidence of life.

The desert was an ever-changing landscape, even at night. Winds shifted and rearranged the sand into a new tableau by morning.

For so long, her life felt shaped by a capricious gust. Losing Papa, her relationship with Mother, and even being whisked away by renegade slaves proved what she believed. Whatever or whoever was in charge, it sure wasn't her.

She was like those desert sands. Hard times shoved her this way and that. They rearranged the terrain of her universe without permission. She blamed her mother, anyone, who blew her here and there with only a disgruntled sigh on her part.

Magi had more than their share of adversity for generations. The dragon burned their home and killed Suzette. Amid all that loss, they carved a kingdom behind a waterfall full of wonder and protection.

Louis left his mountain home and family to help her broken mother in a barren desert outpost. Just that day, he accomplished the incredible and pulled water from the spring with a makeshift well. Its life-giving water gave

Mother a fighting chance and answered the queen's challenge to make others pay with their lives if she didn't bow to her will.

Her grandmother, Alessandra, decreed it in not so many words as they stood in crystal rain behind the waterfall. She would stand, even quaking with fear, to see what she'd never seen before.

Instead of the sand, she'd be a wind.

She'd shape her world with what she had – a gift of freedom.

The oaken door that stood before her inside the Magi cave unveiled a commission on the other side. It was an assignment to return to Darras, to free her mother, the suffering Magi inside those mines, and the Nayeli people.

It wasn't an accident that she was here.

It was the plan all along.

Surely, a calling came wrapped in a lovely bow, clean and bright, like a crystal vase.

No.

It was more like the river that rose from the base of that terrible wall erected around the Nayeli kingdom. It cut its own course, making a way through, around, or over obstacles. As it gushed, it shaped a barren landscape.

Orange lit the sky, spreading like an ominous cloud. Plumes of smoke rose from the center of the city. Explosions, and other sounds of massive fires. Cries sounded as dragon wings flapped, and the stench of sulfur filled the air. The dragon's scream shot terror throughout smoldering darkness, under the cover of untouched stars.

It was the fiery serpent's response to her

disobedience. Cutting off water to the city wasn't enough. It would incinerate the entire city and make her watch.

What did courage look like on her?

Her father answered by riding into the night.

Her mother married the man she loved and moved to the enemy's lair.

Rory and Alessandra, even Maura and Aiden, answered their own challenges when evil threatened.

She used every excuse to deny a gift passed through the generations.

One that brought her before a dragon no human could defeat.

One that was called upon now.

"The breaker, who opens a way through the gate, bursts through doors of bronze and bars of iron."

Someone pounded on the door.

Maybe it was Louis.

She ran down the stairs and peered out the window. Opening the door to the courtyard, she gasped. Flames lit the sky as people poured down narrow corridors and rushed toward the inn. People of every age, some crying in fear, others holding arms around little ones or supporting the aged, streamed toward their doors.

The Gemini was the only building not on fire for as far as she could see. A man with blond hair plastered around a face scorched with heat raised his hand as if to knock again. It was Aaron.

A neighbor dashed out fires along the pathway with a worn sheet. He picked up a smoldering tree limb and threatened to smash Aaron over the head. "Get back to the palace. Before I beat you into dust." He turned to Giselle. "He's one of hers. Enforces her witchcraft

Laurel Thomas

against his own people. Filthy traitor."

Aaron knelt to the ground. "It's true. But no more. I swear. I'm done with her. Let me help."

This Aaron was a long way from the flirty young man with ruddy cheeks and ready laugh. Nothing about him looked youthful. Stripping off his uniform, he stood in a plain linen tunic. "I renounce any allegiance to the queen."

He was a brave knight in not-so-shiny armor, after all. "Stay outside these doors. Make sure no one prevents anyone from entering."

He took his post outside the courtyard to protect everyone who sought refuge.

Would palace soldiers keep people from entering? None of the crimson uniforms were in sight. Maybe they escaped back to the palace, believing they were safe there. Guarding a city under a deluge of fire wasn't worth losing their lives.

She settled the suffering refugees into groups in the dining room, offering them bread and water from a pantry that Louis had filled.

The old woman sat in a corner, holding a trembling child. She whispered, "Hush, now, baby. We're safe here."

"Do you know my friend, Louis?" How many refugees would she have to ask the same question?

"Aye. Of course. He was the one who told us to run to the Gemini. He and his men helped us for days, bringing us bread and water. We wouldn't be alive without him."

He wasn't only her hero. He saved their neighbors without fanfare, without her notice. He didn't need kingly robes or a crown. His heart was a royal one and had been all along. Champions surrounded her. Now it was her turn.

One thing she'd always known.

There would be a confrontation.

At the city gates. Again.

She'd stand. She'd say no to the dragon's dominion.

An imperfect carrier, her heart, and her actions disqualified her long ago. Evidently, the gift didn't care much about that.

It wasn't going anywhere. Somehow it was stamped into her very being.

"What if I can't?"

"What if I won't?"

The dragon itself answered that last question in an all-night trial by fire.

The very air blazed around them. Sparks kindled on door frames, on parched tree limbs and in the broken wooden stalls of the marketplace. Rivers of fire coursed down the alleyways and into open windows.

The dragon didn't care if the whole city burned.

It was proving a point.

It was in charge.

She was not.

People poured into the inn, stuffing every corner. She scanned each person, longing to know Louis was safe.

No one had seen him. No one knew where he was. Everyone gave evidence of a network of provisions and help that wove through the city like a highway of life the queen hadn't discovered.

Hour after hour passed, and still, he was gone. Where was he?

Wailing sounded from upstairs. "Basir. Don't go."

She tore herself away from the masses of people and ran to her mother's room. "Mother, it's me. Giselle."

Her eyes were blank, unseeing. "The dragon…"

Who was she talking to? She reached down to comfort her with a careful embrace and felt limp weight against her arms. Mother's skin was pale and mottled. Her breathing stopped, only to begin again at a random moment.

Wild, erratic fear rushed over her heart. Dashing to the top of the staircase, she screamed over the chaos. "Someone. Anyone. Help!"

Blond curls matted with sweat and soot, Aaron tramped up the staircase and followed her into the bedroom. Without a word, he held his finger lightly on a pulse point on Mother's neck. He removed his hand, then returned it, as if searching. Or hoping.

When he lifted his eyes to hers, she knew.

Mother was dying.

Chapter 24

Giselle pushed aside the blanket she hung over her mother's bedroom window. Gray dawn shifted to muddy red in the eastern sky. The air, full of fire and cinders the night before, remained hot and cloudy with ash. Tiny desert sparrows were nowhere to be seen, as if they, too, were afraid to appear outside the wall that hid homes and businesses charred by dragon's fire.

A sleepless night slowed her steps into determined plodding. She couldn't leave her mother that night or, for that matter, the crowds who poured into the Gemini to search for Louis.

Friends and neighbors were a picture of misery as they poured into the inn the night before. Children cried with parched mouths and swollen bellies. Parents looked at her with eyes blurred in desperation. She handed out food and water until she dropped, exhausted, into bed.

She slept with Mother, her body pressing as close as she could without waking her. Her hand rested lightly on hers, willing her own warmth into the cool, dry skin.

Morning was a tiny respite. Mother was alive.

But this day offered no promises.

She tiptoed around people who slept in every corner to the familiar closet, still full of exquisite dresses. Mother's fragrance lingered there like a gentle love song. The floorboard creaked where the strong chest she'd pillaged before the long trip hid.

She needed the right gown. It had to be a statement of sorts, a display of life that refused to be conquered.

In moments, its fabric met her hands, and she knew.

The gown shimmered in blue, purple, and crimson like a desert sunrise. Its purple was crafted for a queen. Its blue was like the power of rain to quench scarlet fire. It skimmed over her tired body and brushed her skin with its softness.

Her only weaponry lay on the bedside table. She shoved the knife and Suzette's ointment into her pockets and wrapped herself in Leonore's fabric. Then refreshed the cup at the bedside table, broke flatbread into small pieces and placed it beside the water. Finally, she smeared Suzette's ointment on her mother's forehead.

All along, she knew they'd meet again at the city gates. She'd face a dragon equipped with its own weaponry – fire, jagged talons, and razor-like teeth. Enormous, with its own armor, to boot.

She'd figure out a way to defeat it. Maybe use her gifted hands with some kind of flourish.

Like that would ever work.

This was worse.

This was a battle she hadn't planned to face, even though it made a terrible kind of sense.

The dragon said it when she and Tobias were tucked away in the cave. Destroy the one she loved, and she'd melt into a puddle at its feet.

That was true.

She loved her mother and was afraid in a way she'd never known.

This wasn't fear of adventures gone wrong, or even of a romance that fizzled away like smoke.

It was about a sadness that ruled long before.

It took so long to define that grief. Even now, knowing the why didn't matter. Because at the end of it all, one thing was still true.

She'd never been able to save Mother.

It wasn't like she hadn't tried. Except all her childish efforts fell flat. Even tiny forays into peace were pathetic.

Soon, people would rise to the new day and need breakfast. She wouldn't be there to offer it. Others would take charge of the pantry and its coffers. They'd make sure no one was left out.

Mother didn't stir. Her skin was the hue of dingy water, and her breathing came in shallow puffs.

She couldn't leave.

She couldn't stay.

Once again life was a precipice ready to swallow her up.

She turned with a question in her eyes to a dark-haired woman who nursed her child. The young mother whispered in response. "I'll be here. Go."

Gathering Leonore's fabric over her shoulders, she leaned into the metal gates with all her weight. With a clank, then another and another, the doors rumbled open.

The rush of wind pressing sand greeted her. A flock of desert sparrows tittered beneath the olive tree where a lizard dashed by, carrying a scorpion in its narrow mouth.

This was home. Today, she clung to what always grounded her, even when everything inside shouted Run!

Makir's voice called her. He stood by the sundial, dressed in royal robes emblazoned with a crimson dragon. "Where did you go, my love? You left my protection."

"You're no shelter. Not for me. Not for this city."

"You believed a lie, Giselle."

A murky cloud rose from the ground and with it, the familiar terror. It took shape, becoming the queen and her retinue of shadow guard. Queen Naifa's sharp features and hardness were dragon-like. A crimson gown, the color of smoldering flames draped perfectly at her feet. "You came to obey my command."

Giselle refused to tremble. She had her own mandate. "Open the springs for your people. Give them hope for survival after your assault of fire."

The queen's visage didn't waver. It only grew in clarity as if she took on substance with each word. "Their suffering is your fault. Did I not warn you of consequences?"

"You force me to bow by bringing pain and suffering to your people." A sob caught in her throat. "Not only that, you poisoned my mother."

Queen Naifa's mouth twisted into a smirk. "Our best healers were attending her until you stole her away in the night."

"They were killing her the same way you murdered King Abusari."

Early morning chill quickly became a furnace. Was the dragon's presence already nearby? She turned to Makir with a curtsey. "Shall I speak to you, my king, or your mother? Who is in charge?"

"You asked that once before." His words were calm and measured. "My mother and I rule together."

"Which one of you takes the form of the dragon?"

"What are you talking about?"

"The flying serpent that rules here. The one you saw guarding its treasure in your mountain home. It came with you, Makir. You know by now that it is your mother."

The queen shrugged royal shoulders. "Purely a diversionary tactic. Your mother, on the other hand, pays the price for your rebellion. She is Magi, a virulent germ worthy only of extermination."

Sunlight blazed hot even through Leonore's protective fabric. She was without shelter, sand driven by the wind, once again.

"Ah. You're alone." The queen divined her thoughts. "You always were, you know. Never fit anywhere. Forever sure that something better was two steps away from your one." She extended a slender hand. "Join us. Your greatest desires will be fulfilled. We'll rule this great kingdom, together." She paused and mustered a look of concern. "Besides. Don't you want to see your mother again?"

It was the dragon mocking her with the same words she heard behind the waterfall. The words that brought her home on the back of Tobias. The words that pitted her now before the same adversary. "What have you done?"

Had she sent some demonic cohort to deal a final blow? Would she die alone as her daughter faced the very one who murdered her?

History with Mother rushed before her eyes. The lullaby at her bedside, a gentle touch when she was sick. The smallest moments, the most precious ones. She couldn't lose her now. She couldn't let those angry, grieving years rob their future. The dragon had stolen so much. The cruelest weapon of all was to destroy their future.

"Is your disobedience worth the loss of your beloved

mother?" The queen read her thoughts as surely as if she spoke them.

Mother couldn't die. Not at the hands of the one who had plundered so much. She whirled to Makir with a plea. "Open your eyes, my king. Your mother is a murderer. Taking on the dragon's shape only confirms who she is inside."

"That's a lie. I've aligned myself with power. Power to do what is right."

"You can't believe that you're doing an honorable thing. The people of Darras are terrorized, starving, and now without water. The one who controls you is the one who defines you."

Makir's chiseled features turned scarlet. "You left your own mother and, therefore, cannot accuse me. My loyalty is well-placed, believe me."

"Devotion to evil and its lusts is never well-placed. Your mother poisoned King Abusari and many others. Do you think you're set apart? You're as expendable as the previous king, son or not."

The queen hissed. "A vile accusation from one who deserted her own mother and even now would let her die."

"She killed other opposition, Makir." She had to keep talking, longing to reach some kind of truth, some kind of integrity in the young king's heart. "You agree with her every word and carry out her filthy cause. What if you stop? What if your own convictions stop aligning you with a thief and murderer?"

"You hope to put a wedge between us. I'm not a traitor to the Nayeli people, or to my family. Unlike you." Despite his words, uncertainty grazed the young king's face. "I am Nayeli, positioned to serve a higher call. Just as you are, Giselle. Any other thought is a lie. Receive the truth. Return to the Nayeli people."

There were plenty of opinions about both her lineages. Brocagni fairly spat at the sight of her. Even Tobias, her mythical ride, despised her at first. On the other hand, crystal rain drenched her behind the waterfall and revealed a Magi family.

This had to be more than an appeal to King Makir, hoping she could dismantle the wall of lies that separated them. There was only one in charge, and it wasn't Makir. "What is it that you want, Queen Naifa? What treasure do you seek?"

Sunlight glittered against the stone walls of the Gemini. She'd been blind to its sanctuary. There was a mystery she hadn't unraveled that the dragon knew with certainty.

One after another, pieces of a puzzle came together.

The shadow guard never pursued them inside the inn. It was as if the walls and windows were impenetrable to that evil force. She remembered the fateful meeting with Ramaz at the Gemini, long before she recognized his danger. He stood outside the door of the Gemini, waiting for an invitation to enter.

He needed her permission.

The dragon's fire the night before hadn't touched the inn, even when everything around it burned.

Papa's woven star at her window was a sign for all the approaching world to see.

Refuge.

It was the home she longed to escape.

And yet, it protected everyone who entered.

What had Mother transferred? Something real, something touchable, moved from her mother's hands to her own heart. The warmth of that holy exchange returned as an answer.

Mother had given her place as gatekeeper.

Why?

Had she feared that it would vanish if she died?

One thing was suddenly clear through questions that continued to shout.

The Gemini was a prize with her at its door.

She trembled to think what would be lost if she bowed to Makir and his tender admonitions. No wonder he and the queen wanted the Gemini. The inn was like a fortress against anything that came against its inhabitants.

In the hands of the enemy, evil had free, open access.

"I understand. Finally. Our inn is a refuge that refuses to allow you inside. You need entrance. That's why you want me."

The queen looked surprised and then recovered a placid countenance. "True. Although there is more. I require its access to trade in what I love most."

"Do you mean gold? Certainly, your mines produce plenty – at the cost of Magi lives."

"I'm accustomed to using their mortal bodies in the mines. Salt doesn't glitter like a Magi gift, although it makes me rich. There's more. Much more."

"You have plenty of slaves to gather riches for generations. You're a hated serpent, a despised thief of what is really precious. Human lives."

"You begin to understand. You'd think the treasure you carry made you smarter, or at least more aware." She extended her hand to Giselle. "What about your own gift? Why waste it's potential when it can be merchandised."

Giselle's mind whirled, seeking a clear thought. Confusion was a signpost of the queen's witchcraft. She had to resist it.

Queen Naifa took a step closer. "Consider the ability to see the unseen. Wouldn't that be valuable to me?"

"And yet you can't possess it."

"Exactly. You've been deceived, my wayward Nayeli child. You think your hands are like magic. *Voila! Open, Sesame*. All that."

Giselle braced arms against her chest, as if to protect her heart.

"You open not only doors to silver and gold. There's something even better." The queen tsked in disdain. "Silly girl. Can't you see? You unlock supernatural gifts so that I can sell them." Her jaw set in unholy resolution. "Human trade is more costly than diamonds, silver or gold. Magi, along with their gifts, will be ours."

Giselle shook her head in disbelief. "You want the inn as a trading post? To grow rich by selling Magi and their gifts?" This was the very essence of a dragon. "You're a thief like none other."

Makir studied the queen's countenance as if something unnoticed appeared for the first time.

"I have something else that works well. I can make your life on earth miserable by destroying everyone and everything you love." The queen paused for drama. "I am the source of your greatest fear – being alone and unloved. Say goodbye to your dear mother."

"No." She tottered as if against a gale of wind.

"My friends, show Giselle what we have in store for those who oppose my will."

Wispy smoke curled from the queen's mouth as the

shadow guard rushed toward her. Desert heat turned to bone-chilling cold in seconds. Ice careened through her bloodstream and into each life force, freezing them into submission. She fell to the ground, unable to speak or move in darkness heavier than life itself.

A vision of Ramaz rose. His terrible death.

Icy tendrils wrapped around her throat, her chest. She gasped for a breath but found none. Light receded, as if conquered by the evil shadows. Barely aware of the sand beneath her body, her heart slowed to a shallow thump, and then finally gave up.

In what could have been minutes or hours, she stared down at the body that had once been hers.

"Stop!"

It was Makir's voice.

The darkness lifted enough for a gasp of air, though not enough to keep her. The demon shadows had no intention of obeying Makir. They answered only to Queen Naifa.

The queen spoke a simple command. "Leave her."

Inky gloom parted, and she returned to her body in a flash of light.

Makir leaned down, his hands warm against her face. "Come back, Giselle. Come back."

Sunlight blinded her, then cleared as she sucked in a long breath of air. Then another, and another. The frozen grip lifted little by little from her heart, her bones, as if the sun finally had permission to release its warmth.

She was alive.

She rested her hand on Makir's chest and said what he already knew. "The shadow guard listened to her. She is their master."

The young king rose to his feet. He took first one

step, then another toward Queen Naifa.

In a moment she knew.

Makir would bow.

He would submit to what he'd always known.

She'd die.

Mother would die.

Darras would pay for her disobedience. Whatever city rose from the ashes would flourish with slavery and oppression.

She was alone and defeated.

Chapter 25

Cool water pooled around her body. The desert floor was wet. The sand, usually furnace-hot, felt like a refreshing embrace.

Diversion. That's what she needed. She remembered the horned viper at the wall that surrounded the Nayeli kingdom. They couldn't attack it head on. Its destruction required strategy.

Her thoughts ventured back from shadow guard's attack as strength returned. Understanding came with it. She sat upright, feeling warmth flood her body. She faced Queen Naifa. "A dead gatekeeper is worthless to you. You want me alive."

The queen ignored her. "You are Nayeli. Defy that false lineage and join me in your real calling.

"Yours is a kingdom of suffering, veiled in lies. What about you, Makir? Your mother murdered countless people in our city to gain control. What is your part?"

"Nayeli culture must be preserved. At all costs."

"Nayeli culture or dragon's greed? You're merely a figurehead for the serpent's will."

This was ridiculous. She had no plan.

Except to save Mother.

Lifting her hands, the prophecy rang out in the desert air. "You are the door of bronze, the bars of iron. You must bow, Gad El Glas."

As if in answer, a mirage formed against the city gates.

A woman with raven hair walked toward them. She didn't stagger, nor did she hurry. Dressed in a golden gown that shimmered in sunlight and walking with perfect carriage, Mother approached.

Her voice rang out over the desert, and to those who peeked over the wall to watch this confrontation unfold. "Evil crouches at the entrance of our gates, Giselle. It won't win." She turned to Queen Naifa. "Your plot failed. I live to stand with my daughter. I live to destroy you, the one who has plundered so many."

Confusion lifted like a curtain from her mind. She rushed toward her mother with joy, then drew back. "No! Go back to the inn. Go back where you're safe."

Mother was weak and thin, but the veteran warrior hadn't come to concede. "I didn't come to bow."

Giselle groaned. "You don't understand. The Gemini is a refuge. The queen can't touch you there. Go back."

The shadow guard surrounded them as Giselle held her mother, covering the slight woman with her body.

Queen Naifa snarled in contempt. "They're awaiting your decision, Giselle. What will it be?"

"Let my mother go. I'll give you everything you asked. Take me. Not her."

"Don't bargain with the dragon, Giselle." She shrugged herself firmly from Giselle's arms. "It is a liar."

Queen Naifa studied Mother as if she saw her for the first time. "If you haven't noticed, I have you both in attendance. Why should I choose? You can both die."

She longed for Papa so long that she was blind to the mother at her side. The Magi still needed her. So did

Darras. Mother lost her husband and almost lost her faith – but she made the Gemini the refuge it had become.

Was the inn magic?

Not in the way she imagined.

Her mother's repeated, everyday acts made the Gemini a refuge. Her faithful deeds engraved themselves into the very memory of a building.

Compassion came to live in an inn. The place she called home.

As her daughter, her hands were supposedly gifted. It was her heart that mattered all along. What good was a gift when the carrier held a dragon inside?

Not anymore.

Giselle took a giant step toward the queen. "Take me."

Mother placed a delicate foot, clad in magenta, between her and the queen, then stepped into her place with a flourish. "She doesn't stand alone. She certainly isn't defeated. I stand with her." Her eyes flashed. The commander had returned, and she wasn't retreating. "The gatekeeper is a generational gift. We carry it as one. Together, we refuse your entrance into this city."

The queen roared in contempt. "Surely you know that the third link is missing. You have no authority. You cannot defeat me."

"That's where you're wrong."

Giselle whirled around to see Alessandra trudging through the and vibrant with a mass of brown curls swirling around her face.

"I'm here as the third." She grinned, as if they were having a bite of lunch instead of standing before a host of demons.

Placing her hands in Giselle's and wrapping an arm

around Ursula, she raised her voice. "A golden thread runs through the generations, each one stronger, each one more powerful against you, Gad El Glas."

They stood with Giselle in the middle, arm in arm. "If one falls," Alessandra shouted, "we'll help her rise. A cord of three strands is not easily broken."

They were three women of flesh and blood who suffered loss and heartache. Through it all, the enemy hoped they never discovered the wonder they carried.

Gifts to set captives free.

"Are you ignorant of Magi law, O detestable Gad El Glas? With each generation, the gift grows more powerful." Mother's voice rose like judgement decreed.

The queen snarled in response.

Her mother's bold words became iron bars, caging the adversary. Her very soul rose in fearlessness. She was made for this hour. Facing this challenge released life into her body.

Her back straightened and voice rang out as a clarion call. "Ah. You do remember. Strength is built into the very calling itself. Strength to destroy the destroyer."

The queen screamed in rage. "You're the one who lies. No one is more powerful than the Exalted Gad El Glas." Her body whirled once again into a realm where a mortal body no longer bound her. She became crimson and black, rising, and rising into a towering, armored beast.

Beauty no longer obscured her true nature. This was the real Queen Naifa. The one who offered herself to Gad El Glas. The one who chose a serpent's heart. The one who required dragon's might to destroy all who came against her.

No longer a delicate face framed with plaited hair

and flowing dress, razor-sharp teeth jutted from a mouth that drooled with lust. It strode forward, shaking the ground as if the very sand feared it. "A threefold cord, is it? Let's see how it stands against me, Gatekeeper of all." The crimson spot on its throat throbbed with roar after roar.

The city's walls wavered as if the timbre of its voice required their submission.

The three women continued to stand.

Its shadow eclipsed Giselle's frame. A tremor spread through her limbs like a rogue wave. She felt the unshaken foundation of each woman at her side. She sensed their history, one far beyond what she'd known.

She wasn't alone after all.

The very ages upheld her in their wings.

The city within those walls was quiet, but people watched from above its stone blocks.

"Any support you longed for has returned to its holes. The Nayeli are mine." The dragon took a deep breath. The crimson stain grew and expanded like a jar of ink overturned.

"My fire will speak," it cried. "My flames will end this feeble resistance, this paltry defense. I rule over every door that would oppose me. Granite stones cannot stand. Neither will flesh and bones defy me. My flames will overtake you, your family, and this city. Trial by fire. Only the true Gatekeeper would endure."

An eagle screamed overhead, as if in reply.

That made no sense. There were no eagles in the desert. Unless...

In seconds, Tobias swooped overhead with a battle cry. It was lion, it was eagle, and it had come for war.

She knew him. She understood the cost. Tobias

chose a battle against the ancient foe that had once held him captive. This was too much, too hard.

For the mighty griffin, too much and too hard didn't matter. Like Mother and Alessandra, he came when she needed him.

She'd at least try to caution a hero who only knew the mission and its goal. "Go back!" Giselle screamed into the air and shook her fist toward Tobias. "I won't let you do this."

"You're Magi, not a hare running for cover. Gad El Glas will *not* reign. It is a nothing. It is merely a wayward mouse, preparing to flee into its hole." He swooped down between them, taunted the dragon, and then shouted at her as he ascended into the sky. "Remember who you are."

"Go back. Please."

"I'm not afraid. I didn't come to fail. Neither have you." Tobias divebombed once more, soaring over the dragon in open contempt.

The dragon queen only laughed. "Ah. My faithful slave. You missed my company after all. This time your friends will watch as you roast like a bird on a spit."

"Nothing you do bears watching. You have no wonders to perform. You're a dried-up serpent with death in its gut. Die!"

Tobias whooshed overhead and shot away as the dragon propelled himself forward with an enormous cry. "Arggggg. Who are you, insignificant griffin, to mock me? Watch and learn."

Giselle whirled in a frantic circle as Tobias flew away with the fire-breathing she-devil in pursuit. Tobias came to divert the dragon. There was something she was supposed to do. What was it?

A voice from the wall called to her.

It was Louis. He lifted his hand, forefingers crossed. "Remember. Remember the well."

A vision of the well Louis crafted and the water that shimmered inside appeared like a promise.

Water. Why was it so close to the surface?

They never realized that water was possible from sources other than the springs.

It was there all along. Buried, to be sure. But present.

Chronos said it.

Sorcery ruled when Queen Naifa came into power. Witchcraft was there all along. It was the power of Gad El Glas.

She thought Ramaz was its chief henchman. Maybe he was for a time. He ruled over the awful temple, over the terrible mines. He knew what was at stake. So did Queen Naifa.

They understood that water must be suppressed.

Water would ruin it all.

All the deprivation, all the fear and isolation.

Water.

It was the door that must be unlocked.

She thought her mission only covered the city gates and the Gemini. This was an entrance to richer treasure than she imagined.

This door opened to life itself.

Lifting her hands, she cried out. "Water! You've been imprisoned for too long. Hear me. I unlock you. You are free."

Nothing.

She looked like an idiot.

"I said, 'Water. Be free.'" Where was Lucy's

command when she needed it?

The dragon's shriek sounded far away, then closer as it flew back into sight. "I chased your friend back to the cliffs, where he trembles in fear. I return to find you signaling miracles from the ground? You'll have none. My power, the power of fire, quenches every dribble of hope you carry. I am undefeated. You will never prevail against me."

No water. No nothing.

The sun was at its height, hot and relentless. Sweat poured down her back and arms. Her face burned, and she tottered on her legs, about to give out with fatigue.

This wasn't going to work. The dragon had too much fire. Too much everything in its favor. She looked to the ground again and pleaded. "Come on. You obeyed Lucy. What about me? Don't leave me out of this."

A tiny bubble plopped up through the sand.

Then another. And another.

In moments, a narrow rivulet soaked the ground. Giselle stifled a gasp and turned to her mother. "Is it enough?"

Alessandra and her mother stood with their feet in puddles. A smile curved her mother's lips.

The dragon snarled. "This is no escape. You're lost. It isn't enough."

Not enough. Once again. What if she was more than enough? What if she was the extra they needed in this line of gatekeepers?

Her mother's voice was a command. "It's time to sing, Giselle."

Sing? How could that help?

She began a halting, timid, almost song. She raised her hands once more.

Lift up your heads, O gates, lift them up ancient doors.

The gatekeeper must come, and she will not fail.

Over and over, she sang, through tears, until joy began to gurgle inside as surely as the water did outside. Like a picture she saw of the human heart with veins and arteries, a network of water pressed its way through the barren ground.

Streams rose from the earth, as if her song cooled the heat of the dragon's presence, the heat of the noonday sun like spring rain. Her words taunted it in the simplest, sweetest form.

Mother, then Alessandra, joined in. Their melody coursed into the atmosphere and over the desert. It flowed like a stream over the dragon, over Makir, and over the Nayeli who stood overlooking the wall.

The shadow guard shifted to Makir. That couldn't be right. They took their orders from the queen. Still, they hovered near the young king like a noxious cloud with trouble in mind.

For a moment, the dragon was silent, mesmerized by a fragrant aroma that almost neutralized the stench of its sulfur. Then, it shook itself like a dog suddenly drenched in water, as if to awaken from dumb shock.

Smoke smoldered from its nostrils. Bared teeth revealed scarlet embers burning at the back of its throat. A mighty blaze was building.

The city gates creaked open. Chronos exited, carrying a small child and leading a young woman by the hand. It was the woman she'd seen in the mines.

Aaron appeared next. He carried a child on each arm and led his battalion forward. Each soldier carried or led a slave out of the city's gates.

What were they thinking, approaching this battleground?

The dragon roared, enraged at the sight of captives being released. "It won't be hard to get rid of two little women. You're the one I want. The other two are expendable. They are your so-called golden thread. Let's see what fire does to that strand."

Giselle took a breath and kept singing.

The citizens of Darras appeared, like water that first trickled from the massive wall surrounding the Nayeli kingdom.

The cloud of demonic warriors increased in density and formed a circle around Makir. She had to stop, had to intervene.

Without warning, Makir shouted, "Trust your gift!"

It was as if Makir's cry released the floodgates, and the citizens of Darras poured out like the water at her feet. Each of them carried a slave they freed. Limping, broken people streamed out from the city gates as water sprang from the ground.

Makir's face was stricken as the swirling black horde prepared to fall on him like a deadly cloak. "Go, Giselle. Set them free."

The dragon stretched up to the fullness of its height for a mighty howl. Fire sprouted around its gills. With another scream, its claws ignited like a campfire kindled. A tiny groan escaped at the end of its cry. "Makir. Separate yourself from these Magi vermin. This war is over."

Makir rushed to Giselle, instead of the queen, and pushed her out of the way. As he did, the shadow guard overtook him like a stormy mass extinguishing life. He lifted one hand from the ground, but the darkness was too strong.

In a single gasp for air, he collapsed to the ground in a heap of royal robes and crown.

A hush fell over the crowd as Giselle struggled to press through gloom that became a black wall. She knelt and battered the relentless barrier with her fists.

Even the dragon was motionless.

When the shadows finally lifted, Giselle pulled Makir into her arms. Frigid cold sucked heat from her own body as she struggled to embrace his purple skin and unyielding body. The young king was frozen, here on the desert floor, with midday heat blazing.

"No. Makir." She hurried to pull out Suzette's ointment.

"My love…" Makir's words forced through icy lungs trembled, then faded away. A ragged breath shook his body, and he was gone.

"No!" The dragon screamed, gathering steam for a giant blast. A glow shone in its bowels. A flood of scarlet flowed through its body as it opened its mouth to spew fire.

In an instant, she knew.

She had to separate herself from Mother and Alessandra. If they died, the golden thread would be broken. She didn't have a child. There was no one to carry on with the mantle of gatekeeper.

That couldn't happen.

She dashed away to the ancient olive tree. She'd face dragon fire alone where she and Papa had met, anticipating a new day.

The dragon leered as it stomped toward her. In moments, its aim would release a waterfall of flames. She'd be gone, but the line of gatekeepers would remain.

The dragon's shadow overtook sunlight and hovered, as if it relished her fear. It stood, balanced on an armored tail, eyes darting around as if to take in a sight it never expected.

It took a breath. Then another.

What was it waiting for? It could have incinerated her long before now.

It drew air into its serpent's lungs. Soon, its gushing spray would prove its power, its preeminence.

Flames swelled beneath armored flesh. It rose on massive haunches, towering over her. "Pay. I'll make you pay."

A broken cough released a smattering of flame that curled at its razor talons. Scarlet flames spread through its extremities. With another gigantic shake and roar, fire burst out along its armored belly

It shrieked as only a dragon could.

What was going on?

Flames grew and spread inside with each scream. Smoke billowed through its teeth, talons and armor as burning lava coursed through a being impervious to everything except its own fire.

The fire meant to devour them, was devouring it, instead.

It croaked in a garbled plea. "Help me, Giselle."

With one last moan, the fire-breathing fiend, whose name was Gad El Glas, became an enormous bonfire that burned and burned. All the city gathered to watch the impenetrable armor of the dragon, and its inward parts turn to smoldering ash.

Ash that disappeared, without a trace, by a mighty spring that rose in the wilderness.

Chapter 26

Gentle waves lapped the sandy shore of a lake that extended so far to the east its waters rippled out of sight.

It was the lake Papa said was there all along.

For hours after the dragon's demise, she and Louis watched, amazed, as water gushed from its once-hidden place.

Birds arrived to welcome it. Even desert creatures stopped to peer into its depths.

It was the people of Darras who celebrated, though. They played, children and adults, everyone finding an unexpected paradise outside the city that had been dry and barren for so long.

Tobias returned, gliding over an army of Magi who trailed through the desert sands with brightly colored caravans and banners. They arrived, unloading food and more food. More than enough for the whole city.

Rory rushed into the arms of his wife, Alessandra. Then enfolded her and Mother into a long embrace. Maura and Aiden stood at one side, crying with joy as they held each other.

Lucy and Elise appeared from a fancy litter. Even Clarion and Brocagni arrived on the back of camels on a journey so different than the one that whisked her away that night weeks ago.

At the very end, out came Ferdinand and Carnation, wobbly but upright. Ferdinand bowed low. Carnation rushed Giselle, planting slobbery kisses on both cheeks as she twirled her around.

"What are you doing here?"

"We didn't have a proper farewell, did we? We couldn't leave without saying thank you, my dear." Ferdinand straightened to full height and waved his hand with a flourish.

"For what?"

"Aye. Don't be dense, bee-loved." Carnation held Giselle in a rib-crushing hug. "Come back to serve, we have. You and your honey, here. Ruling this fine city."

A big roar of approval sounded from the crowd.

Soldiers, beginning with Aaron, hoisted her, then Louis, on their shoulders and carried them to the city gates outside the Gemini. They formed a cascading ladder of arms and gently lowered them outside the open metal gates and under her bedroom window where the woven star hung.

"We need a new beginning." Aaron was the spokesman of the hour. "Lead us. We'll see a city arise from the ashes. Magi and Nayeli alike, working together."

Louis stood beside her, tall, a commander in his own right. A gentle one, but still… "Together?" he asked, peering down at her. His face was a mixture of longing and a glimmer of what she felt that day by the well.

If he wasn't saying anything, she would. "You're asking me to marry you? Finally? Yes. Yes. And yes."

"One yes will do. Come here, where you belong." He pulled her to himself and planted big smooches on her lips, on her cheeks, her forehead, neck.

"Okay, okay. More kisses, please."

The people laughed and cheered as if they, too, were

a part of this happy development.

"Aye. Time for a weddin', then. No time like the present." Chronos roused the crowd like an aging general.

It seemed right. Why wait when a new chapter rose after the fiery end of another? Who knew where this path would take them? Who cared? They were together.

"Just let me...get a dress. And a bath. You, too, Louis."

Crowds trickled inside the city as she and Louis worked their way into the Gemini with Mother close behind.

Mother's room was no longer a place of sickness and death. Fading afternoon sunlight streamed through the open window and lit every corner as she rummaged through the closet. "This one is yours. I've been saving it." She held out a simple muslin gown, studded with tiny blossoms woven as if they'd sprung from the fabric itself.

Reaching up, she fingered the silver Magi-crafted key Louis had given her the morning of her sixteenth birthday.

Like the necklace, this dress fit perfectly and felt like home. A bath and some much-needed primping were all she needed.

Louis appeared in a new tunic, clean and shaved. Skinny, but handsome, carrying a bouquet of roses that grew near the well in their courtyard. The bush that withered had bloomed again.

Aaron appeared at the door to the city with an entourage of ragtag soldiers. Their uniforms were a variety of singed crimson and homespun brown tunics. Evidently, the palace guard had enough of Queen Naifa, too. "New royalty belongs in the palace," Aaron decreed with a fist pump of victory.

Magi and Nayeli walked together through a war-torn city to the palace. As they approached, the hideous spires of the temple loomed. A cloud bank hurried across the sun as the slightest cast of doubt rumbled through the crowd.

Louis said what everyone feared. "Are the slaves all released? Be sure."

Aaron and his men checked the mines. Everyone was gone.

They stood outside on the giant pavilion, amid devastation all around. Dragon fire swept over even the palace. Soot blackened marble pillars once pristine white. The massive door where she leapt into the masquerade was charred. Smoke and ashy remains lingered everywhere.

She had to say it. "We can't go inside. It stinks with sorcery."

They traveled back through a city torn by flames, each person bent on a determined celebration. After all, Magi and Nayeli walked hand in hand. With Magi gifts and Nayeli hearts, the city would once again spring from the ashes even more beautiful than before.

Giselle and Louis stood on the shores of the lake, which rippled over their bare feet and washed their ankles. Their Magi family was like a royal entourage, surrounded by Nayeli citizens.

Elise strutted like a miniature prize fighter front and center. Her mother decked her out in so many flowers she was the wiggly version of a bouquet.

Aaron walked forward, shoulders straight and proud, from the battalion of soldiers. "Who will marry these two?"

Rory lifted one hand, then the other. A small horde of children trailed around him. "Ahoy, ye landlubbers and bustle-butts. I'm the one for the job."

He pulled Alessandra to his side, drew a quick breath, and bowed to Louis and Giselle. "We're here. Here to celebrate a love purified by fire. A love...."

Alessandra poked him. "Hurry up."

"Okay. Louis. Will you marry this woman who adored you since she first laid eyes on you?"

"Well."

"Okay, will you marry this woman who is figuring things out – finally?"

"Yes. I will. I do."

"Giselle. Will you marry this man who adored you since he first laid eyes on you?"

"Yes. He did. And I do."

Rory laughed. "She's going to find a way to win, you know. She's just like her grandmother."

Laughter erupted from the crowd.

Alessandra came forward. She placed a smooth white stone in Giselle's hands. Rory put another in Louis's hand. They were a commission offered.

There were tears in Rory's eyes as he looked first at his wife and then to Louis and Giselle. "Will you join this adventure? Will you discover what you've never seen before, but trust is unveiled as you travel this road as man and wife?"

"We will," they said as one.

"Will you lead this alliance between Magi and Nayeli, never allowing evil to rage over what belongs to freedom?"

"We will."

Louis's voice rang out as he held Giselle at his side. "We remember waters that bubbled from the sand when it was impossible. We honor the bravery that released its hidden promise."

"May these waters strike fear in the heart of our enemies." Giselle decreed. "May they remind us that compassion overtakes captivity wherever courage requires it to bow."

Louis looked down at her with such love she thought her heart would crack wide open. "May our souls never melt in fear. May our children and children's children run with joy and certain aim into the future."

Rory wiped his brow. His voice rose over the crowd that settled into reverent stillness. "Swear to me now, by all that is good, to carry your gifts into the world. Give each man, woman, and child a sure sign of kindness. Spare the lives of the oppressed. Protect the generations."

He took a deep breath and raised his hands in benediction. "The deep peace of the quiet earth and shining stars be unto you, forever. Rise today through the strength of heaven. May its eternal goodness propel you to the end of the age."

Everyone was still.

Rory cracked a grin. "Err. What are you waiting for, Louis? Kiss her."

She looked into those blue eyes and found what she searched for all along. "You're not going anywhere. Not without me."

"If you travel to the stars, I'll follow. If I must eat your terrible cooking, I will."

Their kiss… Well.

His lips pressed against her softly and kept pressing.

His arms wrapped around her waist and lifted her into a happy twirl. Just as quickly, he lowered her for more kisses. The ones she never wanted to end.

"Hey. Enough already." Rory grabbed Alessandra and planted a big smooch on her lips. Everyone cheered, hugging each other, enveloped in joy that had been absent for far too long.

The indigo bunting appeared and darted around them.

"You're back! Who sent you?"

"I shared my small friend with you." Mother came forward, holding her hand as a perch for the tiny bird. "The queen said she'd kill you if I left the palace. I placed the bunting in your room. It is the child of one who was my ally when we first arrived in the desert."

"You were dying. I…It was so hard to leave you that morning. Then, the queen threatened to kill you. I didn't know. I couldn't…"

"Oh, beloved. Don't you understand? Your courage released me. Your heart set mine free. With every step, strength came." Her fingers grazed Giselle's chin. "You wouldn't be stopped. I lay there in that bed and decided to rise. Death couldn't hold me."

Rory spread out his hands to the cloudless desert sky. "They wanted life, but You have given them more. The days of their blessings stretch on one after another, forever!"

Chapter 27

Louis and Giselle were alone that night. Their Magi family prepared a sanctuary of their very own on the rooftop, complete with embroidered cushions and gauzy veils that obscured everything except the night sky that glittered with thousands of lights in celebration of their marriage.

She cuddled into the warmth of her new husband. "How did you get back to Darras?"

"Tobias. He flew back to the mountains."

"He was so brave to venture back through the danger. *You* were so brave. How did you make it through the demon warriors when you came back into Darras?"

"I had a bit of Suzanne's ointment. It hid my scent over the desert. No bath for days helped." He shrugged. "We lost our food in a brawl with the dragon. Somehow, Tobias skirted that serpent, and it gave up. Probably decided to come back to Darras and fight on its own turf."

"What about the underground? How did you do that?"

"It wasn't hard. Tunnels connect the Gemini with Nayeli homes. They have for generations. Your parents used them to set captives free. They weren't easy to navigate, but the queen didn't know about them. The demon shadows didn't, either."

Suddenly, a star in the east flashed. Light spilled out

over darkness, and the heavens became as bright as day. Its radiance pulsed for long minutes before fading into cloudy debris.

"What. Was that?"

Louis paused for a long moment. He took a breath and found a tasty place on her neck. Finally, he spoke. "A star just died."

"No. Does that really happen?"

"A star has a span of life. Just like us. Lots longer, of course."

"How do you know these things?"

Louis shrugged, then traced his finger from her forehead to jaw, as if memorizing its course. "I know more stuff. Want to hear it?"

She laughed. "Right now? I might have other ideas."

"Oh." He shifted his body over hers. "I'll explain later, then."

"Wait, wait. I'm listening. Really."

"If you're sure, then." He leaned up on one elbow, scanning the heavenlies. "We just saw the 'last hurrah' of a dying star, the biggest explosion anyone on earth will ever see."

"Even bigger than a dragon going up in flames?"

"Yes. Although, I have to say that was amazing. Wonderful. Spectacular. Just want to give that ending the proper gratitude. Every day. Every night." He reached in for a kiss.

"Hmmm." She drew him closer. "I like spectacular. Especially now that it's over."

"This is a leap. Ready?" He searched for words to translate what his heart understood. "Maybe the heavens mirror what we see on earth. Or maybe, the earth is mirroring heaven. Anyway…"

"Go on. I'm listening."

He turned and kissed her deeply, caressing her with each touch, melting once again her heart that was already mush. No more trying to stand alone, to prove what didn't need proving.

Like that ever made sense.

The best part of standing was being surrounded by the ones she loved. Especially Louis. "Okay. More."

"More?" He stretched out with a gleam in his eyes.

She giggled. "Yes, that, too. But tell me first about the star. About us and the heavenlies." "Okay. Massive stars burn huge amounts of fuel at their core. The center gets really hot." "And?"

"A star lives in balance between two opposite forces. Gravity tries to mash the star into the tightest ball possible. But the fuel burning inside its core creates intense pressure. Its outward push resists the inward squeeze of gravity.

"Eventually, a star runs out of fuel. It cools off, and the pressure inside drops. Gravity wins and the star collapses." His fingers stroked a tangle in one curl. "This is a wonder no one will see for generations."

"Like a new beginning."

"Yes. Like that." He sat up, so full of awe it had to spill out. "Stars are like the universe's treasure troves. They hold elements needed to make everything in our universe, like carbon and nitrogen. The biggest stars even carry gold, silver, and uranium. When one of them dies, those elements rain through space. Eventually, they land here."

"The death of a star releases gifts that Earth needs."

"Exactly."

"The dragon wasn't really like a star."

"Kind of, although it was more like a black hole, swallowing everything in its path. It was fueled by an evil energy inside. When that wickedness had to bow, the form that held it died from the inside out. Lots of riches weren't captive anymore. They're free now to bless the earth. Our job is to steward them well."

Giselle had to think about that. It was hard, though, because her husband's body pressed against hers with happy urgency.

This moment was meant for Earth and for them. She wouldn't miss it.

Chapter 28

Louis was still asleep, his long legs stretched akimbo over their bed. The six-point star wavered in an early morning breeze. The days she bounced down the granite walls of Darras to escape were over. Still, the window was just the right place to sit as she watched a camel train wind its way toward Darras.

Tiptoeing down the stairs, she pushed open the metal gates and slipped outside to the waiting sundial. She sat on the limbs of the olive tree, overcome by layer after layer of memories. Papa. An evil queen who vied for a generational gift she'd barely known existed. One who morphed into a dragon and then collapsed like a dying star into ash.

The camel train came closer. A speck in the distant sky rose and then fell as it approached.

It was Tobias soaring on wind currents, just like the morning outside the cave when she wasn't sure he'd return for her.

Unhindered by anything that tied him to Earth, those clear skies were his element. It was the place he was born for and the place he was called to rule. Protector, guardian, all those things, he was that and so much more. He was her friend.

A rider threw out his arms as he flew, reveling in the freedom of Tobias and his wings.

It had to be someone important. The griffin didn't

carry just anyone. Certainly not only for fun.

Joy rushed over her heart. He carried her, though.

At first, she was only a mission from Maura to her dear friend, Tobias. Then, they endured dragon's fire and a trek across miles of desert. His reply to her question as she faced Darras set a course. They adjusted the direction of her heart, like aiming an arrow about to be released.

"What if I can't?"

"What if you won't?"

His response was a challenge that shot light into her confused, fearful heart.

It didn't matter how gifted she was if she didn't act when acting was required. Compassion came on the wings of an eagle with the strength of a lion to prove that a decision of the heart always prevailed.

They were flying closer to the ground, having a great time. Who could the passenger be?

Tobias landed. A figure cloaked in brown stepped off into the sand. He stood, ignoring everything around them – the desert lark, the lake, the animals that gathered for an early morning drink.

His eyes were only on her.

Dark, wavy hair streaked with gray dangled over his eyes. A grin spread across his face, straightening his crooked nose. That brown cloak. It was the one she watched drift away through the sky as the dragon pursued her and Tobias.

Papa.

He held out his arms, and she ran into his strong embrace. He smelled like hope returned and love retrieved. He spun her around just like he had so many years before.

"What? Where?"

They toppled together, laughing, as Tobias took a long drink from the lake.

His presence was almost more than she could bear. She barely breathed as he began to speak.

"I was a captive of Queen Naifa in her desert kingdom. She bound me within the depths of the shadow mountains. I saw her kingdom and knew when she and her son came to Darras. It was a strategic move. One that would place you into their web.

"I agonized night after night." He grabbed and held her tighter for a moment before releasing her again. "Then I knew. You would listen. You would find your way. Your mama and I placed you in the center of the dragon's lair. But we equipped you. You weren't alone. You had a gift that would rise to victory."

"The dragon's fire looked like it was the end. Of everything, Papa."

"Yes. It wasn't, though. You found your family. The ones we love, the ones who love you. Louis led you across those miles when we couldn't. You returned to save your mother. Just as I knew you would.

He paused with a huge smile. "When the dragon died, the prison bars fell away, and the wraith warriors vanished. I was free. The sorcery was broken.

"Tobias came for me. The wall you scaled around the Nayeli kingdom? It crumbled into dust. There was no more sorcery to hold it in place. No more barriers separate the Nayeli and Magi."

A rush of silken fabrics and the fragrance of rose and jasmine rushed from behind. Mother shouted as she ran. "Basir!"

Giselle joined the embrace and then separated herself. This was their time alone.

Louis made breakfast, of course. Soon, the whole family sat at the timbered plank of the same table Sir Damien hurled at the young Magi. Customers would be arriving later, but this hour belonged to family. Her family.

Papa turned to her. His finger grazed the birthmark on her arm. The one he shared. "It was designed to warn you. Did it burn in the presence of Gad El Glas?"

"Yes, although it took a while to figure that out."

"You did fine," said Grandpa Rory. Always the encourager.

Maura spoke up. "The Magi recognized your gift. They just never saw it work in the law of the third generation."

"You talked about that in the cave. It didn't make any sense then."

"The law of the threefold cord has been in place for millennia. It's a calling to deliver captives. More than that, it carries the strength of generations behind it." Alessandra smiled gently. "You noticed that you weren't actually in charge of the doors you opened."

"It was terrifying."

"A safeguard was placed within the gift. The dragon couldn't steal it. I mean, other than stealing you. It couldn't force the gift to work."

"It could only accumulate those gifts like a horde of wealth."

"Exactly."

Rory nodded at Louis. "Your hero here directed the citizens of Darras to open the mines and let the people out."

"Of course, he did." She reached out for a hug.

Papa leaned into Mother. "A gatekeeper doesn't

only open physical gates. A gatekeeper's gift declares *no* to bondage, *yes* to freedom. It offers access or blocks it."

Giselle shook her head, mind spinning with the memory of the dragon becoming a giant bonfire. "I still don't understand why the dragon's own fire incinerated itself."

"I know a bit about that, you know." Rory and Alessandra held each other, as if a memory etched itself in their hearts. "A fire that can't spew consumes from the inside. Your heart didn't give it access."

Hours later, Louis stood by her side at the lake, after people had been fed and family tucked away into their own rooms at the Gemini.

The sun almost finished its course for the day. The beauty of its descent washed their world in hues of crimson, blue, and purple. Just like the fabric of the gown she wore on the day that changed everything.

Maybe life would return to normal, although who really knew what that looked like anymore?

Her ordinary, everyday life shifted when she stepped into who she'd been all along. Not that she was alone in that journey. A host of champions surrounded her. And still did.

A song rose in her heart, one she'd never heard, but knew was for today. It was a song to anoint a new beginning and its hope for the generations.

"O, desert wind, come. For the gifts below and the gifts above have kissed. And Earth shall know it's blessing."

May it ever be. Yes, and amen.

A word about the author…

Laurel Thomas crafts stories about ordinary characters who rise against impossible odds to accomplish the extraordinary. She's written for inspirational magazines, ghosted nonfiction, and currently enjoys her favorite role as storyteller. Three of her novels, River's Call, When Stars Brush Earth, and Stones of Promise have won numerous awards. Through Write Your Heart Out! she teaches and supports emerging novelists with one-on-one coaching, a bi-monthly round table, and small group intensives

https://www.laurelannthomas.org/

Thank you for purchasing
this publication of The Wild Rose Press, Inc.

For questions or more information
contact us at
info@thewildrosepress.com.

The Wild Rose Press, Inc.
www.thewildrosepress.com

www.ingramcontent.com/pod-product-compliance
Lightning Source LLC
Chambersburg PA
CBHW052017020726
47501CB00004B/1110